M000203491

TO MOVE THE WORLD
The Sworn Sisters, Book 2
Copyright © 2021 by Kay Bratt

978-1-7363514-1-3
Published by Red Thread Publishing Group
All rights reserved.
This book or any portion thereof may not be reproduced or used in any manner whatsoever without the express written permission of the publisher except for the use of brief quotations in a book review.
Printed in the United States of America
First Printing, 2021
www.KayBratt.com
This is a work of fiction. Names, characters, businesses, places, events, and incidents are either the products of the author's imagination or used in a fictitious manner.
Cover Design and Interior Format

TO MOVE THE WORLD

THE SWORN SISTERS
BOOK TWO

KAY BRATT

BOOKS BY KAY BRATT

You can find them in Kindle Unlimited, too.

BY THE SEA TRILOGY
True to Me
No Place too Far
Into the Blue

THE TALES OF
THE SCAVENGER'S DAUGHTERS SERIES
The Palest Ink
The Scavenger's Daughters
Tangled Vines
Bitter Winds
Red Skies

LIFE OF WILLOW DUOLOGY
Somewhere Beautiful
Where I Belong

SWORN SISTERS DUOLOGY
A Welcome Misfortune
To Move the World

STANDALONE NOVELS
Wish Me Home
Dancing with the Sun
Silent Tears; A Journey of Hope in a
Chinese Orphanage
Chasing China; A Daughter's Quest for Truth
A Thread Unbroken

SHORT STORIES
The Bridge
Train to Nowhere

CHILDREN'S BOOKS
Mei Li and the Wise Laoshi
Eyes Like Mine

If you have enjoyed my work, I would be grateful for you to post an honest review on Amazon, Bookbub, and any other platforms you use for your books.

To those of you who have left reviews, my sincere gratitude is yours.

I would love to connect with you on Facebook, Instagram, and Twitter. Please sign up to my newsletter to be eligible to win fantastic giveaways, get news of just released books, and get a peek into the life of the Bratt Pack.

PRAISE FOR KAY BRATT BOOKS

True To Me was chosen as one of BookRiot's
**"50 OF THE BEST KINDLE UNLIMITED
BOOKS YOU CAN READ IN 2020"**

"Quinn Maguire has grown up believing that she
knows the truth about her complicated childhood.
But when her mother dies shortly after revealing an
earth-shaking family secret, everything changes in
an instant. Kay Bratt beautifully draws the story of a
daughter returning to Maui—the enchanted land that she
believes holds the key to her past—where she unlocks
a promising future she never could have imagined. Full
of secrets, love and gorgeous settings, *True to Me* is the
ultimate escape." **—Kristy Woodson Harvey, bestselling author of** *Slightly South of Simple*

"*Wish Me Home* has all the trademarks of a Kay Bratt
novel: a heartwarming story that nourishes the soul,
beloved characters, and a plot that kept me turning
pages. Without shying away from the harshness of life,
Bratt has managed to create a world in which kindness
and goodness prevail. My advice to those who haven't
read this book yet? Find your comfy reading spot, get
your beverage of choice, and sink into the world of *Wish
Me Home*. You'll be glad you did." **—Karen McQuestion, bestselling author of** *Hello Love*

"Heartfelt and brimming with lively characters, *True
to Me* is a poignant reminder of the meaning of family,
the importance of truth, and the power of forgiveness.

Perfect for fans of Christine Nolfi and Cathy Lamb."
—**Sonja Yoerg,** *Washington Post* **bestselling author of** *True Places*

"Nothing like a harrowing, life-threatening, and completely unplanned hike through Yosemite's backcountry to make you face years of grief and guilt head on. Kay Bratt pulls this off masterfully in *Dancing with the Sun*, an emotional mother-daughter tale of love, forgiveness, and renewal. Book clubs will love Bratt's latest!" — **Kerry Lonsdale, Amazon Charts and** *Wall Street Journal* **bestselling author**

"For two women who live in paradise, their lives are anything but idyllic. Best friends Quinn and Maggie have spent the past year trying to outrun dangers from their pasts—one a stalker, the other family secrets. But now both pasts have caught up to them, and the two friends will have to decide if they should keep running or stand up and fight. In this page-turning drama, Bratt has created two strong, dynamic female characters who readers will be sure to root for." —**Amanda Prowse, bestselling author of** *The Girl in the Corner*

"Bratt writes a beautiful tale of family which grabbed me from the very first page. Quinn, mourning the loss of her mother, must travel to Maui in search of her roots. Leaving behind her fiancé Ethan, she is drawn to the island's rich history and the locals who welcome her into their world. Woven between the pages is the deep mystery of Quinn's past, and the DNA test that leads her to a family she never knew. Bratt takes the reader on a heartfelt journey of family and forgiveness while Quinn teaches us about those we should let in and those we should let go. For at the very core of the novel is the rare gift of being true to one's self." —**Rochelle B. Weinstein,** *USA Today* **bestselling author**

"*No Place Too Far* is Kay Bratt at her best. Free up some time, find somewhere quiet, and dive into this story of Maggie, Quinn, the challenges they face, and the people who love them. Once again, Bratt tackles complex contemporary issues with remarkable agility and compassion, and it's an absolute pleasure to be along for this ride. And because Bratt is a master of location, it's even more of a pleasure when the ride takes place on Maui. For a few brief moments, I forgot all about errands and laundry and the minivan and soaked up Hawaii, in all its glorious heritage and beauty." —**Lea Geller, author of** *Trophy Life*

"*No Place Too Far* is the perfect blend of suspense mixed with a magical setting and characters we care deeply about. I loved Maggie and Quinn and rooted for them until the final page. Kay Bratt is a masterful storyteller, and the story's pacing and descriptions of Maui left me always wanting more. Highly recommended for book clubs!" —**Anita Abriel, international bestselling author of** *The Light After the War*

"In this delicious drama set against the backdrop of paradise, Kay Bratt weaves a suspenseful story about finding the courage to fight for happiness, forgiveness, and love. I delighted in the enchanting descriptions of Maui, and I rooted for the characters as if they were friends." —**Cynthia Ellingsen, bestselling author of** *The Lighthouse Keeper*

"A baring-of-the-soul emotional story that leaves you with a heart full of love and hope." —**Carolyn Brown,** *New York Times* **bestselling author**

"*In Dancing With the Sun*, a mother and daughter are forced to lean on each other for survival in the wilderness while learning to let go of years of grief and guilt. Readers will relate to Kay Bratt's depiction of a mother's love and her courage in protecting her daughter. Ultimately, though, this novel is a page-turner that will pull on your heartstrings and affirm your faith in humanity." —**Karen McQuestion, bestselling author of** *Hello Love*

"*Dancing with the Sun* is an evocative story of emotional and physical survival in the harshest of terrains. Mother and wife Sadie Harlan is struggling silently with grief when she and her daughter go missing in Yosemite. Away from the world and focused on keeping her daughter alive, Sadie embarks on an unforgettable journey through loss and guilt to find forgiveness, healing, and strength. Book clubs will love the powerful message of this unique novel." —**Barbara Claypole White, bestselling author of** *The Perfect Son* **and** *The Promise Between Us*

"*Dancing with the Sun* is an endearing, emotional tale filled with the perfect mix of poignant family heartaches, unshakable mother-daughter love, and a dose of adventure in a dramatic, vivid setting that will sweep you away until the very last page. Don't miss it." —**Julianne MacLean**, *USA Today* **bestselling author**

"Whether facing the natural terrors of Yosemite or the internal pains of an unforgiven past, this mother-daughter story is beautifully written and relatable as one woman faces a mother's greatest fear—losing yet another child. Kay Bratt delivers on all levels in this emotional and tense story of loss and resilience." —**Emily Bleeker,**

To Amanda

*"Our prime purpose in this life is to help others.
And if you can't help them, at least don't hurt them."*
—Dalai Lama

PART ONE
FEARLESS

CHAPTER ONE

Chinatown, San Francisco 1876

SUN LING SNAKED HER FINGERS through the mare's mane, relishing the unexpected gift of calmness the creature brought her. In her nearly thirty years on earth, she'd never interacted with animals, so no one was more surprised than she when, within days of ownership, she felt a deep affection for the horse that loyally and unwaveringly remained at her side, despite the frequent bouts of danger they'd already faced together.

"Ānjìng, Dulin," she whispered, telling the mare to be quiet. They waited on the opposite side of the street, under a grove of trees. Not completely invisible but at least somewhat camouflaged. After more than seven years of living in the city by the bay, she knew what troubles could befall a woman caught out alone at night, especially now while everyone was so frightened of the smallpox sweeping through the state. But Sun Ling wasn't fearful of the disease. Her father made sure to keep her full of every tea and potion available to keep her healthy. She just hoped the smallpox couldn't be caught by the four-legged citizens of the city.

Thus far, the mare had lived up to the name she'd been given, borrowed not only from a beloved trinket of her childhood, but also from the legendary horse that belonged to Liu Bei, a warlord and ruler of the state of Shu in an all but forgotten past dynasty. Both horses had the same tear mark under the eye and white spots on the forehead, colorations that in Chinese superstition meant the horse would obstruct its owner.

The original Dulin proved an exception. As the legend went, in Liu Bei's greatest time of need, his horse came through, carrying him out of a deadly trap set by his enemy at a grand banquet. Sun Ling gave her horse the same name with the unspoken understanding that if she was ever a hair's breadth from being captured, her own Dulin would carry her to safety.

The mare snorted, and Sun Ling patted her firmly, a gesture meant to tell her to have patience. Also strangely enough, Dulin seemed to understand everything Sun Ling was thinking, even without words between them.

"Good girl," she said.

Yes, she considered Dulin well worth the trade of a bracelet she'd kept hidden for years, a reminder of her past that she was glad to be rid of. She'd slowly rid herself of most of what she'd brought to San Francisco, though the most important piece was still hidden.

A man came near, and Sun Ling pulled down the brim of her hat, hiding her eyes. The bulky jacket and shapeless trousers she wore almost swallowed her up, but the few who looked her way simply thought her a teenage boy trying to score a glimpse at the house across the lane.

They'd never dream that under the man's costume was a woman on a mission. If everything went as planned, one less girl would be imprisoned and treated as less than human—dressed and painted, then displayed to the lecherous and lonely hordes of bachelors in the darkest recesses of Chinatown.

But first, she had to see the girl, to make sure that the

part she played was truly forced upon her. Years ago when Sun Ling had first begun her adventures, she'd been astonished when more than a few times a girl had refused her help, choosing instead to stay and work, to do whatever it took for those who owned her to continue sending money to her family left behind in China.

Familial duty was hard to break, even if the duty was more than what was fair to ask, especially when it amounted to one form of slavery or another. But this case, word was the girl was barely old enough to even know what flirtation and seduction meant. If the rumors were true about the age of the Orchid Princess, as she'd been dubbed in Chinatown, then Sun Ling felt it her own responsibility to skirt the child away in the dark of the night, to protect her until she could be placed somewhere far away from the lecherous paws of those who paid for only a glimpse but wanted much more.

"Stay here, Dulin," she said, then headed across the lane concentrating on using a manly swagger as she took her place in line, her head down and eyes on the baggy trousers of the man in front of her.

Venturing into the sordid world of slavery never failed to make Sun Ling think of her past—her own bondage to a family who'd held no affection or care for her, a household with a master at the helm who betrayed her innocence and that of her sworn sister with his inability to curb his lust. She'd been only a girl then, but her youth had been swallowed up in the belly of the dragon who'd finally forced her to run halfway across the world in search of a measure of peace.

And she hadn't yet found it.

She continued to feel unsettled and unsatisfied, fighting a fire within her that longed to engulf everyone around her in an act of retribution for past transgressions against her.

But at least helping girls who, like her, found themselves sold into servitude that took more from them than they were willing to give—it was a way for her to feel as though her life wasn't wasted. No doubt the title as the most sought-after dressmaker in the city was one thing she could claim, but a dress was just a dress. Her real passion was ignited by more than a needle and a bolt of expensive silk. To get her blood going, she needed to don men's clothing and venture out into the night for an evening of danger. That wasn't asking much, was it?

According to her baba, it definitely was. So thankful was she for the several years of getting to know him again, to be given another chance to show him she is a worthy daughter. However, his stubborn insistence that she marry an established Chinese citizen was beginning to fray the threads of their relationship.

At every Sunday lunch, Baba begged to let him set her up in marriage, repeating his longing for grandchildren. But Sun Ling could not and would not be tied to a husband and household, at least not until she felt she'd done all she could to right the wrongs done to the women in the Chinese quarter. And after all, most of the men she'd known in her life had only wanted to use her. Why would she want to become enslaved to another?

Around her, men stomped their impatience, hollering out for those inside to hurry. The line moved, and Sun Ling found herself on the front stoop, only a few more paces from actually entering.

"One ounce," said a burly Chinese man, holding his hand out. He stood to her right but to her left was another imposing figure just like him, guards put in place to take the money and handle anyone who tried to do more than get an eyeful.

Sun Ling put the small bag into his giant paw and kept her eyes on the ground. When he moved his attention to the next patron behind her, she breathed a sigh of relief.

She'd passed the hardest part.

It wasn't only being thrown out that worried her. If the wrong man caught her at her charade, Sun Ling might find herself in shackles for the second time in her tumultuous life.She thought of Chin Lee, a young man in Hong Kong who was ridiculed for dressing like a woman, even though it was only for the stage. However, in San Francisco there were actual laws against a woman dressing like a man. If she was caught, she'd be severely punished. She needed to be very careful.

With time to wait, her mind wandered to the bewildering subject of men and their lusts. She would bet that many of the men in line with her were married, with wives waiting at home for their return. That scared her off of ever giving her heart to someone. It wasn't that she didn't someday want to find her own mate, but her life was full of memories of men wanting to use or abuse her in some way.

She'd had admirers over the years, though none she encouraged. Thus far she hadn't met a man who she thought would ever be generous enough not to question why she slept little and crept through the night like a silent apparition.

With another surge in the crowd, the door opened and she, along with six others, was beckoned inside. Sun Ling took a deep breath to still her nerves, and followed the man in front of her.

The small ramshackle house was only two rooms, and they were ushered into the front one. The room was nothing new or inventive, sparse with a wooden partition that had a long rectangular opening cut out at eye level to the average man, so that he could peer into it and get his few minutes of paid entertainment at the expense of the fairer sex.

Swallowing past her revulsion, Sun Ling followed suit and stepped up to the peeking hole along with the others. Through it she saw just what she expected, a petite young woman dressed seductively in a Chinese gown, the vibrant gold silk glittering against the candlelight at every move the girl made.

What she didn't expect was the wave of revulsion she felt when she saw that the rumors were right and the girl could be no older than twelve or thirteen years of age.

Slowly and gracefully she danced, twisting and turning, her moves exotic and precise, all expression hidden in her properly demure and kohl-rimmed eyes.

Around Sun Ling the men whistled, panting like animals, begging for more. With each turn, her gestures showing a flash of skin here and a flash there, the fever of the crowd escalated.

For one moment, Sun Ling almost believed the girl to be enjoying herself, but then she turned again, her eyes lifting for a brief second, just long enough for the pain and humiliation to flash before disappearing again under the fine fringe of lashes.

It was with that one look—only a fleeting fraction of a second—that Sun Ling knew her mission would continue. That she would be back when the crowds dispersed and the girl was allowed off the stage, sent to a back room to recover with a few hours of rest before the entire charade was repeated the next night.

And if Sun Ling didn't intervene? Well, then the show would go on until the newness wore off the Orchid Princess and a fresher, possibly younger face replaced her. And then the girl before her would no longer hold court to the observers. Instead she would be sold to the highest bidder either as a concubine to a rich businessman, or as a prostitute to be hired out ruthlessly by one of the famous tongs that held Chinatown in the grips of their unsavory paws. One more piece of human flesh for them to claim as their property.

But not this one, Sun Ling thought, gritting her teeth against the shouts around her, men's voices coming through the shoddy wood, demanding their turn for a gander. No, this was a girl who could and would be redeemed, and if the stars fell into place just right, she would be allowed to return to the childhood yanked from her in a moment of greed.

Sun Ling couldn't do a lot, and she knew the small accomplishments she did to try to tip the scales of injustice wasn't enough to move the world, but she always hoped it was enough to save just one more person.

She steadied herself against a sudden surge from the men behind her, but before she was shuffled out of the room, she whispered through the hole, "Be at your window tomorrow at midnight, and I'll help you," she said, hoping her promise traveled across the room and tickled the ears of the girl with the desperate eyes.

She took the back lanes home, sticking to the darkest streets she could find to maintain her anonymity as Dulin struggled up hilly terrain. Over the years, she'd learned that if one wasn't careful, bravery could at times be confused with foolishness. Each time she traveled the streets, her mind filled with stories of Chinese who'd been massacred at the hands of those who felt them inferior.

The first one that she'd heard of had happened in Los Angeles, but was close enough to send waves of fear throughout the residents of the Chinese quarter in San Francisco. For months, only the bravest Chinese left their homes for work. Her father had begged her not to venture outside—to stay with him at the store, to allow him to protect her.

The reports said that the incident began when two Chinese companies took to the streets to battle over a prostitute that each felt belonged to them. Fighting over prostitutes was nothing new, and a gunfight broke out. Once again men's urge to own women as though they were property resulted in many innocent deaths. The whites took the gunfight as a sign that all Chinese were revolting, giving them the excuse they wanted to retaliate. In all, seventeen Chinese were lynched and two others stabbed to death, the battered and mangled bodies found hanging from various places like the porch rafters of a repair shop, a nearby gutter spout, and even tied to a gate at the entrance of the town lumberyard. Many more would've been killed, but they fled, hiding out in orchards or crossing the Los Angeles River to put distance between them and the mob that had gathered, their hearts set on murder.

Dulin snorted and Sun Ling pulled on the rein, pausing in the street. She listened, and after she heard no one, they continued onwards. Her imagination continued to taunt her with scenes of death and destruction.

Perhaps one massacre could be forgotten, but there had been many more that involved the whites rampaging against her people. Not even a week after the incident in Los Angeles, another squabble between Chinese street gang leaders erupted, and a pack of white men were deputized and told to round up those involved and take them to jail. Others in the community took that gesture to mean their help was also needed, and with pent-up frustration at the Chinese, many Irish and Mexicans joined the mob snaking through town, inciting a riot in their search for victims of Asian descent or, as the New York Times reported, *'the mob's determination to clean them out of the city'.*

Sun Ling felt sick when she thought of the enraged citizens going after the Chinese, climbing houses to cut holes in roofs and pouring gunfire into them, the innocent young Chinese doctor dragged from his home and hung, and the barbaric abuse of the corpses that had lain in the streets. Almost two dozen more Chinese were killed. Many had their queues cut from their heads as trophies. Even fingers were hacked off, a prize she couldn't imagine anyone wanting.

In addition to the senseless deaths, Chinese homes were ransacked. Life savings and treasures families had worked all their lives for were stolen and distributed through the crowds. Stores were broken into, and shop-keepers like her father were completely wiped out, with every last item in stock was either destroyed or stolen off the shelves. Many returned to China, penniless and out of resolve to stay and fight for their rights.

When the dust had settled and the blood had washed away, out of a mob of over one hundred men, only eleven were convicted of manslaughter and sent to San Quentin. If the Chinese had massacred those in the mob, they would've been hung immediately. Justice wasn't on their side, and even with the grand jury declaring the acts an unfathomable human tragedy, a technicality overturned the conviction, and within weeks the eleven were released back to their families.

She sighed at the unfairness of it all. It had to change, for weren't the townspeople the ones always touting the words *freedom* and *fairness*?

Dulin turned the corner and picked up the pace when she saw the Lane estate. Sun Ling was glad to be back, safe from her reconnaissance. It was time to put her thoughts to rest, to focus on something other than injustice and death.

Safe now, she felt the weight of exhaustion and looked forward to falling onto her bed in the attic to burrow under the soft quilts. She glanced up at the attic window, almost expecting to see Bessie's dark face peering down, curiosity at Sun Ling's secret journeys etched in the lines of her face.

She wasn't there.

Sun Ling slid off Dulin and led her into the stable, guiding her to the empty stall before rewarding her with a handful of sweet oats. In her mind she pictured Luli, safe at home and tucked into bed, a small smile of contentment playing across her lips as she slept. The image calmed her, though it also made her more determined than ever that she would never stop fighting for the rights of the Chinese women and children. They had a right to live in safety and not bondage, and a right to make their home on the rich American soil. The intolerant devils could try to purge their communities all they wanted, but they'd never totally succeed.

She wasn't naïve. Sun Ling knew she couldn't change the world. But she could change the world that surrounded the Orchid Princess. She'd changed that of others before her. So perhaps one at time would be enough.

For now.

CHAPTER TWO

THE NEXT NIGHT, SUN LING felt refreshed as she tied Dulin's reins over a branch near where the Orchid Princess was kept. She signaled the horse to be silent, then crept along the lane until she found herself directly under the window of the old wooden house. Everything was quiet, the lines of men gone now that the girl was whisked out of sight. The only sound to be heard was Sun Ling's heart, pounding rebelliously even as she tried to remain calm.

It was still a bit early, so she settled down and tried to make herself as small as possible, hoping to anyone passing by that she would be a part of the dark shadow. She'd made it this far, and that was a feat in itself. For the next part of the mission, she'd need to be calm and alert.

Deep breath. She closed her eyes. Deeper breath.

She could feel her pulse slowing.

Traversing the Chinese quarter on one of the nights set aside for the hungry ghost festival had proven to be a bit trickier. Usually the streets were empty, shops and homes dark after the midnight hour, but on this night, the many candles set out beside offerings of food had made Sun Ling feel as though she had a beam of moonlight shining upon every step of hers and Dulin's.

Superstition held that one must not go out after dark

during the festival, lest they bump into evil spirits, and Sun Ling knew this, but it didn't change her mind about going after the girl. But she did take extra care not to stumble over any offering along the roadside, which would've definitely incurred the wrath of any ghosts nearby.

At one point, the hairs on the back of her neck stood at attention, and she thought surely a wayward ghost must be following her. Who it would be, she couldn't fathom. She'd set out her own offering of fruit and rice for her mother, and she knew of no one else in the afterworld who would be interested in her comings and goings.

She had been relieved to find it was only a young Chinese delivery boy from one of the many laundries in the quarter. They'd taken to delivering at night, since the ordinance that penalized Chinese laundrymen for not using horses or horse-drawn vehicles to deliver the laundry. Their common practice of the balancing the laundry in baskets affixed to a pole across a man's shoulders had been forbidden, which resulted in owners changing delivery times to late night when they could creep through the dark streets undetected, for there were not many who could afford a horse or carriage.

She supposed that was one reason to be glad that San Francisco refused to put any money into gaslights for Chinatown as they had the rest of the city. Only Chinese red lanterns lit the way in an eerie red glow, disguising many a traveler—or delivery boy—as he went.

She'd scoffed at herself then, for jumping at the sound of a mere delivery boy. Suddenly she remembered she was also supposed to stay away from walls, as ghosts liked to stick to them, so she leaned forward until she no longer touched the rough planks of the house.

At dinner that night, her father had once again told her the legend of Mu Lian, a disciple of Buddha, who began the festival when he tried to save his deceased mother. The story went that before she'd died, she was a vegetarian and had unknowingly consumed meat in her soup, then denied it and was therefore condemned to hell and an eternity of wandering, alone and hungry. He'd tried to offer her a bowl of rice, but it burst into flames before she could eat it. Then he tried again, and other ghosts got the food first.

Finally, when Mu Lian sought help from Buddha, he learned how with special prayers and offerings he could relieve his mother's sufferings. From then on, the *Yu Lan Pen*—ghost festival—was embraced by all Chinese.

Baba had a lot of what the foreign doctors called 'phantom pains' where his legs should've been, so he'd been spending less time working the counter at his herbal shop. Yet he still remembered all the stories and legends he'd ever known, and Sun Ling never tired of his retelling them. After so many years apart, she took every opportunity to show him she was a loyal and attentive daughter. Min Kao, Jingwei, and Luli spent the most time with him, living under his roof. Sometimes that made her envious, but Sun Ling had made the choice to stay with Adora and build her future, so she should've had no regrets. She was also thankful that her father had a fulltime companions in Min Kao and Jingwei, and Luli thought of him as her grandfather.

A sound startled her out of her thoughts, and she froze, not sure if it came from within the house or outside, near her.

Then she heard the window above her raising up, an inch at a time. Sun Ling prayed silently that it was not someone put on guard duty. She held her breath until she heard the whistle of a whippoorwill, and knew it came from the girl.

She stood slowly, taking care to be as silent as possible. She held her finger to her lips as she got her first close look of the Orchid Princess.

At first the girl looked startled, but when Sun Ling lifted the brim of her hat a bit, her face softened. The girl's face was free of all paint and powder, proving her to be younger than Sun Ling had even thought. She felt a shudder of disgust at whomever had sold or taken the girl, then put her in the Chinese quarter as the latest object of a working man's desire.

"What is your real name?" Sun Ling asked.

The girl hesitated, searching Sun Ling's face before whispering. "Lian."

"Are you ready to escape this life of hell, Lian?"

"What will become of me?" She looked terrified, and Sun Ling knew she wondered if she would be sold off or bartered once more, perhaps to a worse fate than being forced to dance behind a panel.

"You'll go to a safe place for a few weeks, then together we will determine the best path for you to take," Sun Ling whispered, looking around her again. They needed to get out of there. "But I can promise you that under my protection, you will not be abused in any fashion."

Lian bit her lip, then stepped out of sight.

Sun Ling felt a moment of uncertainty. Had the girl changed her mind? Run for help?

She moved one step away, torn over whether she should run for cover, or try to get to Dulin. She was taking a huge chance, but she decided to wait a few more seconds.

The girl appeared again, then tossed a cloth bag out. Sun Ling set the bag aside and readied to catch her. The window wasn't far from the ground, but could be a rough landing.

First one leg clad in plain cotton sleeping pants appeared, than the other. The girl shimmied out on her belly, and Sun Ling maneuvered her shoulder just under her until, when the girl let go, her backside rested on Sun Ling's back. Gently she lowered her to the ground, and Lian jumped off, then turned to her.

"I think I woke the other girl," she said, her eyes round with fear.

Sun Ling paused, listening for movement within the room. While rescuing more than one victim would be noble, it would also jeopardize the safety of Lian. She put her finger to her lips and beckoned for her to follow.

Lian picked up her bag and moved behind Sun Ling.

A feminine shout rang out from the open window, but that didn't make them stop. Together they made their way around the building, walking softly but quickly.

Sun Ling could smell the fear coming from Lian.

She turned, meaning to give her a word of comfort, and saw a hulking shadow making his way to them from behind them.

"*Tìhng dài!*" he called out for them to stop.

The girl froze in place, and Sun Ling grabbed her sleeve. "Come on, run!"

Her words spurred Lian into action, and together they raced across the lane and into the grove of trees, then shrank against the trunk of a large oak. They heard the guard coming near, hesitated, then ran in the opposite direction as they struggled to catch their breath.

"Come, we have to move now." Sun Ling led the way to where Dulin waited patiently. She took the girl's bag and set it behind the mane, then beckoned for Lian to climb up.

"I—I can't," Lian stuttered, fear evident in her eyes as she backed away from the horse.

Sun Ling heard the sound of the man's boots hitting the pavement behind them. He was getting closer. "Yes, you can, Dulin is gentle-mannered, don't worry about her."

Lian looked at the horse again and shook her head.

Sun Ling knew they had a mere few seconds left. She could even smell the stench of garlic coming off the guard. "Lian, do you want go back in there? Dance for the men tomorrow night?" she whispered, then held her hands together for a step up.

The girl looked behind Sun Ling, saw how close the guard was, then hopped into her hands and threw a leg over the horse. She scooted forward, and Sun Ling hopped up behind her, grabbed the reins, and clicked her tongue.

She leaned down and whispered in Dulin's twitching ear, "Okay, girl, this is one of those times I need you to live up to your name. Git!"

Dulin obeyed immediately, her cantor becoming a gallop as Sun Ling loosened her grip on the reins and let the horse follow her instincts through the other side of the grove and toward the safety of her father's humble home.

"And Xiao Mei, she even refused to help me with my pigtails," she said, making him smile with her exasperation. "Then she said that her father's employer calls us celestials. What is a Celestial, Baba?"

"But I did your pigtails just this morning," he said, looking at her and raising his eyebrows, trying to divert her attention from her question.

"But Baba, you don't do them right, and they fall out by noontime. Tomorrow Mama must fix them, and then they'll stay," she admonished him, her eyes serious. Even with her hair mussed and a dirty spot on her nose, she was endearing. And he had a feeling she knew it.

She knew she was the center of their universe.

"*Hao le,*" he agreed. "If she is here, she will do them. But sometimes Mama is busy helping other mothers bring their children into the world. If she is out late, or gone when you wake up, it is only for that reason. You know if given the choice, she would be here every minute with us."

"I know. But you didn't answer my question."

He sighed. She was much too precocious for her age. "It just refers to us Chinese because many call China the Celestial Kingdom."

She shook her head adamantly. "That's not true. Xiao Mei said they call us Celestials because they think we aren't completely human. What do you say about that, Baba?"

"I say I've heard enough nonsense. Who are you going to believe? The silly Xiao Mei or your noble baba?" he asked.

She pointed at his chest, ready to move on to the next big thing in her life.

"When will Ye Ye wake up from his nap?" She looked toward the back of the shop where Tao Ren's bedroom, now an even bigger alcove than those early days, was still located.

"Soon. For now you go over and work on your penmanship. I want to see your lesson when you are finished." He plopped her down on the floor, though not before kissing her on the forehead, a loud smacking noise that made her giggle.

He couldn't believe his life.

For seven years now, he and Jingwei had been married, tying the knot only a month after courting. Once he'd realized his feelings for her, he could barely eat or sleep when they were apart. Luli also cried when she was pulled from Jingwei's arms, and in a moment of despair at walking away from her one afternoon, he'd turned around and blurted out the proposal.

"Will you be my wife and help me raise Luli?" he asked, then held his breath as his face flamed.

Jingwei had hesitated. He knew she was afraid to believe that someone could actually care for her as he did. By then she'd told him of her earlier life, the isolation and abuse. And he knew of her condition on the ship from China—the devastating loss of her unborn child. She'd called herself soiled, but he planned to spend the rest of her life proving to her that she was perfect in every way. He'd told her that, and then she'd agreed to marry him and help raise Luli, as he'd put it.

Now they were a family. He no longer had contact with his brother, Wei, or his family in China, but Jingwei and Luli—and even the kindly Tao Ren—filled that empty place in his soul. The only issue that still niggled at him was the fact that Luli was undocumented. There was no record of her being born either in China or the States. What would happen to her when she grew older, he didn't know. They'd been able to protect her thus far, but there was talk that soon every Chinese person would have to carry with them approved identification or be exiled.

That was the only thing that made him want to contact

his brother, as Wei probably had contacts who could do the best counterfeiting. But Luli was young, and they still had some time. Min Kao didn't want to admit his pride kept him from going to Wei for help.

Theirs was a silent battle of wills, each waiting for the other to make the first step toward reconciliation. Yet Wei was the one who had wronged him. Not the other way around. So Wei should be the one to fix it. And Wei lived a dangerous lifestyle, one that Min Kao didn't want anywhere near Luli.

With Luli at her desk, Min Kao went back to work on filling the latest prescriptions. It hadn't been easy, especially since other herbalists had come to America in the last few years to find their own fortunes. Competition could be good, though, and finally the store was doing well. These days, Tao Ren only supervised occasionally. Min Kao had learned from the master and felt he could handle almost any need or even emergency. That was why when the opportunity came up with an empty adjacent shop four years before, he and Tao Ren had become official business partners and bought it. They knocked out the joining wall and doubled the size of their shop, as well as the living quarters above them.

They'd kept the walls up there, dividing the space that they lived as a family from the temporary sanctuary for the girls and young women who Sun Ling rescued and brought to Jingwei for a safe place to decide their next steps.

However, a fake wall with a hidden door that led to the sanctuary was the only way that Jingwei was finally able to talk Min Kao into using the space to house those Sun Ling rescued. Their work was dangerous, as many of the women came from the most unsavory of tongs in Chinatown, but helping others was something that gave Jingwei the feeling she was giving back to the gods who had given her a chance at a happy life. He couldn't take that away from her, but he still felt nervous each and every time a new girl was delivered. He rarely saw them, but the unease let him know they were there, on the other side of the wall.

The bell on the door rang, and Min Kao turned.

"Good afternoon, Lao Go," he called out.

The old man shuffled toward the counter, his back bent lower than Min Kao had seen it yet. It was startling what grief could do to a person, and he thought briefly of his mother.

Lao Go held his hand up to return the greeting, mumbling under his breath.

"What can I get for you today?" Min Kao asked.

"I have a smashing headache right back here," Lao Go said, pointing at his temple. "It won't go away, and I can't tolerate it a day longer. What can you fix me up with?"

He automatically held his hand out, and Min Kao took it, then pressed his fingers down to feel the man's pulse. It was rapid. Much too swift for someone who moved as slow as Lao Go.

"Here, sit down," he said, then went around the counter and guided Lao Go onto one of the bamboo stools. "Do you have other symptoms?"

Lao Go shrugged. "I'm weary. Day in and day out—I am so tired but cannot get any rest. It's like my soul is on fire!"

Min Kao studied the man, debating waking Tao Ren from his nap. Lao Go looked as though he was suffering from more than a headache and exhaustion.

Before he could decide, Luli raised her pencil into the air. "Lao Go, your wife said you are feeling poorly because you haven't fulfilled your promise to her."

The man turned, looking at Luli with a puzzled yet angry expression. "Watch your manners, miss. You don't speak of the dead until enough time has passed."

Luli's expression crumbled.

Min Kao waved at her to get back to her studies, though he kept his eyes on Lao Go. "*Dui bu qi*, Lao Go," he apologized. "She doesn't know you are still mourning. She meant no harm."

Lao Go grunted in reply, but he didn't look appeased.

Luli pushed away from her desk, then came to stand before them. "I am sorry, Lao Go. But she won't stop talking to me until I tell you that she said you must hurry and send her bones back to her homeland."

Lao Go gasped. "Well, I've never—"

Min Kao grabbed Luli by the shoulders and guided her around the counter. "You run and wake Ye Ye," he said, hoping she'd stay out of sight until Lao Go left. "Tell him he needs to examine a patient."

"*Hao le*, Baba," Luli said, looking somewhere over Min Kao's shoulders. "But Madame is waving her arms at me. She said her husband is not to send her bones to their marital home. She wants them taken to Foochow and buried next to her mother."

Lao Go stood so abruptly that the bamboo stool he'd sat upon flipped back, clattering to the floor. "Wait," he said, holding his hand up. He'd gone pale, and Min Kao felt a ball of dread lying low in his belly.

Lao Go beckoned Luli to come closer. Reluctantly, Min Kao let her go.

She stopped at the counter, keeping it between her and the old man. He stared down hard at her, scrutinizing her for what felt like hours before he finally spoke.

"How did you know that my wife is from Foochow? We have not spoken of her hometown since the very day she was brought to me in Nanking at the age of fifteen. It's not possible that you should know that information," Lao Go said, his voice slow and disbelieving. "What trick is it that you play?"

"I just repeated what she said," Luli said, her face suddenly fearful.

Lao Go looked at Min Kao, his expression disbelieving. "On her deathbed, my wife asked that I send her
bones home. I just assumed she meant to the home we
had together, but the bone collector hasn't yet been by."

Min Kao avoided the obvious question of how Luli
knew that information, instead trying to steer the man's
attention away from her. "I heard he is in San Jose and
will be by here late next week, then accompany a ship-
ment to China by the end of the month." That was the
truth, too. The bone collector who traveled throughout
California was a busy man, as he was paid often and
paid well to escort the bones of the deceased back to
their family lands for proper burials. He'd be back soon,
and hopefully then Lao Go could complete the oath he'd
made to his wife on her deathbed.

"I can still get Tao Ren to see to you," Min Kao added,
"He might prescribe something for your pain."

Lao Go turned, looking around the room as though
searching for someone lurking in the shadows. Then he
returned his gaze to Luli, his eyes wide with fear. "Tell
my wife I will follow through. And demand she take this
pain from my head, for I can't think one simple thought
with all this pounding."

"She heard you," Luli said. "She says the pain in your
head is coming from your liver and if you'd stop drinking so much *báijiǔ*, it would calm your yang and you'd
recover."

"Luli—that's enough," Min Kao scolded, though now
he smelled the liquor on the man's breath and had a feeling it was indeed causing most of the symptoms. He
pointed at Luli. "Upstairs with you. I'll be up shortly."

She ran off, her lip out from hearing the reprimand in
his voice, and Min Kao felt guilty. She was only trying
to help—he knew that. Yet what she'd done was startle
the man half to death.

"I only drink to forget that I'm now a lonely old man," Lao Go said, most of the words unintelligible under his breath. "She never allowed me to have the liquor in the house before."

"Lao Go, please sit back down."

He shook his head and went to the door. "I must go find the bone collector today. I'll borrow a wagon and head out to the last place he was seen. I can't delay, lest my wife's ghost decide to never give me peace again." Then he hurried out as though his wife held onto his coattails and he was trying to dislodge her.

Sighing heavily, he turned to find Tao Ren behind the counter, sitting tall in his chair.

"I can explain," he said, holding his hands out.

Tao Ren wheeled forward until he was only a few feet from Min Kao. "There's no explanation needed. Luli did what comes natural to her, what feels right. We can't change who the child is, we can only hope others don't perceive her for what she isn't."

That was the difficult part. With a heavy heart, Min Kao turned to go upstairs and find her. He'd do his best to comfort her, but he knew that today was the beginning of a long road of heartache for a girl who didn't understand that she possessed abilities that most didn't.

Hours later, Min Kao watched from the doorway as Jingwei tucked the coverlet around Luli, taking every effort not to miss any part of the nightly routine they'd established over the years. First, a glass of warm milk as Luli allowed Jingwei to brush, then braid her freshly-washed hair. Then Luli crawled into bed and readied herself for her bedtime story. Sometimes she asked for something new, but more than not she wanted a repeat of an old favorite. But tonight she had something else on her mind.

"Mama, why did Lao Go get so angry with me?"

Her words struck him deep in his heart, and he almost went to her. But he'd already said his piece, and it was Jingwei's turn to do what she could to soften the blows of reality their daughter had felt that day.

Jingwei stroked Luli's hair out of her eyes. "Because sometimes people are frightened of what they don't understand. Lao Go would very much like to believe that his wife was here today, but since he could not see her, it was hard for him to trust it was true. Lao Go wishes for his wife to go on to her place in the afterworld, where she is supposed to wait for him. That's why he burned the paper money, house, and even a paper carriage. He provided for her journey, and he doesn't want to think she is stuck here, tethered to a world where she cannot be seen or heard by those she loves."

"But his wife just wanted me to give him a message. She said she'd go on once he does what he promised," Luli said, her lip quivering.

Jingwei gathered Luli up in her arms and hugged her close. As she rocked her back and forth, she spoke quietly. "I don't want you to be sad, Luli. You have a gift, and though sometimes it may not seem like it, your abilities can bring people peace. But your baba and I want you to wait until you are older before you deliver any more messages. But this time you did what Lao Go's wife asked of you, and now you can be at peace with it. *Hao le?*"

Luli pulled away and nodded, though Min Kao could see she was still upset. He left the doorway and joined them on the bed. "What do we have here?" he asked. "If my little empress is going to shed tears, please let me get my gold-encrusted carafe so that we may catch them."

She smiled through her tears.

"Because," Min Kao said, his tone teasing, "We all know that tears from the infamous Empress of Chinatown are very valuable, and if we can only catch a few of the tiny gems, we will be rich indeed."

Luli laughed, the episode with Lao Go forgotten for now. "Mama, tell me how you got your name."

"Yes, tell us, little bird," Min Kao agreed, settling his back against the wall. He was glad Luli was back to the routine, and requesting a story she knew by heart.

"Well," Jingwei began, "in the ancient works of Shan Hai Jing, he tells a story of a little girl born to the majestic Sun God. Her name was Nvwa, and every morning, she was sad as her father left her to go to the East Sea and direct the rising of the sun."

"She wanted to go to the East Sea, too," Luli said.

Jingwei nodded. "Yes, she did. But her father said she wasn't yet old enough, so one day after he'd gone, she took a row boat and tried to follow."

"The sea rose up like a monster, and the waves swallowed her up," Luli said.

"The end," Min Kao said.

"No, Baba," Luli said, exasperation in her voice.

Jingwei gave him a scolding look. "No, that's not the end. Is it, Luli?"

Luli shook her head, and Jingwei continued, "Nvwa died, but she came back as a big bird with red claws and a white beak. She was so angry at the sea that she vowed she would fill it up. Every day from morning until dark, she worked, using her beak and claws to carry stones and branches, throwing them into the sea."

"And she cried out, '*Jingwei, jingwei!*' as she worked," Luli said.

"Yes, she chanted the word to encourage herself to keep going. Year after year, she kept working to try to fill the sea, and she became a symbol to the Chinese people that one should never give up on a dream," Jingwei said, then stood.

"Determination can reduce an iron rod to a sewing needle," Min Kao added, with a wink at Luli, "but you won't help a new plant grow faster by pulling it up higher."

"Baba, do you know every Chinese proverb there ever was?" Luli asked.

Jingwei laughed. "Yes, Luli, I think he does, and through your baba, I've heard them all, too. That one means determination is a great quality to have, but patience is also needed." She kissed Luli on the forehead. "Good night, and I hope you sleep soundly, with nothing but lovely dreams."

Min Kao kissed Luli on the nose, then tucked the blanket tighter around her. "See you in the morning, Empress."

He led Jingwei out of the room, and they crossed the hall, to their own bed. She sat first, and he joined her. She'd put up a good act, but he could see that Luli's distress had gotten to her.

"You know what Luli asked me this morning?" he said, trying to break her out of the mood. When she didn't answer, he continued, "She wanted to know how old she needed to be before she should get a job and help us with the family finances."

Jingwei looked at him, her eyes questioning.

"I told her at least sixteen," he said. "I don't know how she even knows we have finances or what that even means. She should be worried about dolls and homework, not what it takes to survive in this foolish world."

"We have to protect her, Min Kao," Jingwei said with a rush of breath, as though the words escaped from her uninvited.

"I know we do."

"But if we tell her to hide her gift, she'll grow up to feel ashamed of it."

He nodded. "I agree. It's a very complicated problem. Because Lao Go doesn't want his business talked about, he'll most likely say nothing. But if Luli reads the wrong person, news of her abilities will spread like wildfire, and who knows how that will affect her?"

Jingwei sighed loudly. "I'm fearful that one of the whites will learn of her. In their religion, they don't take kindly to this sort of spiritual talk. It could be dangerous."

They'd talked about the danger before, years ago when Luli had first told them of one of her encounters. It was only after the third or fourth episode that they'd finally realized she wasn't speaking of simple imaginary friends. They'd thought they had years before others would think anything of it, but today—she had convinced Lao Go she did indeed speak to his wife, and that scared Min Kao to no end.

The day she was born, a woman in the marketplace had claimed Luli was marked. Min Kao had pushed the prediction aside, but it turned out the old woman was right. He could only imagine the terror a Chinese soothsayer could bring to the American whites. And if anything happened to Luli, it would crush both he and Jingwei. He'd survived a lot while building a life in a new place, but it was all for Luli.

"I'll talk to her tomorrow," Min Kao said. "I'll make her understand."

CHAPTER FOUR

JINGWEI DRESSED QUICKLY IN THE worn tunic and trousers, then stood in front of the mirror. These days she didn't have time to waste looking at her reflection, but it was impossible not to immediately notice the tired rings around her eyes, or the pinched look of her mouth. It had been a long night of little sleep, her mind on Luli and Lao Go.

She was so worried that the old man would have loose lips and cause them trouble. Many people in the Chinese quarter longed for a piece of the homeland they'd left behind, and if there were rumors of a soothsayer—even a child one—Jingwei had a feeling others would come calling.

At the crack of dawn, Min Kao had urged her to stay in bed, telling her he'd take her morning duties and get Luli off to school.

Jingwei examined the expensive jade bracelet that had been given to her by her sworn sister, Sun Ling. She didn't know if they'd ever be able to bridge the emotional gulf between them. They still saw one another for Sunday dinners, as well as for brief moments during the handoffs of rescues, but it was different now.

She couldn't quite pinpoint what had changed in their relationship, but Min Kao said it was the fact that Sun Ling tried so hard to fit into the white world. It was true that Sun Ling no longer wore Chinese fashions, and that she was fond of the foreign hairstyles and strange shoes, but deep down Sun Ling hadn't abandoned her people, and that was the most important thing. So what was it that made them less comfortable in one another's company?

Jingwei didn't know, but some said that those destined to be in your life forever were attached by an invisible red thread. She believed that was true, so she vowed to never give up trying to regain the relationship they'd once had. After all, they were sworn sisters, and nothing would change that. For now, they'd continue their cloak-and-dagger work together, and perhaps one day, everything else would fall back into place.

She picked up the brush from her bureau and pulled it through her hair. Her eyes lingered on the colored bottles lined up along the scarred wood. Each bottle held its own tantalizing scent—Jingwei's work from the last few years that she was still trying to perfect.

Luli loved to line the bottles up and play with them, taking surprising care even as a toddler not to spill one single drop, as though she believed they contained magical potions. Jingwei smiled when she thought of how fast Luli had grown. Sometimes she looked at her and wished she'd have been there from the very moment she'd taken her first breath—that she had born her from her very own body, though she couldn't love her any more than she already did.

Jingwei longed to have another child, to experience giving birth and to present Min Kao with a son. But after the loss of her first child, her body was obviously no longer able to produce.

She needed to get over it. Her life was full of fortune. She had Luli! And the gods might not appreciate her constant pining over what she couldn't have.

She hurried to the secret door at the back of the closet

and, once through it, went down the short hall, the smell
of the morning congee already filling her senses. A simple meal for simple—but grateful—people. Never once
had anyone dwelling in the small space complained of
the meager fare or the crowded accommodation. To
them, it was a sanctuary, no matter how humble.

Most of the women were already seated in a circle,
each holding their bowls in one hand as they scooped
the rice porridge into their mouths with the other. They
were dressed in the loose, comfortable wide-legged
pants and tunics that Sun Ling provided, outfits that
were the total opposite of the revealing, flamboyant
clothes most of them arrived in.

"*Zao*," she said, giving them the usual morning greeting. She kept conversation in Mandarin, the language
of her childhood. Some of the girls were reared with
Cantonese, but they all did their best to communicate,
and somehow, they got by.

At her greeting, one or two smiled above the rims of
their bowls, but others, still too traumatized to make eye
contact, didn't look up.

"If the delivery boy makes it by this afternoon, we'll
have bok choy and rice for dinner," she said, hoping
to cheer them. She could get the familiar Chinese cab-
bage at the market if she wanted to pay top price for
it, but the vegetable men from the city's outskirts made
their rounds once a week, bringing overloaded carts of
not only better quality, but cheaper-priced produce. It
helped them save on the mounting bills of feeding so
many houseguests.

The announcement got her a few nods and one smile.

"No babies today?" one girl asked. The girls knew if
she didn't show up, it meant she was busy with her other
work.

"Not that I know of," Jingwei answered.

Over the years, Jingwei had built a reputation as a

sought-after midwife. She wasn't sure if it stemmed from the memory of her own miscarriage so long ago, but she worked passionately, trying everything she could to keep the expectant mothers from feeling the guilt and sorrow that came from losing a baby.

Kitten moved in and around the women, meowing for a morsel of food. The cat was older now, having come with them from the ship they'd taken to America, but still hadn't lost her need for constant attention and affection. She made a good mascot to the atmosphere of ever-changing residents, always curling up in the laps of the most needy to share comfort and warmth.

Jingwei scanned the room for the newest addition to their small group, then saw a mound under a pile of blankets in the corner. Most likely exhausted from what Sun Ling had called one of her closest calls yet, Jingwei wasn't surprised that the girl hadn't roused. There would be time to comfort her later, when she decided to join the others. For now, if she was awake, perhaps she listened. Jingwei made a mental note to speak louder than usual.

She sat at an empty stool, a place of honor always waiting for her. Kitten crept over and hopped into her lap, settling herself into a circle of fur.

"We cannot change what we don't acknowledge," Jingwei began, then took a deep breath. "In us, we all have a story, and it took a long time before I gave voice to mine. Now, I hope in this circle of sisterhood, we can all expunge the poison that is our past. Spit it out, examine it, and then learn from it before we move on to a healthier path."

Some nodded. Nobody spoke.

"While a few of you have heard it before, I'll share my story first. Then you can think about if you'd like to share yours today. Once we are through with today's healing, we will work on writing our letters and speaking basic English words."

That got a few grimaces, but Jingwei would not let them procrastinate the lessons. They were in America, and if they planned to build better lives for themselves, they'd need to be smarter and shrewder than the average Chinese immigrant.

"So," she began again, "I come from a village in Canton, China. As I remember from so long ago, it was situated on the banks of the Si-Kiang River. My home was a one-story brick house with a stone wall surrounding it, and at all times we had dogs, cats, and chickens running free. I felt the most happy when I was with the animals, and I, along with my brother and two sisters, chased them at all hours of the day. But my favorite memory is of the mornings with my mother, when she took me with her to the flower garden and taught me the names of every bloom."

She almost smiled thinking of the ease in which she used to run around her childhood home, or squat in the garden among the blossoms, her feet strong and steady and free of pain.

Jingwei could no longer remember their faces, and speaking of her siblings after so many years of keeping her secrets was difficult, but she reminded herself that the women before her likely had stories very similar, and over time, she'd learned that keeping it all to herself only resulted in a burden too heavy to bear. She didn't want that for them, and she didn't want it for herself any longer.

The truth shall set you free. Wasn't that what was always said?

If true, she should have been soaring above the clouds because people were finally learning who she was and where she came from. "During my youngest years, my mother was allowed to keep me at home, but soon my days of chasing animals and playing in the flowers were cut short. I was made to stay in a big house with my sisters and the other girls from the village."

"It was the same in my small town," said a young woman named Yung. "The boys were gathered under one roof, the girls under another. I slept in a room with more than thirty others. I was jealous of my brothers because, while we were made to stay indoors, at their communal house they played outside all day. What was it? Some sort of game with a ball—I think they called it yin."

Jingwei smiled. It wasn't all bad being separated from her parents. Some memories of the house of girls were fond ones. But that wasn't what she was here to discuss. "We had a farm, but it was located a good walking distance from the village, and my father went out there every day to work, then returned home in the evenings. When we fell into hard times and could no longer hire laborers, my father took us back and set all of us to work. Many days we carried tureens from the canal to the gardens from sun up to sun down, watering the many lines of sweet potatoes, beans, peas, and others crops."

"Were you the oldest daughter?" one of the girls asked.

Jingwei shook her head. "At the age of eleven, I was in the middle. And when the drought came and the crops shriveled to nothing, my birth placement was the reason given for my father selecting me as the daughter who would save the family from starvation."

At this part, her voice got quiet, and she saw the bundle of blankets in the corner raise up and lean forward.

Jingwei cleared her throat and continued, "I was told that, if I didn't agree to be sold, we would all die. I believed it, too. At that point, we no longer owned any animals. They'd all been eaten long before. When I looked around and, for the first time in a long time, saw how skinny and malnourished my siblings were—my dear mother was—I knew what my answer would be."

"You had a choice?" another girl asked.

Jingwei shrugged. "I'm not sure. If I had said no, my father could've sent me anyway. But I could not refuse. My baby sister had dark circles under eyes and cried in her sleep from the pains in her empty stomach. My mother was a bare slip of herself, as she gave everything she had to her children. It pained me to see her so thin and weak. When my father said the price for me would feed the family for a year, I stepped forward."

"There's another drought been going on in China for two years now, and even more children being sold," one of the girls said.

"Were you a *jì nǚ*?" another asked.

"No, I wasn't sold as a prostitute. I was bonded as a *mui tsai* and sent to work for a wealthy family in Hong Kong." Jingwei still remembered that day, and though faces were now a blur, she could feel the anguish her mother held as Jingwei was pulled from her grasp, then handed over to the woman who would be her travel partner until Hong Kong.

"A bag of silver was placed in my hand, then in turn I gave it to my father." It didn't need to be said that this was the ritual long held in selling off a person. That the girls took the money willingly, then gave it to their fathers was an unspoken contract of agreement from all parties involved, even when in reality the one sold wasn't always in agreement. Some not even old enough to comprehend what was happening until they were ripped from their mother's arms.

"Rich family in Hong Kong?" called Xiao Xong, a woman who still held much anger. "Sounds to me like you led a very easy life."

Jingwei shook her head. "No, it was never easy, though I'm sure many of you had it much harder than I. Tomorrow I'll talk about when the mistress had my feet bound, but today, who would like to share part of their journey with us?"

A young woman who'd been with them a few months lifted her hand, then her face. It wasn't her fault, but the newer girls flinched. Bei Ming's skin was shocking, the scars puckered and faded, but still a vivid reminder of the acid she'd been assaulted with when the man who thought he owned her body had a moment of anger at her expense.

It had taken a long time, but she was one of the first Sun Ling had wanted to rescue—someone she'd known of during her short time in the city jail and had not forgotten. Out of all the girls who came through their doors, only Bei Ming knew that their boyishly brave rescuer was Sun Ling. Unfortunately, with Bei Ming's scarred face, she stood out, and thus far they weren't able to find a place that she could blend in enough to hide from her captors. So she stayed. And as they sought somewhere safe for her, Bei Ming's story was always a good way to get others to open up about their own.

"Yes, Bei Ming." Jingwei looked at her timepiece and determined she had a half hour before she had to report to the mission, where they knew only of her work for them, helping the Chinese write letters home and working with the children to learn English. She needed to keep the connection to have an additional resource for the women who came into her care, but Mrs. Montgomery would faint away if she knew that Jingwei herself housed her own flock of rescued doves.

"I was only seven when I was sold," Bei Ming began. "The journey was long and hard. After I arrived, they spent five years grooming me before I was forced to be a *jì nǚ* in the Chinese Quarter. You probably can't imagine it now, but in the beginning I was lovely enough to draw the biggest crowds and the most coins." She looked down at her feet for a moment before meeting their gaze again. "I ran away and found work in a laundry. But they found me after only a short time, and I was punished. They brought me back, and these last years, I've been made to work for the most sordid and depraved customers in the city."

She stopped for a moment, catching her breath. "After the accident, I was too fearful to step out against my keepers. I thought I was owned by a tong in the city, bound to them until death. Then, like all of you, I was rescued. And now I am here to tell you all that no matter what they try to make you believe, you never again have to belong to anyone other than yourself."

When the other girls didn't say anything, Bei Ming reached up and touched the place on her face that was ravaged. "And I don't mind this anymore. It's proof to me that I'm still here. I went through hell and came out alive. I consider it a battle scar."

Jingwei sat back on her stool and gave the young woman an encouraging smile. Finally, years after her wounds on the outside had healed, Bei Ming was beginning the process on the inside. Just as Sun Ling had promised, Bei Ming made an ideal addition to their work. She had a long way to go, but she'd eventually recover from the invisible wounds inflicted on her. Jingwei only wished she could say the same about Sun Ling.

CHAPTER FIVE

EVEN AFTER YEARS OF LIVING in Pacific Heights, it felt so different from Chinatown that you'd think it another world—at least, that was what was in Sun Ling's mind when the carriage pulled up the driveway to Adora's home and came to an abrupt stop. Before the driver settled the horses, Sun Ling admitted to herself she was tired. Emotionally as well as physically. Maybe even a little lonely.

Something had to change. She just didn't know what.

The door to the carriage opened, and she was surprised to see Adora's brother, John, poke his head inside and look around.

"Brother!" Adora exclaimed, interrupting their exchange with her outburst of delight. As always, she was John's biggest fan, especially since the early death of his late wife.

"Good afternoon, ladies." He put his hand out, helping Sun Ling down first, as she was nearest the door. His gesture brought back the memory of the first time she'd arrived at the Lane home, and how the driver had refused to offer his hand to her and Jingwei, disgusted by the color of their skin and the slant of their eyes. But here, so many years later, Sun Ling was treated more like family than hired help, though she still maintained some of her duties and probably received much more pay than the ill-mannered man from so long ago had.

"Sun Ling," John said, a light smile twitching under the handle-barred mustache.

"What are you doing home?" she asked, stepping aside to let him assist Adora.

"I'm in town for a conference," John said. "After hours of arguing with the city council about the stricter building and fire codes they should implement, I'm beat."

Adora shook her head. "We were just discussing those exact sentiments at the tea that Cousin Betsy gave last week. You would think, after all that Chicago suffered only a few years ago in that great fire, that those in charge would make sure San Francisco is better protected."

"My thoughts exactly, Sister. However, it's hard for them to set aside budget for something they can't imagine. I only wish they could've gone to Chicago like I did, and witness the devastation and loss of life. That would change things, to be sure. We most likely wouldn't be in this great depression now if there hadn't been so much related property loss there, which—on top of the post-war inflation and dislocations in Europe—continue to strain the bank reserves."

"Yes, Papa has been in the most turbulent mood ever since he's not getting top dollar for his imports any longer. If he'd listen to me at all, I'd recommend he stop his voyages to Asia and concentrate his efforts here in San Francisco with some other sort of business that can improve our economy as a whole."

"I agree. But enough talk of that," John said, then his expression changed to one less somber. "While I was here, I thought I'd stop by and see how the two loveliest girls of San Francisco are faring."

Sun Ling looked down at her outfit, hoping it wasn't too wrinkled. Today she wore a dark brown silk day dress with velvet floral designs down the sides. Over the years, she'd adopted fashions similar to Adora's, except every dress she wore was stitched by her own hand and not store-bought. She patted her hair, confident the French twist was still in place because of all the pins she'd added to hold the weight.

That morning, she'd fixed a long braided hairpiece around Adora's small bun, making her hair appear thicker and more elegant than it really was, but Sun Ling's hair was so thick on its own that no hairpiece was ever needed. She did, however, try to use Adora's Marcel iron on her hair, working for far too long to put some bend into her stubbornly straight hair before finally giving up after the second burn to her fingertips. After all her efforts, only a few strands had retained any curl whatsoever.

Not that John would notice. He looked weary, and she wondered if he was still up at all hours of the night, pacing the floor in guilt. A marriage of responsibility, he'd told her repeatedly. But that was before his slight wife took the fever and then her deathbed, without even a child to show for their few years of matrimony.

John didn't have to tell her that he felt his inability to really care for the young woman was what weakened her and made her susceptible to the illness that, after several weeks, took her in the dead of the night. He thought if he'd been more devoted, more passionate, then perhaps she would've fought harder for her life.

Sun Ling felt sorrow for him.

"I should be thoroughly peeved at you for staying away so long," Adora said, taking John's arm and leading him toward the house.

Sun Ling followed. She and John were colleagues of a sort now, bound together in their fight against the persecution of the Chinese in San Francisco. But they didn't talk much of their work around Adora and the rest of the family.

He looked over his shoulder and nodded at her. "Sun

Ling, if we can meet in the garden in half an hour's time, I'd appreciate it greatly."

"Of course," Sun Ling said, diverting her path and going toward the back of the house. She hated that, since his wife's death, he'd adopted a more formal attitude with her. Gone was the easy comradery and friendliness between them, his guilt spilling over into every aspect of his being.

What he wanted her for today, she did not know, but she hoped it was good news.

John didn't know of her late-night escapades. He thought she only served as a confidant and witness to her people's plights. He'd helped her once, saving her from prison time and possibly even death, and he wouldn't be keen on doing it again. She would never want to cause him trouble, but she hoped he never learned of the danger she was putting herself in and asked her to stop.

She busied herself picking weeds in the flower garden as she waited. She didn't acknowledge the sudden boost in her mood.

Finally, he arrived and beckoned for her to come sit at the bamboo bench. He knew the sitting area to be her favorite, a place Sun Ling came often to gather her thoughts. The bench faced the koi pond that the new Chinese gardener had put in place the summer before. Ah Kow, an elderly friend of Sun Ling's father who came to him seeking employment, had worked his magic and arranged a sanctuary infused with peace and tranquility. With the variety of lotus flowers and lily pads, and the gurgling made by the water flowing over the rocks and into the pond beneath, it reminded Sun Ling of a gentle Chinese garden. Sometimes Min Kao brought her father to visit, and the garden was the perfect setting for them to reminisce about the past, and work on rebuilding their future.

John ran his hands through his hair, sighing heavily.

"What is it?" she asked.

"I need your services," he said, looking around as though to be sure no one listened.

Sun Ling stifled a tremor within her brought on by the satisfaction that he felt her intelligent and worthy enough to come to for anything.

She nodded, encouraging him to continue.

"I've received a letter, and I have no one I trust enough to translate." He pulled a weathered envelope from his inside his jacket pocket and thrust it at her.

She took it and examined it, confused. Then she met his gaze. "It's addressed to you in English. And it was posted from a city called Truckee."

He nodded. "Someone wrote that part for him. Inside it's only in Chinese characters. Open it."

Sun Ling pulled the letter from the envelope and unfolded it. She skimmed over the crudely scrawled scripts before reading it aloud. "Please come quick. The Chinese need your help. A life-and-death matter. Signed, Jack Yan, proprietor of Truckee Laundry."

She returned her gaze to John. "What does this mean?"

"I heard from one of my colleagues that a few weeks ago. The citizens of Truckee tried to burn out the Chinese. Most of their Chinatown has been decimated, along with the businesses of a number of whites unfortunate to be located next to the Chinese. The only reason any of the town was saved was by actions of the quick-acting bucket brigade."

"But those responsible should have to answer for this!" Sun Ling said.

John shook his head. "Not only are they not being held responsible, they are blaming the Chinese. They've formed a committee called the Caucasian League, and they're boycotting all Chinese businesses and labor. They are even stopping shipments of rice and other supplies, trying to starve them into leaving. But I have my suspicions that the Chinese are not going quietly. "

Sun Ling felt sick at her stomach. "But what can you do from here?"

"I'm not sure what I can do at all, but I feel that it's my civic duty to at least travel there to see how this Jack Yan thinks I can help. I don't even know how he heard of me, but he must have gone to great trouble to find where to post a letter to me. The least I can do is see if I can be of any service at all. Perhaps he wants to be advised on his rights as a property owner."

"But you can't go alone. What if there is no one there to translate?" Sun Ling asked. "I'm sure this Truckee place doesn't have as many educated Chinese as here."

He looked at her, raising an eyebrow. "Are you offering?"

Sun Ling felt heat flush through her face. She thought quickly, searching her memory for anything that would help her appear less eager. Finally, she thought of something.

"I only ask because I have a friend who is looking to move away from here. I thought perhaps I could accompany you, and she could come, too. That way I can translate for you, and in return, you can help me give her a new start. She has experience with laundries, too, so perhaps this Jack Yan could use her."

They locked eyes. Could he tell that she was in dire need of a break from her dual life as a seamstress and a rescuer? Or that more than anyone she knew, it was his company that entertained her the most?

If he did, he didn't show it.

He nodded. "I think that is a very good trade-off. But I should warn you, Sun Ling. Traveling to Truckee will not be pleasant. There is some rough country to get through, and we're headed into summer, so it will be ghastly hot."

"I can handle any conditions," Sun Ling said, thinking of the sweltering Hong Kong summers and the long hours of working from daylight until dark. If he thought a carriage ride through the country was going to put her off, he didn't know her too well. "And my friend can, too. When shall we be ready to go?"

He took the letter from her and folded it, then pushed it into the envelope and set it back into his jacket pocket. When he looked up, his face held that determined look she'd come to know. She respected that even though it was unlikely he'd make a penny from the client, his own sense of right and wrong made the trip to Truckee necessary. Sun Ling hadn't met any other white men like him.

"I will need at least a week to wrap up my current case load, then I will be back for you. If you can take care of gathering provisions for at least two weeks, that will help me out. Just tell Bessie you are accompanying me to a conference to speak on behalf of your people. Don't mention Truckee, in case my father has heard of the unrest there."

Sun Ling nodded.

A journey with a change of setting. That was what she needed. And perhaps after a few weeks spent with Adora's brother, a compilation of his irritating ways would be just the thing to get him out of her head once and for all.

PART TWO
FIGHT OR FLEE

CHAPTER SIX

SUN LING FELT NAUSEOUS AGAIN. Outside the window, the scenery was a blur, if not from the bumping and grinding of the carriage on the uneven dirt roads, then from the boredom of long days traveling within the small confines of the stagecoach. She could feel the perspiration gathering under her stays. The temperature outside was mild enough, but inside the closed-in coach, it bordered on unbearable.

They hit yet another rut in the road.

"Damnation!" If she wasn't such a lady, she'd reach around and rub at the soreness in her backside, but instead she bit her lip, trying to focus through the pain.

"I see your grasp of the English language just keeps getting better and better," John said, a small grin playing across his lips.

Bei Ming clutched the leather handle hanging from the ceiling and let out a small laugh at Sun Ling before launching into yet another topic, a flurry of Cantonese filling the carriage.

Turning away from them both, Sun Ling wished yet again that she could ride in the box with Clyde, their plump driver, to at least feel a bit of breeze on her face. But that wouldn't be appropriate, and therefore John would never approve. But he shouldn't have anything to say, since he didn't warn her about how June in the

Sierra territory could be tricky—warm days with nights that could surprise you by turning bitterly cold.

Why had she ever agreed to accompany him on such an arduous journey? Every muscle upon her body ached with a vengeance, reminding her of her younger years when she was worked to the bone by the family she was bonded to. Her years in San Francisco had obviously made her soft, because she felt every jolt and thump as though a personal affront to her person.

On the other hand, Bei Ming had turned out to be quite the hardy adventurer. So relieved was she to leave San Francisco that she'd kept up a steady stream of Cantonese in Sun Ling's ear, telling her far too many stories of her life under the strong hand of the tong. At times, though, Bei Ming slipped into talk of other, more mundane subjects.

More than once Sun Ling had lifted her eyes to see John wearing a smirk, one eyebrow raised at her. He knew how she disliked idle chatter and didn't always feel comfortable in close confines with another female.

Jingwei was different. They were like sisters and knew one another as much as one human could. Sun Ling never felt uncomfortable in Jingwei's presence, even with long periods of silence. At least not until lately, when she'd felt attacked about her preference to live with Adora rather than her own father.

But that was all behind her for now, and all that stretched in front of her were more miles and probably at least more than a few more sleepless nights in questionable layovers.

She didn't even want to ruminate on the boardinghouses they'd been forced to stop at along the way. After the first few proprietors had refused to accommodate her and Bei Ming, they'd skipped by any others that looked like white establishments and looked instead for the Chinese parts of town.

Sun Ling's pride was greatly damaged that she'd been treated in such a way, but John took it in stride and seemed to gain a new friend in each small poorly-constructed home, among dozens of Chinese who'd settled in the tiny towns that dotted the Sierra. With his smattering of Cantonese and Mandarin, the Chinese immediately embraced John as a friendly comrade, and he was given their best rooms.

Among the Chinese, once they'd made clear they were under the foreigner's protection and not some shipped-in prostitutes, Bei Ming and Sun Ling were treated like spinster aunts. They made quite a colorful pair, she in her foreign traveling gowns and Bei Ming in traditional Chinese tunics with flowing pants, with her hair arranged to cover most of her scars.

At least their suppers in the Chinese dwellings were made up of tantalizing dishes, simple but authentic and delicious fare that had John begging for more. With his gushing compliments, the cooks beamed and offered dish after dish to the tall, wild-haired foreigner who had to duck to enter their homes.

The sound of wood splintering followed by the worst jolt yet sent Sun Ling out of her seat, landing her sprawling across John's lap. Across from them, Bei Ming held on tightly, her fear very vocal in a flurry of Cantonese curses.

"Whoa, whoa," Clyde yelled.

It felt like they'd left the road and were careening across a rocky prairie as Clyde tried to get the horses under control. Sun Ling struggled to get loose from John's grip even as he fought to keep hold of her. Just as she thought they were doomed, even headed for death, the rocking carriage came to an abrupt stop, leaning precariously to the right.

John extracted himself, and Sun Ling straightened, finding her seat even as she blushed scarlet.

"What the hell was that?" John asked, peering out the window. "You two stay in here until I see if it's safe."

Before anyone could answer, he threw open the door and climbed out.

Sun Ling, never one to be told what to do, followed, with Bei Ming right behind her. They stepped out into the dust cloud that hadn't yet settled, coughing immediately. She half expected to see bandits and would almost welcome the respite from her eternal boredom, but it was a much less dramatic scene.

The horses huffed, their heads bobbing in panic as Clyde stood between them, speaking gruff words as he stroked their flanks.

"What's going on?" John said. "You just about killed us in there."

Clyde pulled his rumpled hat off his head and used it to wipe the perspiration from his red face. When he looked up, he was obviously miffed. "On the contrary, I think I did a damn good job of keeping control and saving your lives. I just about got thrown out of my perch," he said, pointing at the far side of the carriage.

Sun Ling felt sorry for the man then. He looked quite shaken, and he had kept the horses from bolting, after all. But what had caused it?

"Oh bloody hell," John said, shaking his head.

She pulled the scarf from around her neck and held it over her mouth, trying to filter the dust from her lungs as she peered around him and saw the source of his irritation. The wheel was broken completely through, only shards of it still attached to the carriage.

"We're lucky it's only a wheel and not the chassis," Clyde said, stating the obvious.

"Can it be fixed?" John asked.

Clyde nodded. "I've got a spare, and we can try, but I'm not sure if it can be done with only two men. We might be camping out here tonight or until another traveler comes though."

Nearly an hour later, Sun Ling watched as John and Clyde tried once again to lift the carriage enough on one side to get the pieces of the old wheel off so they could fit on the new one. She and Bei Ming stood next to the horses, comforting them as they grazed a few feet from the shoulder of the road.

"It's too heavy," John said.

"Can we please help?" Sun Ling called out. "I might have some ideas."

"No, stay over there in case it falls," he replied.

The carriage still sat cockeyed, but they'd tried to stabilize it by stacking a trunk under the corner with the broken wheel. Everything else they'd brought was still piled on top, and Sun Ling was sure the bulk of the sacks of rice and flour were contributing to the impossible weight of the carriage.

"I still say we should unload everything," she mumbled to Bei Ming. "That's a lot of weight they are trying to lift."

Before they'd left San Francisco, John had made some inquiries and heard that some of the Chinese were having a hard time getting supplies in Truckee, so he'd decided to bring some with them. He said he'd distribute it only if the rumors were true, and he'd rather have it than not, in case the need was there.

"Why is he so stubborn?" Bei Ming asked. "All white men are that way, aren't they? They like to think and act alone, instead of compiling knowledge and efforts with others."

"John isn't like most white men," Sun Ling said, unable to keep herself from defending him even though she also was irritated at his pigheadedness. "He cares about—"

"C'mon ladies, come help unload?" John asked, unknowingly interrupting what might have become quite the spat over his honor.

Sun Ling fought back the urge to tell him he should've listened to her from the start. Instead, she positioned herself a few feet from him, beckoning Bei Ming to stand opposite her.

"This is the life of adventure, wouldn't you say, Sun Ling?" John said, grinning at their eagerness.

Despite his attempt at humor, Sun Ling noticed he was tired enough to finally accept their assistance. What he didn't understand was that they were a lot sturdier than most women he knew.

Clyde climbed to the top of the carriage and handed the rest of the suitcases down to John. John passed them to Sun Ling, who passed them to Bei Ming to stack by the roadside.

It was exhausting work, and once they got to the heavy bags of rice and flour, Sun Ling and Bei Ming took them from John together, working as a team to set them on the ground.

Next, Sun Ling stood ready with the new wheel while both Clyde and John leaned on the tongue of the carriage, trying to lift the vehicle up enough to allow them to dislodge the broken wheel from the axle.

There was a cracking sound, and then the trunk that was propping up the carriage buckled and split right up the side.

"Look out, girls!" John said.

Sun Ling was quick enough to recover when she recoiled out the way, but Bei Ming was knocked backwards by the jolt, and she caught her fall with her hands behind her.

Sun Ling helped her up and saw the trunk belonged to John.

"That trunk wasn't strong enough," Clyde said, easing off the tongue.

John glowered at him. "You don't say?"

They all stood back, eyeing the forlorn carriage as though it were a creature buckling under their disapproval.

Bei Ming pulled on Sun Ling's sleeve and leaned in, whispering in Cantonese. "We will have to wait for help. This is using up all their energy for nothing."

John held a hand up, waving it toward them. "Don't tell me what she said. I can only imagine, and yes, we need to stop and think about this."

Clyde walked a short piece away, taking cover behind a scraggly bush to relieve his bladder. He came out smoking a cigarette. "We're near Trout Creek, so it isn't far into town. I could try to walk it and come back with some help."

Sun Ling and Bei Ming sat on a few sacks of rice, and John paced around them. He was furious, probably at himself because he couldn't fix the situation, so Sun Ling stayed silent. Any more advice would only make things worse.

"No, I think we'd be better off waiting for someone to pass by. Anything could happen to you on the road alone," John said.

"As you wish," Clyde said, squinting up at the sky. "But it's getting dark. I say we make camp in case we are out here all night."

John threw his hands in the air, then pointed at Sun Ling. "The ladies can't sleep outside on the ground! I'm not going to put them in danger that way."

"John," Sun Ling said, "we can sleep outside just as well as you can. I promise we won't wilt like a couple of flowers."

"I've got bedrolls," Clyde said to John. "You and I can sleep next to the fire, and the women can keep to the inside of the carriage."

Sun Ling would've rather slept by a warm fire, but she held her tongue, knowing by the expression that John wore that he was almost at the end of his patience. Finally, he nodded, and Clyde unloaded another bag or two that was in his box.

"First things first, and we've got to find a better way to support this carriage," John said.

"We'll go gather some kindling for a fire," Sun Ling said, glad to get away from the two men for a moment or two. She reached into the carriage and grabbed her bonnet that had flown to the floor. She put it on and tied it beneath her chin, then set out.

Bei Ming followed, and they stepped off the road, walking toward the sound of rushing water. They began to gather small sticks and twigs.

"Clyde can find the bigger logs we'll need," Bei Ming said. "He probably ran the wheel over a rock and put us into this predicament. Let him sweat a bit."

Sun Ling agreed, just as her stomach let out a loud rumble. She hoped he had something in his bags to make a simple dinner, though she hated the thought of what would probably be a can of beans, if they were fortunate. Then she remembered the bags of rice and smiled to herself. Perhaps one of the sacks would accidently get a tear or two.

They worked together, and after they had what they thought was plenty of kindling, they returned the way they'd come.

John sat near a pile of larger pieces of logs one of them had collected. Clyde was beside him, cursing as he did his best to light a fire. The carriage still sat askew, but the chest had been removed from under it and now a larger tree trunk was there. Sun Ling couldn't imagine how the two of them had dragged it over there, but she was glad that at least it was a temporary fix.

They approached and dropped the kindling next to John. He looked up, raising his eyebrows at Sun Ling, with an imploring expression. She shrugged. Making fire was not on her list of skills, and she'd bet it wasn't on Bei Ming's, either.

"Let's get inside," Sun Ling said to Bei Ming. Their abilities wouldn't do any good until there was a fire, when they could try to put together a supper.

Carefully, trying not to upset the carriage, they climbed in and settled themselves amidst the personal valises that still remained. Sun Ling sighed. It could be a while before they were needed again.

Outside, Clyde let loose another colorful string of words. Sun Ling saw Bei Ming lean her head back and close her eyes. She followed suit. They might as well get a bit of rest before dinner.

Two hours later, Sun Ling and Bei Ming still sat in the carriage, shivering with cold and wracked with hunger. John, being the city boy he'd been raised to be, didn't know the first thing about making fire. As for the driver, he had no such excuse, and Sun Ling felt like wringing his incompetent neck. Without a fire, they'd been left to bundle up in as many clothes as they could while they nibbled on crackers.

"I don't like this," Bei Ming said, her Cantonese dialect heavy with discontent.

They sat together as close as possible, sharing their warmth. Sun Ling worried for John, out there on the ground with only a small blanket. She doubted he and Clyde were sharing anything, other than a few frustrated and colorful words.

Without the fire, they couldn't even boil drinking water, and their reserves were long empty. She didn't know what they'd do the next day when the sun was high in the sky, the temperatures warm again, and they were all even thirstier.

John just hadn't thought of packing for emergencies. Of course, bringing in staples in case they were needed in Truckee was a smart thing, but he'd neglected to consider them being stranded along the way.

"I'll never be able to go to sleep," Sun Ling said. She was beyond exhausted, but much too cold to relax.

"Wait—" Bei Ming leaned her head toward the window.

"What is it?"

"I hear something," Bei Ming whispered.

Sun Ling wasn't sure she wanted a visitor now. They'd hoped for someone passing by during the daylight hours, but in the dark, it could be anyone. What if they were about to be robbed? She listened and thought she heard the sound of hoof beats.

She leaned forward, pulling the canvas to the side to peek from the window.

At first, she didn't see anything, but as her eyes adjusted to the dim moonlight, she could make out Clyde standing outside the carriage, his stance protective as he held a rifle toward the impending visitors.

John wasn't in sight, but as he didn't have a gun, Sun Ling imagined he was hanging back somewhere.

The hoof beats got louder, and a few seconds later, a group of three horsemen came to a halt, their dust covering Sun Ling's view so that she couldn't make anything out.

"Get on outta here!" Clyde hollered, raising the rifle higher.

John came into view from the side, stepping between Clyde and the visitors. He lifted his hands as though to try to calm Clyde down. The dust began to settle while they argued, and Sun Ling gasped, then clutched Bei Ming's arm.

The shadows outlined in the moonlight were clear. She saw feathers. And a strong profile with a very distinct sort of nose.

Her gut lurched, and she jerked the curtain back as though she'd touched a rattler. They might never see Truckee, after all. One of her worst fears was about to be realized.

Indians.

CHAPTER SEVEN

IF JINGWEI HAD KNOWN THAT morning that her world would be turned upside down—she would've crawled into bed with Luli. Instead of waking and dressing her for school, she would've held her daughter tightly, refusing to allow fate to cause her grief once more.

But it was too late for such regrets.

She felt a wave of dizziness and backed against the counter, dropping her chin to her chest. This wasn't happening. She couldn't go through this again. She wanted to wake up and find that all was as it should be. The alternative was too horrifying to contemplate. Girls of Luli's age were often dragged into the dregs of society—some straight from China.

Min Kao put his hands on her shoulders, giving her a shake.

"Stop it, Jingwei," he said, his voice barely penetrating the roar in her ears. "We'll find her, but I need you to be strong."

"Someone has her," Jingwei whispered. Then she lifted her face, glaring at Min Kao, and shouted, "Someone has her!"

"We don't know that, child," Tao Ren said, the authority in his voice calming her when the desperation in Min Kao's couldn't. "Let's think through this and plan each step carefully."

Jingwei couldn't help it. For the first time in their marriage, she felt rage toward Min Kao and wanted to lash out at him. It was *his* responsibility to make sure their daughter was safe. He was the one who'd convinced Jingwei that Luli was old enough to walk home from class, joining other children her age. He'd reminded her that all the children in the Chinese quarter were allowed to be out without adult supervision—that some of them even played in the streets at all hours while their parents worked.

Min Kao should've been waiting at the door of the small shop that served as the local school. She thought of Luli, out there alone—or worse, not alone—possibly being sold this very minute to some depraved monster intent on buying children and doing terrible things with them.

Sun Ling! She had to get a message to Sun Ling to come home. Her sworn sister would turn San Francisco upside down if she had to.

She felt Min Kao shake her again.

"Jingwei, I need you to stay with me. Don't let your fears overtake your common sense. I need you. Think—did Luli say she had any sort of after school activity today?"

"No," Jingwei said, feeling numb as she realized it wasn't Min Kao's fault. It was hers.

When she'd braided her daughter's hair that morning, Luli had asked if Jingwei would be there when she got home from school. She would've too, if only the grocer's wife hadn't gone into labor! And then she should've come straight home after she wasn't needed there any longer, instead of going to the mission to help the illiterate to write letters home to China for an hour.

She was flooded with guilt. Because of all the other responsibilities that Jingwei had put before her family, she hadn't been home, waiting. She was the worst mother in Chinatown. Luli should've been her first priority, not her last.

"What about the girls upstairs?" Tao Ren asked.

"I've already been up there," Min Kao answered. "They haven't seen her."

Jingwei didn't know why he'd even asked that. Luli knew she wasn't allowed into the secret quarters. They barely even talked about the girls in front of her, as the less she knew, the better. Luli wasn't even aware that Sun Ling arrived in the deep hours of the night, the handler of the beginning of each girl's journey. Min Kao barely knew much. Tao Ren, as wise as he was, might have known more than he let on, but he didn't speak of it.

Everyone involved knew they played a game of life and death, especially because of those rescued from the tongs. So she and Sun Ling kept as much of it to themselves as humanly possible. There was less chance of their secrets being spilled that way.

Anyway, it wasn't as though Luli could get lost up there. They were down to only three girls hiding away, the rest of them having been sent off to their new lives or back to China, if that was their wish. The remaining three would have to remain until Sun Ling returned with more funds to help finance their futures. That was the way it went, sometimes—some leaving quite quickly if Sun Ling was able to sell more dresses or find more money somehow, however she always managed it. But when the coffers were low, the houseguests stayed until they weren't. As Sun Ling was often finding more girls she could rescue, at times the upstairs was quite full.

She knew her thoughts were circling in chaos, her mind refusing to latch on to the truth that her gut told her, that Luli was in danger.

She thought of something and straightened, feeling a

wave of hope.

"Min Kao, you must go to Lao Go's home. What if he took Luli to communicate with his wife again? She could be there. You must go. Now." She turned, gathering her bag from the counter. "I'll go with you."

Tao Ren put his hand on her arm, stopping her in her tracks. "But Lao Go didn't want her to talk any more to his wife. He was afraid."

"It's a start, Jingwei," Min Kao said, giving her an encouraging smile. "Perhaps he said something to someone else about her. He could give us a lead, even if Luli isn't there. And if she is—"

Jingwei saw the clouds cross his face, an expression she'd never seen him wear. She hoped that Luli was with the old man, but if she was, she felt a shiver of fear for what Min Kao would do to him for taking her.

"You wait here. I'll go there now," Min Kao said. "I can't imagine he would be that foolish, but maybe he was drunk and not thinking clearly. You should stay in case she comes home."

"I will not," Jingwei answered, lifting her chin, feeling a burst of strength now that they had a plan. "She's mine, too."

Tao Ren waved his hand at them. "Go together. I'm more than able to watch out for the child to return here, and if she does, I'll make sure she stays put. You two hit the streets before it gets dark."

Dark? Jingwei felt sick. Luli was afraid of the dark. They had to find her before the sun went down. She took a deep breath. She would not cower and buckle when Luli needed her.

She turned to Min Kao. "Let's go find our daughter."

Min Kao went to the door and held it open. Together, they stepped out into the street and were immediately engulfed by the lively mid-afternoon hustle and bustle of Chinatown.

Jingwei looked from left to right, scanning the literally thousands of dark heads, big and small, short and tall. How would she ever find one tiny girl in the raging river of humankind that flowed from one street to another, from the docks to the hills and back down again? It appeared an impossible task.

She prayed that Lao Go had Luli and was simply peppering her with questions about his deceased wife, with all intent of letting her leave.

CHAPTER EIGHT

L AO GO DIDN'T ANSWER ON the first knock, or the second, so Min Kao opened the door and went in. Jingwei followed, then went around him, her determination obvious as she searched the small, stuffy front room. She was on a mission, and Min Kao couldn't have stopped her if he'd tried, so he stepped aside and let her go.

Like many small houses in the area, the main floor was not only the daily living quarters, but also held a bed for sleeping and a small counter in the corner for cooking. An old wok and wooden spoon were next to a large container of what appeared to be cooking oil. The wire basket that hung over it was empty other than a few fallen onion layers, proof that it once held vegetables. Taking center court, though, was an emptied bottle of *bai jiu*. The room reeked of it and of unwashed clothes. Min Kao thought of Mistress Go and how disgusted she would be at how low her husband had sunk and the disarray her house now lay in.

"Where is he?" Jingwei said, looking toward the stairs. Even they were piled high with piles of unwashed clothing and blankets.

"Right here," a muffled voice said, coming from between the old iron bed and the wall.

Min Kao went to investigate and found the old man

wedged in there, one hand up as though in surrender.

"What are you doing?" he asked. "Have you seen our daughter?"

Lao Go struggled to get up, then let himself fall back again.

Min Kao pulled him up, and with his help, the old man managed to squirm out. When he got to his feet, he was out of breath, and he backed up until his knees were against the bed and sat again.

"I thought I had hidden another jug back there, but when I went to look, I couldn't get back up," he said, a drunken grin spreading across his face. "I've been wedged in there since about midnight last night."

Jingwei wrinkled her nose, and Min Kao guessed that the stench, stirred up by the sudden activity, had reached her. The combination of the liquor and the man's urine overpowered the room.

"He's drunk," she said.

"No, I *was* drunk," Lao Go slurred. "But I've slept it off in my hours of captivity. But I don't mind—at least the ghost of my wife couldn't find me there."

"Have you seen our daughter?" Jingwei said.

"No, and I don't want to. Why ask me that?" Go said. "If you ask me, that girl shouldn't be doing those things she says she can do."

Jingwei ignored him and took the stairs at a run.

"Hey—" Lao Go said, holding his hand up in protest.

"Stop it," Min Kao said, slapping his hand from the air. "Our daughter didn't come home from school today. We've come to look for her."

"So, what are you saying?" he asked, looking bewildered. "What kind of man do you think I am? You think I took your girl?"

Min Kao looked at him doubtfully.

Jingwei reappeared, and she shook her head. "She's not here."

"See," Lao Go said. "I told you. I might have me a little drinking problem, but I still have honor. I didn't take your child."

"I apologize, Lao Go, for the abrupt intrusion," Min Kao said, feeling ashamed. "As you can imagine, we're quite upset. We don't know what to do."

Lao Go looked at Min Kao as though he were daft. "Go to the police!"

"We can't," Min Kao said. "The first thing they'll do is ask for her identification papers, and we don't have any."

Jingwei descended the stairs and stood next to him.

"Now what?" She looked at Min Kao as though he held the answers.

Helplessness threatened to smother him. It was his job to protect his family, and now they were back to square one, and he didn't know where to look next.

"Now you get out of my house," Lao Go said, starting to look angry.

Min Kao felt guilty for being so suspicious.

"We're going. I hope you won't hold it against Tao Ren that we violated your privacy, Lao Go. He considers you a good friend and loyal customer. Come, Jingwei. Let's leave the man alone," Min Kao took Jingwei's arm, leading her to the door.

They were almost through it when the old man's voice rang out. "Yeah, you do that. I told your daughter just yesterday that if she wanted to keep her little trick a secret, she was hanging out in the wrong place."

Min Kao froze midstride. He let go of Jingwei and turned around.

"Yesterday? How did you tell her anything yesterday? That was a week ago that you were in the shop," he said, feeling his stomach drop. Maybe the old man did have something to do with Luli's disappearance, and he'd just slipped up.

Lao Go didn't respond.

"Min Kao?" Jingwei said, her voice heavy with uncertainty.

"Shh," he said to her, then strode back into the room and stopped in front of Lao Go. His hands shook with the need to squeeze an answer from the man. "I asked you how you told her anything yesterday. What do you mean?"

"I saw her at the undertaker's office down on Sacramento and Waverly. I went in to make a payment on the fancy funeral he threw for my wife. Your daughter and another child were there, working on paper banners. Not a good place to send your daughter to work if you don't want her talking to ghosts, I'd say," Lao Go said, shooting them both a disapproving look.

Min Kao looked at Jingwei and knew his expression was incredulous. "Do you know anything about that?"

She shook her head. "Yesterday, I knew she was going to be late, but she said she stayed after school to get extra help from the teacher on her final grade essay."

"But... she turned her essay in last week," Min Kao said slowly.

"What are you waiting for?" Jingwei said urgently. "Let's go."

Min Kao struggled to make sense of Lao Go's words as he and Jingwei weaved in and out of the crowded walkway in their rush to the undertaker's office. The idea that Luli could even be there was so far-fetched, it couldn't be true. But Lao Go had declared it so confidently—he had to know what he was talking about.

"Remember the other night?" Jingwei asked, "She asked how old she needed to be to get a job. Maybe he's not lying."

"She's seven."

"I know, but why else would she be there?"

Min Kao didn't know, but he hoped she was indeed there, safe and sound. The alternatives could be so much worse than Luli being drawn to a place that organized the remembrance of the dead.

Back out on the street, they didn't speak much. They moved through the crowds soundlessly, Jingwei in the lead, determinedly clearing the way for Min Kao.

When they arrived, Min Kao immediately saw Luli sitting on the floor with a boy a few years older, cutting around an outline of a funeral banner. The sight of her huddled in a room with funeral urns, incense, and even a few caskets displayed for sale was startling.

"Luli," Jingwei cried. She dropped to her knees and gathered her up in her arms.

Of course, Luli looked frightened, her glance from over Jingwei's shoulder meeting his with an expression that said she knew she was in trouble.

Min Kao glowered at her, ready to give her a piece of his mind. Before he could, though, the undertaker emerged from the back room, taking in the scene before turning to Min Kao.

"What is going on here?" he asked.

"That's what we want to know," Min Kao said. "Why is our daughter here instead of at home?"

Jingwei stood, pulling Luli to her feet. She gave her a small shake. "You have some explaining to do. You know you are to come straight home after school. You frightened me half to death."

"Your daughter asked if she could help Peso, and I said yes," the undertaker said. "I've got a funeral tomorrow, and we're behind on getting everything ready."

"Peso?" Min Kao asked.

"That's me," the boy said, looking up briefly before returning to his work. The ease with which he spoke their language was confusing, as his features—and his name—suggested that he was from a Hispanic heritage.

Min Kao returned his attention to the man. "We haven't given permission for our daughter to work anywhere. *Aiya*, she's only seven years old!"

"Luli, come on," Jingwei said. "We're going home. You should've asked us before coming here. What's gotten into you?"

"But I feel comfortable here, Mama," Luli said. "The people like me."

He wasn't even going to ask *what people*. Now that he knew she was safe, Min Kao felt irritation take over and smother the fear he'd held in his chest for the last few hours. He was done talking. He went to her and plucked her off the floor, put her over his shoulder, and headed out of the shop.

"You'll be feeling my strap across your backside when we get back," he muttered, struggling to keep Luli still as she squirmed in his arms.

Min Kao saw fear cross the boy's face as they passed him, but he didn't move from his place on the floor. Peso? What sort of name was that supposed to be? And how had a simple boy convinced his daughter to be so disobedient? He couldn't believe Luli's actions and disregard, worrying them so.

At the door, he shot the undertaker a scowl.

"She won't be back," he said, then headed out to the street.

Jingwei followed, and they both ignored the undertaker's words as he yelled at them that Luli wouldn't be paid if she didn't finish.

CHAPTER NINE

L ULI KNELT NEXT TO TAO Ren's chair, his hand
  stroking her head as she sobbed. Jingwei had to fight
herself not to go to her daughter and gather her up, con-
sole her that everything would be fine. But Luli had to
learn. San Francisco could be a frightening and dangerous place. She'd given them quite the scare.

"But he doesn't have a family," Luli wailed. "And I'm
his only friend."

Jingwei raised her eyebrows at Min Kao, who leaned
against the counter, his arms crossed.

"What do you mean, he doesn't have a family?" Tao
Ren asked.

Luli was smart. When they'd arrived home, she immediately ran to the old man for refuge. Now Min Kao
waited for her crying session to subside so that together,
he and Jingwei could decide how to discipline Luli
appropriately.

She looked up, tears staining her face.

"Peso's mother died, and the undertaker lets him stay
under his stairs. If he doesn't get enough work done
each day, he doesn't eat. I wanted to help him."

Well, that's concerning. Jingwei studied her daughter.
She had to admit, she was moved by Luli's emotion.
Not enough to ignore her behavior, but enough to be
curious as to what had driven their normally very obedi-

ent daughter to misbehave.

"Min Kao, I think we need to investigate this further," she said.

"Investigate what?" Min Kao said. "What I know is this: our daughter decided to partake in an activity without our knowledge or permission. That tells me she has a lot of explaining to do, and tears are not going to sway me from her blatant disrespect."

Jingwei went to Min Kao, leaning in to keep her words between them. "Just do this one thing for me first, Min Kao. Go back to the undertaker's shop. Just see if the boy is still working or if he's at least been given a rest and dinner. It is our duty to at least make sure he is being treated properly. Then come back, and we'll finish this."

Min Kao looked at her, locking eyes in a silent battle.

He let out a long sigh, then pointed at Luli. "Fine, but I'm not done with you yet, young lady. When I come back, there'll be no hiding behind your Ye Ye's arms. If you want to make grown-up decisions, you need to face grown-up consequences."

To Jingwei, he shook his head, then went out the door. She knew he would go. He might be full of anger, but it was driven by the fear that something had happened to Luli. Now that she was safe, he wouldn't ignore doing the right thing. It was the very thing that made him who he was, and it had drawn her to him in the first place.

Less than an hour later, Jingwei handed Peso a bowl. The first thing he did was pluck the green vegetables from the top of the rice and drop them into his mouth, smiling with pleasure. When Min Kao had returned with him in tow, the boy had gaped in incredulity at the quality of their home. His comments made Jingwei wonder just what type of squalor he and his mother had lived in, considering 'luxurious' was a description far from the reality of what their home really was.

His name was strange, his features even more so. His eyes were dark but rounder than others in Chinatown. His mouth full and shapely. He was tall for his age, as well.

The boy put the bowl down for a moment, then used both hands to scratch. Under his armpits, down his legs, and back up to his head—he clawed before shaking like a dog, then returned to his dinner.

"After you've bathed, I have some ointment I'll mix up for you," Tao Ren said. "It'll settle your itching."

Jingwei prayed it was just a skin issue and the boy didn't have lice.

"How did you get the name Peso?" Min Kao asked the boy.

Peso talked with his mouth full, a few grains of rice escaping and landing back on top of the bowl. "From Mama. She said me and one measly peso were the only things she ever got from my father before he disappeared."

Min Kao looked over the children's heads at her.

Jingwei blushed. She wondered if Peso's father was a Mexican, which would explain his appearance. How sad for the boy to have that story as the only knowledge of his father. She hoped Luli didn't understand the boy's proclamation.

"Let's get back to how you came to be with the undertaker," Min Kao said.

Peso looked saddened. He swallowed and put his bowl down. "Mama knew she was dying, and she made arrangements with him to have a proper funeral. She asked if he'd take me in, and the old man said yes, if I'd work for my keep. But I didn't know what a rude ogre he was until Mama died."

"How so, Peso?" Jingwei asked gently.

"At first he let me stay in school," Peso said. "Your daughter was my only friend."

Jingwei's heart swelled with pride at Luli's kindness, but she nodded for the boy to continue.

"But then he said I had to do more to help him ready the dead, and to make more paper banners. Then he put me in charge of digging graves. He gave me so much to do I don't have time for school. Most days, he said I didn't do enough to have dinner."

"When he didn't return to school, I went to offer help," Luli said.

"Don't you have any other family?" Jingwei asked him. She couldn't imagine the small boy digging a hole deep enough to lower a casket. But looking at the muscles that sat atop his wiry arms like ripe plums on a branch, she didn't doubt his story.

He shook his head. "My mother's family is in China."

Jingwei felt terrible that Peso was trying to get over the loss of his own mother even as he was surrounded by death.

"Baba, there was a funeral yesterday, and you should hear the ladies in the white dresses," Luli said. "They cry like there's no tomorrow."

Min Kao smiled. "They're paid to do that, Luli. They aren't really sad."

Luli looked confused, and Tao Ren reached over and patted her hand. "Don't worry, little one. It's only that some people come here from China and don't have enough family with them to make for a proper funeral. So the undertaker arranges for people from the community to participate and help send the deceased to the afterworld."

Min Kao put down his own bowl and took a long sip of water before turning his attention to Peso again. "You are welcome to stay with us for as long as you need," he said, looking at Jingwei for agreement. "What the undertaker did was not right. Here in America, many are taking advantage of child labor—especially when it comes to the Irish immigrants' children. But whether Irish, Chinese, or white, a child should not be worked like a mule. Cutting out banners is one thing, but keeping you out of school to dig graves, making you suffer for your supper—that should be a crime."

"I told you, Peso. I knew my baba wouldn't ever do something like that. We should've come to him, and he would've helped you earlier."

Peso had stopped eating and sat staring down at his bowl, leaving the remains of the rice untouched.

Silence settled around the table until Tao Ren cleared his throat. "You can sleep downstairs with me, and you'll go back to your studies. As long as we have a roof over our heads, we'll share it with you."

Finally Peso looked up. "I can work to pay for food and shelter here. I swear, I'll get a new job tomorrow."

"You'll do no such thing," Min Kao said, his tone making it clear there'd be no argument. They didn't have much, but what they did have, they could very well share with one small boy, without expectation of anything in return. "You'll return to school."

Peso looked at him, nodding. In his eyes, Min Kao saw tears of gratitude. The boy was strong-willed and hadn't wanted to admit it, but he was obviously relieved to be free from the place of so much grief and drudgery.

CHAPTER TEN

SUN LING NEARLY DOVE OUT of the carriage when she saw John plant himself firmly between Clyde's rifle and the Indians. The hefty man was practically shaking with fear, his finger on the trigger, ready to blow someone away.

Sun Ling would not let it be John. She stumbled out so quickly that she lost her footing and fell forward, tripping on her skirts and bracing her fall with the palms of her hands. She stood, brushing them off.

"Wait," John said to Clyde, his hands in the air. "They're not dangerous. Don't shoot!"

The Indians didn't look in the least frightened. The obvious leader, an elderly man, didn't flinch at the sight of the gun. The two women with him were equally as calm.

Sun Ling stumbled over until she was back to back with John, facing the trio on horseback. She didn't want him to get an arrow through him while his attention was on Clyde.

"Move out of the way," Clyde said. "They're savages and will scalp us and leave us for dead."

They didn't appear as though they were prepared for battle, and Sun Ling didn't think they were looking for any trophies to take back to their tribe. She could've been wrong, but the feeling she got was they were harmless.

"No, they won't," John said, his voice low and calm. "He does not appear to be a warrior, and if you hurt him or his maidens, we'll have an entire band of Indians at our feet by morning, and yes, then we'll be dead. Let's see what they want, and perhaps they'll go peaceably."

The Indians still didn't flinch, but the youngest female caught Sun Ling's eye and held it. She looked curious, her gaze going from Sun Ling's hair twisted up behind her head, down her traveling gown and all the way to the embroidered boots on her feet.

The elder Indian took his time looking around, first at the broken wheel, then at the each of them, before pointing at the ring of logs and kindling, tilting his head inquiringly.

"John, he's asking about making a fire," Sun Ling said.

Clyde must've been colder than he was scared because he lowered his rifle and stepped back, muttering to himself or saying a prayer—Sun Ling couldn't tell which.

The elder man said a few unintelligible words, and the two women slid off their horses and disappeared into the dark. Sun Ling noticed then that the Indian carried a long lance lined with feathers. He wore many layers, some of the outer ones made from animal furs. His solemn face held no war paint, but the deep lines and grooves indicated a long and potentially traumatic life.

"What are they doing?" Clyde said, "Where are they going?"

"Just be still," John said. "Your paranoia is going to make this into a dangerous situation."

The two Indians returned, carrying handfuls of leaves and moss that they dropped on top of the gathered logs. The younger of the two women went to the elder, and from his robes he pulled out a stick and a small square piece of wood and handed it down to her.

She returned to the logs and knelt down, pushing her skirt to the side. She began to spin the upright stick into the small square.

After only a few minutes, a small puff of smoke arose. The other female gathered the leaves up in her hands and blew gently, urging the smoke into a tiny flame that grew stronger until suddenly it erupted and she put the pile back down on the logs.

Sun Ling could've embraced them both then, but she thought of the bag of rice and went to retrieve the pot stored under her seat.

"Bei Ming," she said, opening the door to the carriage. "You can come out."

"Are they gone?" Bei Ming asked from behind the lap blanket where she'd hidden her face.

"No, they're friendly. We have fire! Hand me the pot, and I'll go to the river for water."

Bei Ming brought the pot out from under the seat and handed it to Sun Ling. She peeked out the door and, seeing the elder still on his horse, retreated quickly again.

"I'm not going out there," she said, her voice shaking with fear.

"Well, stay here, then," Sun Ling said. "I'll bring you some supper as soon as we have it."

When she returned to the group, Clyde hadn't moved. He leaned against the carriage with the gun resting across his arms. John, however, was doing his best with hand signals to thank the Indian. He rubbed his stomach and then pointed to the pot Sun Ling carried, then used his hand to make an eating gesture.

The elder nodded, then soundlessly slid from his horse. He went to his bags, pulled out the contents of a small leather bag, and offered them to John.

Sun Ling waited for the water run, wanting to see what it was.

John held his own hand out, and the elder dropped

what he was holding into it. John smelled it, then pulled one small dark piece from it.

"Chicory root," he said, his smile evident in the fire glow. "Let's make coffee."

The youngest of the Indian women came to Sun Ling then, gesturing for the pot. Now that she was closer and there was light from the fire, Sun Ling could see had a very kind face and was very young, just at the cusp of becoming a woman. A single turquoise feather dangled from a tiny braid in her hair.

Sun Ling handed her the pot, and the girl set it down, then went to her horse and untied a basket. She quickly disappeared into the shadows, headed toward the river.

Not to be left out of the activity, the other Indian woman—possibly the girl's mother—disappeared, too. Sun Ling felt useless, even as she stood rubbing her arms, cold from head to toe.

John noticed and came to her, removing his jacket and placing it around her shoulders, then gently guiding her to get closer to the fire.

"I'm going to go try to get Bei Ming to come out and warm up," he said, then went to the carriage.

Clyde emerged from the shadows with his coffeepot and a skillet, shaking the beans around in the pan before setting it down next to the fire. Then he actually made himself useful and pushed rocks closer around the fire, then constructed something from sticks that he could hang the water pot from.

The elder watched him, his face completely impassive and possibly unimpressed.

Before long, the two Indian women returned, one with a basket filled with water and the other with a large trout hanging from a tiny string. How she had caught the fish in the dark, in such a small span of time, was beyond Sun Ling, but she was grateful. They'd have fish with their rice.

Sun Ling took the basket from the girl, marveling at how much lighter it was than toting a heavy pot. It was woven tighter than any other basket she'd ever seen, and no water escaped from the seams. She filled Clyde's coffeepot before dumping the remainder of the water into her pot, then hung it over the fire. They'd boil water for drinking first, then fetch more from the river to boil rice. She was light-headed and so thirsty she could barely even make moisture in her mouth, and she eyed the water, urging it to boil.

Beneath the pot, Clyde set the skillet on the fire and poured the coffee beans into it, letting them sizzle. When they'd cooked enough to cover the area with a strong but tantalizing smell, he removed the skillet and set it on the ground, then used his ax handle to crush the beans before scraping them into the coffeepot.

John returned, guiding a terrified Bei Ming to stand beside Sun Ling. He then handed Clyde the chicory, and Clyde added it to the coffeepot, then set it on the fire.

At the sight of the fish, John clapped his hands, bowing in front of the Indian holding it in a gesture of thankfulness. She nodded, then took the fish over to a rock and pulled a knife from her belt. She sliced through the fish and began cleaning it.

John gestured for the elder to join them, and the old man complied, coming over to squat next to the fire. Sun Ling didn't know what to do—the women worked so quietly and diligently, taking care of everything—so she stood behind them, waiting for the water to boil.

"Bei Ming and I would like to cook up some rice after we get more water," she said to John. "It will go nicely with the fish and make dinner go further."

They would obviously need to share the dinner with the Indians, a thought that made her a little fearful but also excited. She couldn't wait to tell Luli of her adventure. Who did they know that had survived an encounter with Indians?

John nodded and went to the stacked sacks, pulling the top one from the pile. He brought it closer to the fire and used his knife to cut a small slit in the top corner.

"Rice will be good," he said.

The woman returned with the fish, now sliced into bite-sized pieces, and she ignored the skillet, choosing instead to lay the meat on the rocks closest to the fire.

They all gathered around the fire, warming themselves as they waited.

"I know a bit about these Indians," John said. "Their territories have been flooded first by those seeking fortune in the gold rush, and then when the dream faded for many, the men became loggers and have been stripping the forests to help build up all these new towns popping up."

"Doesn't that hurt the Indians' chance of survival?" Sun Ling asked.

John nodded. "Of course it does. I believe these Indians are from the Washoe tribe, and their usual diet consists of things they gather from the woods—seeds, wild onions, currants. They also eat rabbit and fish, but unfortunately for them, the lakes that were once bountiful are now becoming depleted."

The elder let out a grunt, as though he agreed with John.

Sun Ling wondered now if this was a grandfather, his daughter, and granddaughter, and what they were out doing alone without their tribe. She felt sad for the Indians as a whole, forced to share their own land with the whites who tended to lay claim to everything, including what wasn't theirs to claim. She had no doubt that once the lands were completely populated with the whites, the Indians would be driven out.

The water finally boiled, and the Indian girl took it from the fire, using her skirt to hold the pot as she poured it back into the basket, before disappearing into the shadows with it again.

"She's going to go cool it in the river," John said.

Sun Ling grabbed the pot and followed. She wanted to get more water so she could get the rice started. She would've been too frightened to go to the river alone, but with the obvious competency of the Indians, she felt secure.

Sun Ling tried to stay close to the girl, following her shadow through the brush. She paused once, then when Sun Ling caught up, she continued.

At the river, she knelt on the bank and placed the basket of water into the river, holding it carefully as rivulets swirled around it. Sun Ling moved in next to her, tipping the pot sideways to catch enough water to boil rice. After she filled it, she set it on the bank and waited for the girl, marveling at the miracle of a basket woven so tightly that it would hold water.

With the moonlight brighter now, Sun Ling could see the girl was looking at her, searching her face.

Sun Ling smiled, and the girl reached up with one hand, touching her hairclip before smiling back and once again holding the basket steady.

"You like that?" Sun Ling asked, then carefully removed the pearl-encrusted clip, letting her hair fall around her shoulders just like the girl's, except for the small intricate braid that held her hair back from her young face.

Sun Ling held the clip out, cradling it in her hand like an offering.

The girl eyes widened as she set the basket of water on the bank, then reached out and touched Sun Ling's hair, running her hand down it before doing the same to her own. Then she touched her eyes, and pointed at Sun Ling's.

"No, our eyes are not the same, but you are right, our

hair is," Sun Ling said, laughing gently. She wondered if the girl had never seen a Chinese before now.

A laugh rang out, an imitation of Sun Ling's. Then the girl took the clip, sliding it into a pocket hidden somewhere within the skirt she wore. She then reached down and pulled the moccasins from her feet, handing them to Sun Ling.

"Oh no, I couldn't," Sun Ling shook her head. The moccasins were well worn, but could possibly be the girl's only thing of value. They appeared to be made of deerskin, and the dangling beads made a slight tinkling sound when they moved.

The girl nodded emphatically, pushing the slippers into Sun Ling's hands.

They felt soft and so pliant and luxurious. Sun Ling didn't want to take them—she didn't want to leave the girl shoeless in the cold temperatures—but she also didn't want to insult her by refusing again. She gathered them close, exclaiming over the workmanship.

"*Xie xie*," she said, reverting to her own language to thank her. She then pointed at her own chest. "Sun Ling."

Then she pointed at the girl and tilted her head in question.

"Dubuda," the girl said, slowly enunciating the name, her hand on her chest.

Sun Ling felt a kinship with the girl, a sisterhood similar to that she knew with Jingwei, something felt deep in the soul. Emotion overwhelmed her, and she swallowed past the lump in her throat.

Together they stood with their water, pausing to look at one another for a moment before silently returning to the campsite. With a few traded gifts and a moment in the moonlight, a friendship was born.

CHAPTER ELEVEN

SUN LING WATCHED JOHN AS he pointed out the carriage window, exclaiming over something. Whatever it was that he saw, it made him squirm in his seat like a small boy. To Sun Ling's dismay, he barely looked tired, a direct contradiction to how she knew she appeared, worn and exhausted from being on the road all night to make up time lost with the wagon wheel.

"What is it?" she asked, barely caring. She was lost in thinking about all the work that awaited her back in San Francisco. A wealthy family friend of Adora's was planning a gala, and thus far, three young women had commissioned Sun Ling to make them something unique to wear. Just what design she'd use, she hadn't yet decided, but after she returned, she would have to work like a fiend to get them completed in time. She hoped to be so secure one day that she'd only have to dress herself, not half of San Francisco.

"Just look," he urged.

Sun Ling expected another sunset, tumbleweed, or random coyote to be staring back at them. For the entire journey, John had exclaimed over the different aspects of nature and wildlife around them, enjoying the contradiction from city life.

Without San Francisco's organized crisscross of streets and lanes, shops, and manicured lawns, Sun

Ling's world felt out of control. A country girl she was not, and she hoped to get their business done quickly and get back to civilization.

But it wasn't another tumbleweed or starving coyote. Outside the window was a small township, but this time she saw a hand-painted sign welcoming them to Truckee, with population numbers carved above it that Sun Ling couldn't make out.

"What is it?" Bei Ming asked. She couldn't yet read much English.

"We made it," Sun Ling answered, unable to keep the relief from her voice. Her eyes lighted on the many great piles of sawn logs, dotting the landscape between the steep-roofed houses. Made of sun-bleached clapboard, the homes and buildings were placed haphazardly down the length of the dusty main road. On plenty of the worn porches, men congregated, some of them smoking, most of them swigging from brown bottles of what was most likely the infamous white devil moonshine she'd heard talk of.

"We sure have," John smiled widely. "Four days, almost two hundred rugged miles, a half-dozen changes of horses, an encounter with Indians, and finally we've arrived in Truckee. Let's hope Mr. Lau is still here and in need of my services. We wouldn't want this trip to have been for naught."

Sun Ling didn't answer. Her mind was on the encounter with Indians that John spoke of. On Dubuda, her new friend.

After they'd returned to camp, the girl had retrieved another pair of moccasins from her bag and pulled them on her feet. Then they'd gathered for supper, but before they'd eaten the rice and fish, the elder had set aside a small portion, then bowed over it and gave thanks. He hadn't allowed them to eat the portion he'd set aside, and John said it was an offering to their maker, asking forgiveness for taking the life of the trout.

Sun Ling had never thought of meat that way and felt shame for her years of indifference when it came to where her meals came from.

After their dinner, the elder had worked with the horses, guiding them to drag the carriage to rest on a large rock that was on the side of road. With the solid support it gave, John and Clyde—and the Indian women—had been able to put enough weight on the tongue to lift the carriage high enough for Sun Ling and Bei Ming to pull the bad wheel free and replace it with the new one, their actions directed by the elder.

It was still dark once the carriage was repaired, so they all decided they'd stay put until morning to ensure no more accidents happened.

After that was settled, they began their goodbyes to the Indians, and John pointed at the bags of rice and flour. The elder accepted, and John and Clyde loaded their horses with as much as could be carried. Even Clyde had warmed to those he'd first declared savages, and he had gifted the elder a small bag of coffee beans.

Dubuda had held Sun Ling's gaze as long as she could before the small band headed off the road and into the countryside, all evidence of them having been there— and rescued them—gone without a trace.

But the memory would stay.

"This town must be doing very well," John said, pointing out the window to a sparkling silver fire engine parked near the road. "It will take the calmest team of horses to pull that monster, though."

Sun Ling thought of Dulin and felt a wave of home-sickness. Ah Kow, the gardener, had promised that he'd ensure the stableboy took care of the horse, and that he'd give Dulin an apple a day and plenty of affection. Sun Ling hoped he held up his promise and that Dulin didn't feel abandoned.

They hit a bump, and John leaned nearer. "You both stay near me. I've been told this is a rowdy place. We'll most likely see it all while we're here—gunfights and all sorts of nonsense. I don't want either of you getting caught up in any trouble. I checked into things, and I know there is some anti-Chinese unrest going on, so stay on guard."

Sun Ling sighed. "I can take care of myself, and I'm sure Bei Ming can, too."

Bei Ming might have been intimidated by the Indians, but from what she'd confided in Sun Ling, she'd held her own for years in bawdy saloons, opium dens, and probably worse.John stared at her intently for a moment. "I almost wish I hadn't asked you to accompany me. I hope I haven't put you in more danger than I'd imagined."

He had told Clyde what to look for, and soon, the carriage stopped in front of a tall but narrow wooden building, with a neatly printed sign over the door stating *Truckee Laundry.*

Clyde jumped down from the box and came to the door, opening it and allowing the whiff of freshly laundered sheets to swirl around them. John climbed out first, then held a hand out to first Sun Ling, and then Bei Ming, to help them down. He led the way, and they followed up the wooden ramp to the porch.

Across the street from the laundry was what appeared to be a small general store. A pair of men leaned against the tying post, peering between the horses to watch them. Both looked rugged, one sporting a long, shaggy beard and the other a mop of rusty-colored hair sticking out from under his hat.

"Hey mister, you got you two Chiney ladies instead of one, huh?" the redhead called out, then spat a long stream of tobacco from the side of his mouth. "How about sharing?"

Sun Ling turned and scowled at them.

"Ignore them," John said.

"Oh—lookie there at that dirty look she done gave us. One of them is a she-heathen!" the other man yelled. "How much for her?"

"Barbarians," John said, standing aside to let Sun Ling and Bei Ming pass him by so he could be in the rear. "Not worth a response."

On the porch hung a sign with prices on it, and Sun Ling paused to read it.

Shirts 7cUnderdrawers 7c

Shirts Plain 12cShirts w/starch 14c

Undershirts 7cPajamas Suits 18c

John pushed open the door and the bells attached to it clanged loudly. They were immediately hit with the heat of the steam. They entered and let the door close behind them. Sun Ling felt prickly within two seconds, and she pulled her collar, trying to loosen it.

Bei Ming lifted her nose and inhaled. "Nothing smells finer than the inside of a laundry," she said, her words fast and choppy.

"What did she say?" John asked.

"Doesn't matter," Sun Ling said. The bells on the door had alerted the proprietor, and he hurried out, his face shiny with perspiration.

"How can I help you?" he asked, leaning against the counter. He took a handkerchief from his pocket and wiped his brow. He appeared exhausted, almost as though without the counter there to lean on, he would fall down.

"Are you Jack Yan?" Sun Ling asked, quickly taking position as translator.

He nodded.

"This is John Lane, the lawyer you wrote to in Oakland," she said.

The man looked from Sun Ling to Bei Ming, then to

John. When the realization hit him, he put his arms on the counter and laid his head down, hiding his face.

"Uh, Sun Ling," John said. "What did you say to him?"

She shook her head, confused by the reaction.

Bei Ming went to the counter and put her hand on the man's back, leaning down to whisper in his ear. When she rose, he did, too.

He wiped his eyes and murmured some words.

"He say he heard of you and his letter sent on wings of fate, he ask gods to send you here. He very glad you come save him," Bei Ming said, her English halting but heavy with emotion.

The back room had a small living area, and after he locked the front door, Jack Yan took them there. It wasn't much, just a tiny table to eat at, a few stacked boxes with kitchen tools, bowls and cups, and a cot pushed up against the wall where he'd obviously been sleeping. All around the room were worktables, stacked high with freshly washed and folded linens, and racks of hanging shirts. On the other side of the room, a fresh basket of sheets awaited to be folded and probably ironed, too.

Sun Ling was startled at how much work it appeared to be, and that obviously the man did it all alone. "Do you have help?"

Now that he'd pulled himself together, he moved briskly, a wiry bundle of energy that seemed to sprout from nowhere. "I used to have a few young fellows, but they finally had enough of their delivery baskets being upturned into the mud, their stacks of clothing strewn around, and the veiled threats left on their doorsteps with piles of burning horse dung. They've scattered to other areas where the anti-Chinese sentiment hasn't spread yet."

Jack Yan offered John his only stool, and for the girls he pulled up some overturned crates, then got busy making tea on a small gas stove in the corner. John had been around Sun Ling and other Chinese for years. There was a process of etiquette to get to before starting a meeting, and after shooting Sun Ling a knowing look, he waited patiently.

As the minutes passed, John talked and Sun Ling translated about the state of the entire country and how the situation against the Chinese had turned dire in many places, mostly because the economy was collapsing and bitter struggles between white laborers and officials wasn't helping matters.

While many white men no longer had jobs or ways to feed their families, the Chinese were continuing to keep their heads above water by selling vegetables from their wagons at rock-bottom prices, and working as domestic help so cheaply that those who'd never had servants before were taking advantage and hiring them. The disparity between those wanting the Chinese out because they were working too cheap, and those who continued to use their labor and laundering services, was like a fire keg, igniting and spreading from state to state.

How it was affecting an isolated community like Truckee, Sun Ling supposed they were about to find out.

Finally, Yan delivered each of them a cup before finding his way to another crate and sitting down with his own.

"Ask him to tell us what is going on," John said.

As Jack Yan spoke, telling them of the troubles he was facing, he paused for long breaks, allowing Sun Ling to catch John up. She felt sad as she relayed all the man and other Chinese in town and the outskirts had been suffering at the hands of those who wanted them driven out. Not only had Yan been working ten to fourteen hours a day to keep his business going, but in the midst of his exhaustion, he was hit from all sides with notices of eviction, late-night taunting, and even attacks on his person when he was out for deliveries. Supplies were also getting low for the Chinese, as the store owners were beginning to refuse to sell them flour, rice, or any sort of staples to survive on.

"If most of this is caused by city leaders, ask him what he thinks I can do," John finally said.

"He need white man on his side," Bei Ming spoke up.

Sun Ling nodded. "Jack Yan is a very smart man, but he does not know the American laws and feels the only way to stop these uprisings is to use their own rulings against them."

"Who owns this land?" John asked.

Sun Ling turned back to Yan, asking him. The narrative he shared was so shocking it was almost unbelievable. Even Bei Ming shook her head while he talked, and Sun Ling thought she'd seen much during her time in America. But this—what the so-called respectable citizens of Truckee had done to the Chinese—was reprehensible.

"A rich timber and railroad baron named Charles Crocker," she said. "And everything you see on this street, including this laundry, was burned to the ground just over a year ago by a fire that mysteriously sprang up from nowhere."

John sighed, rubbing his beard.

Yan rattled off more details about how it cost him his life savings to come to America and start the laundry, how it had been a success before the uprising started, but then it had taken every bit of profit he'd made over the last few years to rebuild it after the fire, so now he was worth nothing once more and couldn't even send money home to support his village.

At this point he had to stop talking to collect himself again.

"The fire burned all the Chinese homes and establishments, and before the fire train could put it out, it burned some white businesses, as well," Sun Ling said. "The town stable was demolished, along with a saloon and some other places."

"I'm sure their fire train of hoses and the bucket brigade didn't work too efficiently until the white part of town started blazing," John mumbled. "Perhaps they got what they deserved."

"He said he and others asked for a fire company to be placed in Chinatown, to guard against future fires, but the city officials refused."

John sat up straight. "But what about that shiny new steamer fire engine I saw as we came into town?"

Sun Ling asked Jack Yan.

"The whites purchased it from Virginia City, but only for their part of town."

Yan spoke more, telling of the vigilante committee that sprang up to try to prevent the Chinese from rebuilding—of their boycotts and ongoing demands on the community to refrain from hiring Chinese for anything or from using their services or buying their goods.

"Who is this committee made up of?" John asked.

Sun Ling could tell from the thunderous look on his face that Jack Yan had hooked him. John didn't like maltreatment in any form, to any class of people.

"They call it the Caucasian League," Sun Ling said.

John stood. "Well, tomorrow this Caucasian plans to pay them a visit. Ask him where he thinks we can find accommodations for tonight. Somewhere that won't turn away a Chinese or two."

Before Sun Ling could ask him, Bei Ming spoke in Cantonese. "I will stay here tonight and help him with all of this." She waved a hand in the air toward the piles of unfolded linens.

The grateful look that came over Jack Yan's face

almost brought tears to Sun Ling's eyes. She thought of her father then, a man who had worked years for the railroad and then walked away with a broken body, the efforts worth almost nothing. But he'd built it all again with his herb shop, one coin and one loyal customer at a time. Why was it fair for the white man to practically be born prospering, but the Chinese to continually fight to survive?

"We will help you, Jack Yan," she said, speaking for them all.

CHAPTER TWELVE

"IF YOU HAD COME INTO town from the other direction, you would've seen the plot of land the Chinese have grabbed to grow their vegetables. Some of the richest soil out there, and they've claimed it and enclosed it with a mess of sticks, stones, and gunny sacks," the official said, his jowls flapping with the impact of each bitter word.

Sun Ling pushed back her impulse to retort. She'd promised John she would behave herself, but it wasn't easy. She was already irritable from being awakened in the dead of the night by a bunch of drunks firing their pistols into the air. Even from the small boarding house in the Chinese part of town—a good distance from the saloon on the main street—the shouts and rounds could be heard until the wee hours of the morning.

Truckee was a not a reputable town, that much had been clear as she'd struggled out of bed a few hours before, exhausted and cantankerous.

"But doesn't the town benefit from the vegetables the Chinese grow and sell?" John asked calmly. "And who is going to wash your clothes and iron your sheets? Be honest with yourself—haven't the Chinese been fair with their prices for items and services? Haven't they worked hard to build their businesses?"

Reed slammed his hand down on the counter. "That's

not the point! That plot is land that we could be using to grow our own vegetables. Chinatown sits on ground that we could use to maximize our commercial areas of town. It's all land that was settled by our ancestors. It should be ours."

"Is that so?" Sun Ling said, unable to keep silent any longer.

"Sun Ling," John admonished, then turned back to the official. "If your ancestors settled it, then why was it empty when the Chinese came to town? Why was their money taken in exchange for deeds?"

Reed turned red, his face flaming even as he blustered in frustration. He clutched his suspenders, snapping them in display of his irritation.

John had asked for a meeting with the Caucasian League, but only one had agreed to speak to him, and that had taken three long days to even get the appointment. She and John had taken rooms at a Chinese boardinghouse, and Bei Ming stayed at the shop with Jack Yan, insisting he still needed her help.

After Sun Ling and John had divided out the supplies they'd brought and disbursed it as widely as they could to the Chinese who flocked around their wagon, they'd spent their time discussing the news that was filtering in from other counties. The anti-Chinese sentiment was moving across the state like a prairie fire.

In the midst of her turmoil of all that was happening, Sun Ling couldn't get her father out of her mind. Usually she kept thoughts of him compartmentalized, only giving him attention when he visited her or she came to eat Sunday dinner with them, but for some reason she could not stop the monologue in her head that berated herself for being a spoiled and disobedient daughter.

That didn't mean she wanted to give up her place with Adora, or the secret work she did in the late evenings, but she did make a promise to herself that when she returned to San Francisco, she would grant him more of her time. If she could only stop trying to prove to herself that her life meant something—that she needed to continue trying to undo the bad done to women like her, then perhaps she could become more of a filial daughter.

The appointed morning of the conference, bright and early, Sun Ling and John had hurried to the meeting room located over the top of the general store. On the porch, a young man tended to a row of barrels with mackerel and brine, and he gestured for them to go on in.

Once inside, they'd passed shelves lined with items like cutlery, charcoal, and tin cooking pans. Stacks of rice and flour stood in one corner, but a crudely written sign tacked to the wall above it read that it would not be sold to the Chinese.

A trio of men stood around a coal cooking stove, sipping coffee and watching them. One guffawed behind his hand when he saw her and John pause at the sign.

John had put his hand on the small of her back, leading her away from them to the back of the shop. Carefully they climbed the stairs and entered a small room where a smooth-faced, pudgy man sat at a table, the only piece of furniture in the room. He fiddled with a deck of cards, turning first one over, then the next, until he saw them in the doorway.

It took only a few minutes after introductions were made that it turned fiery between the two men. The official—Reed, he called himself—was irate that Jack Yan had sent for legal representation, and John insisted to him that every person, regardless of color, had a right to be treated fairly. From there, the words flew, and it was all Sun Ling could do to keep up with their conversation, as each belted out his opinion at every turn.

Finally, John paused, taking a deep breath before starting again.

"Let's cut to the chase here," he said. "It is rumored that you have cut off access to supplies for the Chinese. Is this true?"

Reed didn't answer.

"What is the matter? Can't speak now? What about employers holding owed wages from them?" John asked. "That's illegal."

"Their contracts have been terminated," Reed said, his voice smug.

"You owe them back wages."

"We want them out of our town."

John pointed a finger at Reed. "Then you should've thought of that before they were welcomed here and people like you made a profit from them. Tell me, were you one of the landlords that charged them rent for the last few years? Or did you, like many here, use their cheap labor to build your business? And someone in this town made a lot of money off the real estate transactions in the last seven or eight years, we all know that."

"Jack Yan and others like him own their land and property," Sun Ling said. "You can't take it from them."

"Who taught this chink to talk?" Reed said, gesturing at Sun Ling as he directed his question to John. "And why is she all fussed up in our women's clothing instead of the garb the rest of her people wear? What are you trying to pass her off as, a real lady? Is this one of them yellow concubines you men in the city keep?"

"I think we've said enough today," John said, rising from the table.

Sun Ling stood too. She could see the tic in John's jaw—the one that usually preceded his temper exploding. She wouldn't react to the man's insult, as that would make him feel validated. And she didn't want John getting into legal trouble, either. Especially not over her honor.

"John, you are right. We should go," she said softly,

putting her hand on his shoulder.

"I have one more thing you ought to hear," Reed said, looking at Sun Ling with disdain. "If you care for your people, you will encourage them to leave Truckee before it's too late."

"What is that supposed to mean?" John demanded. "Is that a threat?"

Reed pushed his chair back from the table and stood. "I'd say it's more of a promise."

With that he stomped out of the room, a whiff of an expensive cigar lingering behind him.

"Well, that went well," John said, looking at Sun Ling. She gave a small laugh.

John ran his hand through his hair. "I'm not sure if I can do much more than bluff the officials, but I need some time to think. This isn't over yet."

"Let's go talk to Jack Yan," Sun Ling suggested. She wanted to get John out of the general store in case Reed came back. The man had avoided seeing John at his most angry and didn't realize how close he'd come to real danger.

John let out a long breath of frustration, then followed her out the door.

At the laundry, Sun Ling and John entered to find Bei Ming hanging shirts across a long line of cable. The front of the store was just as neat as the previous day, but Jack Yan wasn't to be seen.

"*Jóusàhn*," Bei Ming greeted them, wishing them a good morning.

At her elbow was a bowl of congee, half emptied, and a small tin saucer of oil-fried breadsticks.

Jack Yan came through from the back room and gestured widely. "She is a very good worker," he rattled off in Cantonese, smiling at them. "Much better than boys who take off to the mountains, afraid of the whites."

"Mr. Yan, we spoke to a man named Reed this morning," John said, then paused for Sun Ling to translate.

"Mr. Reed is a bad man," Yan spat out before Sun Ling could say more.

She nodded. "Yes, that much was obvious. But let me tell you all that he said." She then caught him up on the conversation, stopping occasionally to ask John what else he wanted to add.

"All this, nothing new," Jack Yan gestured into the air as though dismissing the man's threats. "Tell Mr. Lane I have more Chinese coming here this morning. We talk."

Right on cue, the bell over the door rang, and a few Chinese men came through, dressed in loggers' clothing and looking around nervously. One carried an ax, and Sun Ling guessed they were a part of the large woodcutter population around Truckee.

As though she'd been mistress of the shop forever, Bei Ming gestured for them to follow her to the back of the store. The men pulled their hats off, nodded respectfully, and obeyed.

Sun Ling looked at John. He raised his eyebrows at her, then held his arm out to let her go first.

"I have nothing to tell them yet," he whispered into her hair.

"You will think of something," she turned slightly to reply as she passed. The feel of his breath against her skin sent tingles through her body, and she moved away quickly.

In the back room, she noticed a row of crates had been brought in and turned upside-down. The three men took seats upon them.

Against the far wall, Sun Ling saw a pile of white shirts, a large barrel of steaming water, and a washboard set up. She looked at Jack Yan again. His arms and hands were reddened.

John stood in the corner, and Sun Ling took her place beside him, ready to translate. Before they could start, the bell up front rang again, and two more men entered, taking seats and nodding at the others.

They decided to wait a bit longer, and soon, they had more than a dozen men lined up on the crates, looking at John and Sun Ling as though they held the resolution to all their predicaments.

Just exactly how they thought he could do them any good when even the town officials were against the Chinese, she didn't know. But at least John was open to discussing it and hadn't turned tail and run.

One of the men stood and went to Jack Yan, whispering fervently. When he finished, Jack Yan turned to Sun Ling. He looked stricken.

"This is my friend who works in the lumberyard for one of the white men who are not against us. He's been given a secret warning that tonight a group is forming to try to burn us out again."

Sun Ling gasped. What had they fallen into? What would happen to these people? Quickly, she translated to John. With each word, he looked more alarmed.

"We must get you and Bei Ming to safety," he said.

"John, don't think about us. These men need you right now," she said. "Go talk to the constable, or whomever is in charge. Surely he won't let this go on in his town."

The men began to chatter amongst themselves until John held his hands up, silencing them. He turned to Sun Ling again, his face grim.

"You need to explain to them that I can only try again to negotiate with the Caucasian League, but I give no promises that my words will not fall upon deaf ears. Let them know that it is not only they who are experiencing such travesties for being Chinese, but also their countrymen all around the states. Our priority today must be to gather water to have on hand for fires, and if these men have families, to get them somewhere safe."

Sun Ling nodded, ready to pass along the message. But she'd also tell the group one more thing—that they should be grateful because, thanks to the hopes of Jack Yan and his trust in fate, they'd secured the most honorable and trustworthy legal representative that could be found in the skin of a white man.

CHAPTER THIRTEEN

M IN KAO DIPPED THE RAG in the bucket of cool water, then wrung it out and put it across Tao Ren's forehead. June in California was usually warm, but this season was proving to be hotter than any he'd known since coming to America. There couldn't have been a worse time for the smallpox to come to their door and strike the oldest and frailest of them all.

Outside the sickroom, life moved on. Customers had lined up day and night before Tao Ren fell sick, and now Min Kao wondered if perhaps more than one or two of the loyal people they served was already sick and carried the pox to them, handing the virus over on each bill that changed hands and thereby exposing the lot of them.

He thanked the gods for Peso, as the boy knew the streets of Chinatown and had taken over all the deliveries, even venturing up into Nob Hill and other white neighborhoods when the occasional order came in. For such a small lad, he'd become integral to keeping things going as Min Kao tended to Tao Ren. Min Kao hated to put so much responsibility on him, but saw no other alternative if they wanted to survive.

But the fear against the pox was growing, and Min Kao even heard that some of the elder generation had resorted to the old tradition of inhaling pox scabs up their noses to keep the disease at bay. He'd discouraged each customer from such a drastic action, but something told him a few refused to listen.

It would seem that San Francisco in its entirety, not just the Chinese quarter, was in panic mode over the latest smallpox epidemic.

He didn't know what he'd do if it got to Luli or Jing-wei. Or even the boy.

"Water," Tao Ren said weakly.

Min Kao checked the water with his own lips to be sure it was no longer scalding before he held it out for Tao Ren. One of his first lessons from the old man had been about the benefits of consuming hot water to balance cold and humidity within the body, and to assist with blood circulation and toxin release. Even in the hot temperatures, Min Kao was sure Tao Ren would've scolded him if he'd brought him cool water.

After Tao Ren had sipped enough, Min Kao set the cup down and checked his pulse.

It fluttered erratically.

Min Kao picked up the paper fan and waved it over Tao Ren, trying to stir a breeze to cool him. The illness had started with a headache, then within a few days, Tao Ren hurt all over. None of his own remedies or even the concoctions made by Min Kao had brought him comfort.

At first they thought it a passing virus, but then the rash came and struck terror into both Min Kao and Tao Ren. Immediately the old man insisted on being isolated to keep from spreading the illness to the rest of the family. They were fortunate that all the rescued girls upstairs had moved on except one, and Jingwei had taken her to Adora and asked that the girl stay there at least temporarily. And with Sun Ling out of town, there would be no need to house any new guests.

Tao Ren had first sent Min Kao to find someone to

nurse him who'd already fought the pox and survived, but Min Kao had come up empty. All survivors either had left town or were nursing their own clans. Even if Min Kao had offered a copious amount of money—which he didn't have—no one would've agreed to accompany him to the shop to nurse one sick old man.

So it was up to Min Kao.

Tao Ren had remained stoic and determined, even when bearing the indignity of being carried up the stairs like a sack of rice. He'd insisted a pot of boiled water and a bar of lye soap be kept outside the door for Min Kao to wash up with after each visit.

Now the room felt large with only Tao Ren as its lone inhabitant. It would be a matter of days before they'd know if he'd pull through or not. Once his blisters erupted, if they scabbed over, there was a good chance of survival. If not, Min Kao didn't know how he'd cope, but arrangements would have to be made.

He heard a shuffle at the door. "Don't come in! Who is it?"

Luli's small voice rang out. "How is Ye Ye this morning, Baba?"

"He's better," Min Kao lied, his gaze on the raised blisters that had days ago been only a rash. "Now go back downstairs and help Mama with the customers."

"There aren't any right now," Luli said.

He heard her whispering and knew Peso was there, too.

"Go." Min Kao knew Luli and the boy were very worried. For all Luli understood, Tao Ren was her grandfather, having taken the place of those she couldn't or wouldn't ever know. The connection between them was strong, and Luli was full of fear for his declining health. And Peso—the old man had treated him as though the boy was a long-lost grandson.

He heard the sound of their footsteps receding on the

stairs and breathed a sigh of relief. Next time, he'd have to remember to lock the door. With both Peso and Luli so worried about Tao Ren, they could become anxious enough to disobey and sneak in to see him.

"Has she returned?" Tao Ren asked, opening his eyes for a moment.

Min Kao shook his head. He didn't have to ask who Tao Ren was referring to. It was all he'd mustered strength enough to speak of in the last few days. "She's on her way."

He'd lied again. Sun Ling probably hadn't yet even received the telegram that her father was sick. It would take a few days after she got it to make the return home. He just hoped she made it before—

He stopped himself. He would not think that way. Tao Ren might not have the strongest body, but his willpower was more than any man Min Kao had known. He would beat the pox and recover. There was no other option. They all needed him. The success of the shop was nothing without the man's wisdom and calm presence. And with him at the helm, the little family they'd constructed was whole.

Min Kao often thought of his own father and wished that man had possessed half the character and compassion that Tao Ren did. Min Kao could see his father now, standing beside his mother's bed and ordering for Luli to be taken away—abandoned at a wall, where no one could imagine what would befall her. How could any man do that to his own child? To then send his sons overseas to manage a drug-smuggling venture—the man had no scruples at all.

Did what his father had done with Luli compare to what Tao Ren had done with Sun Ling?

Min Kao didn't think so. Their father hadn't cared for Luli's future or well-being, while Tao Ren had thought placing his daughter in the house of the influential in

Hong Kong would be an avenue toward a better fate. He had been wrong, but his intent had been noble.

Perhaps Sun Ling still held a nugget of bitterness toward her father for how her life had gone in that house. Why else would she insist on such distance from them? Why would she continue to try to integrate into the whites' world with her accommodations, clothing, and hairstyles? Was it a silent reproach against the Chinese? Against her own people and customs?

He felt a burst of anger at her. She needed to be there and give her father strength to recover! Didn't she know that the city of San Francisco was already reporting almost a thousand deaths from smallpox?

Tao Ren moaned, and Min Kao murmured softly to him, then stood.

"I'll be back with broth," he said. He rolled his shoulders, exhausted and sore from the bedside vigil. "And I'll read to you as you rest."

He held silent about his plan to slip some opium oil into the broth. It was the only way he could get something into Tao Ren that could ease his pain, but the man would never agree to it. Min Kao left the room and used the key around his neck to lock it behind him. He bent over the barrel, scrubbing and rinsing his hands and arms all the way to his neck, then putting the rag he used to dry himself in a bag on the floor to be burned later that night. They were already down to the last dozen or so, and he would have to go out and find more to use for himself, as well as to bathe Tao Ren.

As he descended the stairs, he heard Jingwei arguing with someone.

"No, that will hurt our business," she said.

"What is going on?" Min Kao asked, his foot on the last step.

Two men were there, one white and one Chinese. The white man wore an official suit and in his hand was a yellow flag and a hammer. It was obvious what he was there for. Min Kao had expected them any day, with the way rumors spread around Chinatown.

The white man muttered a few words.

"You have a case of smallpox, and you must alert the public to stay away," the Chinese man said. He looked at the white man, then lowered his eyes to ground. "They think the smallpox came from the Chinese quarter."

"I understand their fears," Min Kao said, though he really didn't. "But we are keeping him locked away upstairs while he recovers. He will not be in contact with anyone."

"Yes, your wife told us. My boss said that's not good enough," the translator said, then apologized.

"Your boss will kill all our business," Jingwei said, her voice heavy with tears. "Everything we've built will be gone. Our customers will never return."

Beside her Luli clung to her waist, arms wrapped tightly, disturbed at the commotion.

Peso watched from his perch behind the counter.

Min Kao put his arms around Jingwei and patted Luli's head. "We'll figure it out," he said. "At least we can still do deliveries."

The men ignored them and went outside. The white man then turned and tacked a yellow flag to the overhang, letting it wave over the door, a visual warning to all in Chinatown that the shop held contagious people.

At least his translator had the decency to look ashamed, and Min Kao couldn't fault him from trying to make a living. He wasn't in charge of shutting down businesses—he was only the messenger.

"Baba, my arm hurts," Luli said, rubbing her upper arm.

"Jingwei, please get her a cold compress," Min Kao said. "I must try to get Tao Ren to sip some broth."

He was worried. Even more so now, but already that

day he'd taken his family, including Peso, to a white doctor in the poor part of San Francisco. The rumor that was making the rounds was that the doctor would inoculate the Chinese for a price. It had taken almost a month's profits, but Min Kao didn't care.

But now with the swollen redness on Luli's arm, he wondered if the doctor was just another swindler, selling fake medicines and injections to desperately terrified residents of San Francisco. The doctor had pointed to his certificate on his wall, and truly, what choice did Min Kao have? He wanted his family safe, and their Chinese herbs just were not strong enough to combat the evil disease. After all, Chinese medicine was focused on prevention of disease. Sadly, they weren't always successful in creating medicines that would cure what hadn't been prevented.

But it made him so angry that the officials were saying the smallpox originated in Chinatown, when everyone knew the numbers of cases and even casualties were higher in the white neighborhoods.

"Min Kao," Jingwei said, putting her hand out to stop him from moving. "You are getting worn out. I think you need to rest."

He studied her face, making sure it was clear of any spots before he shook her arm off.

"Just be sure the candle doesn't go out," he said.

They'd made a shrine to the T'ou-Shen Niang-Niang, goddess of disease, and he'd instructed everyone to not refer to any blisters as anything other than 'beautiful flowers' once the candles were lit, so as not to offend her. Each morning they prayed and offered sacrifices of food and paper money. And after some coaxing, Luli was wearing a paper mask at night to fool the god into thinking Luli was not a pretty young girl, to move on to the next home.

Even if Min Kao had to check his daughter ten times

a night, he'd be sure her mask stayed intact as she slept.

His brother, Min Wei, would most likely laugh and call him too superstitious, but Min Kao cared not what anyone thought. No, there would be no rest for him until he knew his small family would be spared. He'd come to this herb shop with nothing but his sack on his back and empty pockets, but now within its four humble walls was everything he held dear.

CHAPTER FOURTEEN

SUN LING HAD NEVER SEEN John look as alarmed as he had in the back of the laundry and because of that, she declined arguing with his latest order, as she'd have done any other time. Now they were on what was supposed to be a secret trail, and despite the circumstances surrounding them, she found herself amused at the sight of Bei Ming in front of her, struggling to stay atop her mare as the horse swayed from side to side.

Straddled atop the horse, dressed in an extra pair of Bei Ming's wide-legged trousers and a billowy tunic, Sun Ling was indeed perspiring from the high temperatures, but she still felt free from the cumbersome burden of her corset and skirts. She loved wearing the dresses of her own making, copying the latest styles and sometimes using a unique design, but she'd forgotten how light she could feel in a traditional Chinese day outfit. She was now glad she'd forgotten to pack her riding clothes. She wiggled her toes in the soft moccasins, marveling yet again at the difference between them and her fancy boots.

However, Bei Ming was showing signs of not being comfortable at all. From the awkward way she moved up there, looking quite ridiculous, she might as well have been bundled up in San Francisco's latest fashions.

"Wouldn't you rather sit behind me and let me do the

work?" Sun Ling asked her yet again. "We can easily tie your mare to mine and move much faster."

This time, Bei Ming gave in to her distress and nodded. Why she'd thought she could handle a horse without any instruction was beyond Sun Ling. Thus far, her ineptness had only slowed them down, though Jack Yan never complained once. Alternatively, he'd showed much concern about Bei Ming's struggle, and he would likely have a crick in his neck from all the turning around to check on her that he'd done.

"How do I stop it?" Bei Ming asked.

"Just gently pull back on the reins and tell her to whoa." They'd gone over this before leaving the stable, but obviously Bei Ming hadn't listened, and now the pain she was feeling was evident. Sun Ling had tried to tell her that if she didn't sit on the horse in the correct manner, it would not be a comfortable ride.

As for herself, she was enjoying the escape from the dusty streets of Truckee. The mare behaved like a gem. Not as well as Dulin, of course, but good enough that it made her miss her own horse dearly.

"Jack Yan," Bei Ming called.

The man stopped and turned around. "We must hurry," he said. "What is it?"

"Please help Bei Ming dismount and join me on my horse. Then we'll be able to move faster."

He nodded and slid off his own horse, tying it to a hanging branch before coming back to them.

They'd been on the trail only about half an hour or so. While others were in town, taking stock and preparing more water barrels, John had appointed Jack Yan to lead them out of Truckee to a cabin in the woods that was shared by a few other Chinese. There they would be safe, Jack Yan had promised.

Sun Ling wasn't happy about being taken out of the line of fire, but John had come close to having a con-

niption until she'd agreed to go, at least while he tried
to negotiate with the thus-far resistant members of the
Caucasian League.

As much as Sun Ling wanted to be with John, taking
part in the negotiations, she knew her and Bei Ming's
presence would only hinder him if the situation turned
dire.

Bei Ming did a very ungraceful slide off the horse
into Jack Yan's arms. Sun Ling could've sworn a look
not meant for her eyes passed between them before he
guided her the few feet and helped her up onto Sun
Ling's mare.

"Now, put your arms about my waist," she encouraged Bei Ming.

Jack Yan took the reins of Sun Ling's horse and led it
around the abandoned one, then tied them together. He
headed toward his own mount, then stopped and turned.

"*Aiya,* Sun Ling," he said, pulling a small slip of paper
from his inside pocket. "In all the excitement, I forgot to
give you this. My apologies for the delay."

"What is it?"

"You had a message at the post office, and the boy that
helps deliver packages brought it to me this morning.
He said it's been there for several days, but the white
men there threw it aside because your name is foreign."

He held it up to her and she took it, then unfolded it.

Across the top it read *The Western Union Telegraph
Company.*

Under that was her name and then a short paragraph:

*Tao Ren smallpox. Situation Dire. Come straight
away.*

Only a few short sentences, but reading them made
Sun Ling feel as though her appendages had turned to
mush, and she could no longer sit upright.

"What is it?" Bei Ming asked, tightening her arms
around Sun Ling's waist.

Of course, she couldn't read the telegram though she peered over Sun Ling's shoulder. It was in English.

"It's my father. He's contracted smallpox. I must leave Truckee at once."

Three hours later, Sun Ling sighed, peeking through the old gunnysack that served as a curtain. It was still and clear out there, and she was having second thoughts about her decision to continue on to the cabin and not turn back to Truckee.

Behind her, Bei Ming chatted with the three lumberjacks that lounged on their bedrolls. Jack Yan had sworn they'd be safe with the men, but to be sure, he'd taken the trio outside and had a serious talk with them. He'd most likely told the men that she and Bei Ming were under the protection of John, and they all knew who he was and that he was in town to help them.

Now she barely listened as, one by one, they told their stories to Bei Ming, speaking of their journeys to America and their early excitement of plenty of work—even with the low wages—but then their disillusionment as the whites slowly began to resent them. From the bits and pieces that she did pick up, Sun Ling understood that the last year had been a hellish one for every Chinese man in and around Truckee.

"The man I tried to buy a horse from told his daughter right in front of me that I wasn't quite human," one man said. "He told her that if cut, I would bleed black instead of red."

"I went to pick up my earnings, and the foreman tossed the bills into the outhouse hole, making me dig through the shit to fish them out," another remarked.

Sun Ling's problems up until the telegram were miniscule compared to what the men dealt with daily. But now she felt a sense of panic at the distance between her and her father, though it wasn't possible to secure a driver to leave immediately. Even if she could, John would never allow her to take the trip back to San Francisco without him as an escort.

On the trail, she'd been torn, but ultimately she'd let Jack Yan continue to lead them to the shack in the woods, making him swear upon all he held dear to take the telegram to John and ask him to make travel arrangements as swiftly as possible.

Now she paced in front of the window, ignoring Bei Ming's coaxing to come eat her share of the rice before nightfall. She couldn't bear to eat. All she could think about was her father on his sickbed—his already worn and lacking body now even more fragile. He probably wasn't eating. Why should she?

She tried to calculate the days the telegram sat unheeded, compared to how long he might have had the pox. Was he in the spots stage? Or blisters? Could he somehow miraculously be recovering by now?

Not only those thoughts but also waves of guilt washed over her, telling her she should've never left him. That she'd once again put others in front of her family's well-being. But if her father had known what was happening to his fellow kinsmen in Truckee, wouldn't he want her to do what she could to help?

And John. Where was he? Was he in danger? Surely as a white man, he would be safe if there indeed was rioting in Truckee. Oh why had her life turned so complicated? Just a week ago, she'd been plaiting Adora's hair and helping her to plan the next gala. And, of course, sneaking away at the midnight hour to rescue those in need.

So perhaps her life was never simple, after all.

Sun Ling went to her bedroll and sat down, then slipped off her moccasins and set them next to her. She'd become accustomed to the idea of a pillow, and she arranged her small cloth bag of belongings into a roll, then lay down.

As the last shadows began to fall through the window and the sun dipped below the tree line, Bei Ming lit a candle and set it atop their makeshift table. Silence began to settle around the room as first one man fell off to sleep, then another.

The last one named Wan Li kept talking, his voice low and melancholy as he told Bei Ming about the girl he'd left behind in Hong Kong. He was the youngest in their group, even a few less than Sun Ling's twenty-eight. Perhaps he saw Bei Ming as a mother figure because, with the other men sleeping, he seemed eager to talk more. He told Bei Ming he planned to ask his girl to marry him soon and bring her over to America, then he expressed worry that someone else would ask for her hand before he was able to save enough money for the wedding and the passages back and forth.

He talked of his plans to start his own business and build an empire that could be handed down to his children and grandchildren.

Sun Ling finally allowed her thoughts to be swayed from her father as she listened to Wan Li, his youthful voice and wishes for his future lulling her into a state of relaxation.

Then he told the story of meeting his girl, his voice rising and falling as he described the way her hair fell around her shoulders in waves of ebony, and her voice rang out like the morning birds playing in the soft rain. A romantic, he was, and Sun Ling had to smile as she listened to him go on and on as though the girl he left behind was a mythical goddess that fate had put in his path.

She imagined him standing at the wedding altar with a young bride, their costumes vibrant and red, with gold tassels strung throughout the room. There would be solemn oaths, then loud celebrations as they pledged their futures to one another.

With the fantasy Sun Ling wove in her head, she allowed herself a moment of yearning. Oh, to have a man fall in love with her that way. But she'd passed that stage in her life when she would be the most attractive to the best suitors, and anyway, women like her were practical—and certainly not the type to embrace in the moonlight or whisper longings to anyone else.

Simply put, marriage wasn't in the tea leaves for her. Sun Ling knew it, yet she couldn't help feeling a pang of regret for the life she'd never lead. Her father would have to remain disappointed at her reluctance to settle for a good match that would give her stability in her old age, though she had to admit she felt guilt that she'd never be able to give him a grandson.

As if on cue, Wan Li chuckled when he spoke of the jolly fat son he'd have someday, and then the line of daughters he'd sire and provide huge dowries for.

"We will wed in China, and then I will escort her to America and we can begin this journey," Wan Li said wistfully. "Our family will be grand, and I'll have many descendants to carry on my name."

"Have you already expressed your love for her?" Bei Ming asked, playing the part of counsellor. "Has she promised to remain true?"

The two other sleeping men began to snore. Sun Ling sighed, fearing it would be another sleepless night, even in the cabin so far from any possible uprisings in town.

After Wan Li softly answered Bei Ming, she comforted him that a girl of any sort of honor would never go back on a promise, and for him to be patient and work diligently so that the months would pass more quickly. She assured him that if their bond was true, nothing could come between them.

His response was interrupted by a shout outside.

Sun Ling shot to her feet, slipping them into the moccasins as around her the others also sat up, looking around in bewilderment and possibly fear.

"Blow out the candle," Sun Ling hissed to Bei Ming.

The cabin was suddenly pitch black, so much so that Sun Ling couldn't see her hand in front of her face. But she heard the movement and knew that the men had scattered, taking their places on either side of the door with their weapons in their hands. Shovels and picks—a ridiculous defense against men outside with firearms, but all they had.

As though she'd willed it to happen with her line of thought, a shot rang out just as Wan Li leaned around the window, attempting to see what was happening on the other side.

"Get back," she shouted, but it was too late.

The young man gasped, then fell backwards.

Bei Ming screamed. The other men cursed, their tools clanging together as they tried to position themselves in safer locations.

Sun Ling ignored their shouts as she crept closer to where Wan Li had fallen before stopping to allow her eyes to adjust.

The moonlight filtered through the window, casting a glow against the scarlet stain that was spreading across the pale tunic he wore.

He didn't move. It wasn't even clear if he breathed.

All Sun Ling knew in that moment was the cabin wasn't as safe as John had expected, and Wan Li was not going to be given his wedding altar, after all.

Then again, with the scene unfolding before her, it was most likely that none of them would ever have that chance.

CHAPTER FIFTEEN

WHEN THE FIRST TORCH FLEW through the window, Sun Ling found the situation almost too surreal to believe. Only a week before, she had been in civilization, taking tea with Adora as they calmly discussed the latest styles and a book that had the San Francisco ladies' secret reading group all aflutter.

Now here Sun Ling was, out in the wild, with her life being threatened by a band of narrow-minded hooligans.

The gunshots had stopped, and she bent over Wan Li, holding a wad of clothing pulled from her bag against the hole in his chest. She tried to push away the nausea and concentrate on staunching the blood.

One of the other men screamed and grabbed a blanket and tried to smother the fire. Wan Li moaned.

"You'll be fine, Wan Li. Stay with me and don't go to sleep," Sun Ling said. She felt the warmth of his blood already soaking through the material and onto her palms as she pressed down.

He blinked slowly, his eyes telling her that he didn't believe he'd make it. The sorrow on his face said that his mind was on the girl he'd left behind.

"We have to go," one of the men shouted.

Bei Ming rocked back and forth on her heels, sobbing as she begged Sun Ling to do something to save Wan Li. "He's barely more than a boy," she cried. "We mustn't let him die."

The men stomped at the torch, one of them using his shirt to smother it before yet another torch came sailing inside, filling the room with smoke.

"Sun Ling, the others are right. We're sitting ducks here," Bei Ming said, finally coming to her senses and squelching her crying. "Let's get him wrapped up, and then we will try to go out the back before this whole shack goes up in flames."

"Leave him," one of the men shouted, then began choking on the smoke. "We must go now!"

Both Sun Ling and Bei Ming turned and shouted back. "No!"

Neither she nor Bei Ming would leave Wan Li. If he were to perish, it would not be alone in a shack burning around him.

Sun Ling stood, straightening to her full height before turning to the two men scrambling on the other side of the room. They were gathering their things, preparing to flee.

"Too risky to get to the horses," one of them muttered. "We'll have to go on foot."

"You will help us carry Wan Li to safety, or I'll make sure that you hang," Sun Ling said. On what grounds, she didn't know, but she'd be damned if they were going to scurry out like cowards and leave a young man behind to bleed to death.

The men paused, looking at one another. Sun Ling could almost see their minds working, comparing their current predicament with the fact that she was closely linked with the foreigner they were all depending on to help them.

One dipped his head toward the other, and they whispered, then he turned back to Sun Ling. "We will take him as far as the creek. If you want to remain with him, then that's on you," he said, and he even had the decency to look ashamed.

"*Hao le*," she agreed.

He pulled the plywood from the top of the barrel that had served as their table and lay it beside Wan Li. Together, the two men rolled Wan Li onto it, then hefted it into the air. Sun Ling could barely see the boy through the now-thick smoke that permeated the cabin.

"Get the back door and follow us," one of them said.

Sun Ling turned to Bei Ming and saw that she'd already gathered their things and was holding the two canvas bags. She thrust Sun Ling's at her, then clutched her own. In the dim light of the moon, her eyes were wide with fright.

"It will be fine. Stay calm," Sun Ling urged her.

Bei Ming maneuvered around the men and opened the door, then stood aside as they carried Wan Li out. The men didn't waste time. As soon as their feet hit the grass, they ran for the trees, Wan Li bouncing with each stride and his moans increasing.

Sun Ling and Bei Ming followed, and in seconds, they were in the trees and on a narrow trail. The voices behind them faded, and they moved as quietly as they could to get deeper into the woods.

"Perhaps they will think we are all in there, burning alive," Bei Ming whispered before being shushed by the men.

The men tripped over a fallen tree limb, and Wan Li almost rolled off the board. They paused, letting him settle before moving forward again. Sun Ling watched the trail in front of her, taking heed not to stumble and draw more attention to their run for freedom.

She knew it was unlikely that they would be allowed to get away, but she focused on putting one foot in front of the other, instead of letting her thoughts wander to what would happen if they were caught.

A few minutes later, they emerged from the thickest

part of the trees. The men set Wan Li down under the wide leaves of a wild bush, then pointed north, where Sun Ling heard the slight gurgling of water. The men had said they'd only take Wan Li to the creek, and she hoped it was far enough from the cabin for them to hide until morning light. It was all they could do, and they would have to tend to Wan Li as they waited for John to send someone to them. Wan Li might not make it, but at least they'd given him a chance.

Before she could get her bearings, another shot rang out. The sound was coming closer. The two men froze, straightened and nodded at each other, then fled back into the woods.

"Wait," Sun Ling hissed, but the men didn't turn.

"We are going to be captured," Bei Ming said, looking from the men's retreating backs to Sun Ling.

"Go with them," Sun Ling said. "They'll lead you to safety, and you can make sure someone sends help. I am not leaving Wan Li."

She bent over him, whispering for him to stop moaning and be quiet.

Bei Ming didn't answer, but when they heard the sounds of horses coming from where they'd emerged, Sun Ling could see a tremor in the dark form of her shadow.

"Go, quickly," Sun Ling urged again. "If we are both caught, how will that help this young man?"

Her words spurred Bei Ming into action. She threw her arms around Sun Ling for a split second, then whispered an apology and fled.

The horses were getting closer, but no more shots were fired, and Sun Ling prayed that they would not be seen. She hovered over Wan Li as though the protection of her body over his would be enough to keep him alive.

They moved quietly but it was at least two horses, she was sure of it as they came closer. With all the strength she could muster, she took hold of the plywood and pulled Wan Li even further under the bush, then crawled in beside him. She didn't have time to find fallen foliage to cover them.

"This is it," she whispered, squeezing the boy's hand. "They will come through, and if you make a sound, they will harm us. Please—please, Wan Li, do not stir if you have hopes of ever being betrothed."

He went silent, and she thanked the gods for at least that small miracle, but it would take a bigger one for them not to be seen.

She listened harder than she ever had in her life. She held her breath, knowing the horsemen would also be listening for clues as to their whereabouts.

After she finally heard them begin to emerge from the line of trees, she bent over Wan Li again and closed her eyes. She thought of her father and how he'd probably never know that, if she had been able, she would've come.

The hoofbeats came closer, and Jingwei and Luli came to Sun Ling's mind. She would miss them, but she was glad they had each other.

When the two horses were upon her, Sun Ling still refused to look up into the barrel of a gun or at the evil of the man who held it. She would not give them that satisfaction. Remorse filled her, the regret of not being able to save Wan Li and deliver him to his fiancée heavy on her heart.

"*Du bu qi*," she whispered in apology.

She had to look. To allow someone to take her life without looking him in the eye would be letting a coward off without justice. But it was too difficult! At least with her eyes closed, she could focus on the faces of those she loved—those who had loved her.

She waited for the blast.

It did not come.

No one made a move, and finally, Sun Ling opened her eyes and starting at the horse's hooves, she let her gaze travel upward to see who would be her executioner. She braced herself to look upon pure evil as she tried to stay the quaking that had taken over her entire body. If she were to die, it would not be as a trembling flower. She was strong. She was courageous.

She was Sun Ling.

CHAPTER SIXTEEN

THE SPOTS SOON SPREAD FROM Tao Ren's face and neck down to his torso and arms, then turned back into blisters like the first round. Min Kao felt hopeless to turn fate and make things go back to the way they were before.

The shop below was quiet, and Min Kao wondered what the others were up to. He'd left Jingwei and Luli sleeping, but it was past time for them to be up and around.

Peso had a few deliveries scheduled that morning, but by now he should've heard the bell on the door ringing to indicate the entry of at least a few of their regulars. He'd have to get down there to see for himself as soon as he could. He also needed to eat breakfast. Juggling the constant bedside vigil with keeping up with herbal orders was wearing him thin, and he needed sustenance to keep going. Normally Jingwei would've sent something up by now.

He'd go see about it all soon.

But first, he finished with the bathing, then worked slowly and gently to wrap the clean strips of sheets around Tao Ren's hands, layer upon layer like a heavy set of mittens. Only once did the man's eyes open, glittering with a quick flash of pain before glazing over again, but Min Kao worried that one day the man would be bitter at the efforts they had to take to keep him from scratching and spreading the blisters more.

Tao Ren was a firm believer that health was a person's greatest possession, and only now, in the midst of watching someone he admired and respected fade away in such a damaged body, did Min Kao finally appreciate the sentiment fully.

At times Tao Ren opened his eyes and tried to speak, but his delirium usually resulted in a jumble of words that Min Kao tried hard to decipher but usually failed.

Both he and Jingwei were anxious to see the blisters scab over, a sign that the old man would improve. But thus far, the *beautiful flowers* continued to bloom, and the prognosis was grim.

Now the focus was on pain management, and Min Kao had mixed up several different concoctions, all in an effort to find the combination that would ease Tao Ren's suffering the most. Min Kao could only imagine how painful the blisters were. Only the day before, he'd noticed that lesions had erupted inside of Tao Ren's nose and mouth, and they made it nearly impossible to get more than a teaspoon of broth into him every few hours.

The old man had already been slight because of his confinement to his chair, but now he barely made a bump under the thin coverlet. If he didn't soon recover, he'd fade to nothing.

At least he'd stopped asking about Sun Ling, and Min Kao didn't know if it was because he'd given up on her or that he was just too delirious to know what was going on. Jingwei had sent another telegram, but they had yet to get a response. It infuriated Min Kao that Sun Ling hadn't yet answered—especially considering how expensive it was to send each message. Surely she'd made it to the town by now, and Jingwei was talking of sending another letter by post.

At times he wondered when Sun Ling would com-

pletely turn her back on them and immerse herself
totally in all things white. She'd taken it so far now that
to him, it appeared she was trying to blend in with her
benefactor, Adora. Possibly even become her! Sure, he
and Jingwei—or even Luli—weren't blood related but
they were still family. And what about her father? From
what Jingwei had told him, during their years in Hong
Kong, Sun Ling had never stopped dreaming of finding
Tao Ren, and now she had him she didn't spend nearly
enough time with him.

He felt she was always trying to prove something.
When she got back, he was going to sit her down and
make her see that she was enough—that she did not have
to continue traipsing around in dangerous situations to
prove that she was no longer the poor bondservant that
embarked on her journey so long ago.

He would make her listen, he thought as he worked. If
Tao Ren made it through the pox, he had every right to
really know his daughter and feel her loyalty. Min Kao
would convince Sun Ling to make her father a priority
before it was too late.

After he'd done all he could for Tao Ren, he picked
up the soiled cloths and retreated from the room. He
no longer had to lock it, as the seriousness of the man's
illness had finally sunk in with Peso and Luli, and they
knew not to come near the sick room.

Min Kao had to force himself to keep his movements
slow and methodical as he scrubbed his hands and arms,
then he removed the cloth he'd tied across his face and
added it to the bag to be burned.

He turned to the stairs, but something made him hes-
itate. He paused to peek into their bedroom, just to be
sure Jingwei wasn't still there, cleaning up or making

the bed.

The bed was not made, and the scene within the room made Min Kao catch his breath. Jingwei was in the bed, and she met his eyes, the fear in them evident.

Within her arms lay Luli, who looked asleep but feverish.

"Jingwei, is she…?" He was unable to voice the words.

His wife nodded, and he came closer. When he looked upon Luli, then back at Jingwei and saw the spots that covered them both, terror clutched at his throat.

Not his family, he prayed. Anything—anything in the world he would give up, but he couldn't lose them. He fell to his knees beside the bed, dropping his head upon Jingwei's shoulder. The tears fell, and then her arm come around, patting his back and giving him reassurance. He could feel the heat of her skin, burning through his clothes, the fever already on a rampage through her body.

And yet, she gave him comfort.

He knew it should've been the other way around, and he gathered himself, standing and blinking back the sheen from his eyes. Jingwei still hadn't spoke, but he knew—and he suspected she did too—that they were about to enter a battle of life or death.

I will not lose them. I will not lose them.

With that mantra swirling through his thoughts, Min Kao turned to get the bucket of cool water and some clean cloths. He would have to depend on Peso even more than he did now, because there was no one else.

And if Peso was to be struck with the pox, then what? Could Min Kao care for them all? Would he have to make the impossible decision of which one to save? And if he himself got the pox, then what?

He shook off the dark thoughts, not letting his mind linger on the vision of them all laid up with fever and blisters, dying slow and painful deaths as Chinatown hustled and bustled right outside their shop door, oblivious to the fact that his world was falling apart.

"Leave me be," Jingwei whispered, then pointed weakly to Luli. "Care for her."

"I will care for you both," he said. "We will get through this."

When they'd first met on the ship to America, Min Kao nursed Jingwei through illness. He knew she was strong and would use everything in her power to hold on for Luli. On that same ship, she'd nursed Luli back to health when they'd thought she was all but lost.

Miracles did happen and could come again.

He would accept no alternative.

CHAPTER SEVENTEEN

MIN KAO STOOD OVER THE basin of murky water, staring down at the fragments of his reflection that swirled in pieces. He raised his gaze to the small mirror pegged to the wall. Jingwei had hung it there so that she could see to braid her hair. Now, he wished he had the nerve to take it down and smash it, for the reflection didn't lie.

He was a man barely hanging on.

Four days and three nights. That was how long he'd been going with only minutes of sleep here and there, stolen between the vigils he was keeping between the two sickbeds. He'd carefully moved Jingwei and Luli to a bed in the sickroom with Tao Ren so that he could keep them all in his sights at all times.

At first, Jingwei had continued to try to comfort him, speaking soft words of encouragement and hope as he administered to them. But she was soon too ill to talk, and now he missed the quiet confidence she instilled in him. She was not only his wife but also the closest comrade he'd ever had, and now, when he needed her the most, he had to remind himself that this time, she needed him more.

Seeing them suffer was killing him, but he hadn't been surprised when their spots had turned to blisters. He felt only resignation that it was not going to be easy to save them. But he had determination on his side. And yes, exhaustion. But determination could beat out exhaustion any day. At least, that was what he continued to tell himself.

The candle that burned to the goddess was inside the room, now. When Min Kao wasn't softly encouraging Jingwei, Luli, and Tao Ren, he was soundlessly praying that the gods would have mercy upon his family.

He put his hands down into the water, holding them there a minute to refresh him—and hopefully rejuvenate him.

He heard footsteps coming up the stairs and turned to find Peso, his small face etched with concern.

"How are they today?" he asked.

"The same." Min Kao was still astonished that the boy had been spared. He was thankful, too, as Peso was now his hands and feet for the boiling and fetching of fresh water, cloths, and a multitude of other errands.

"We are out of clean cloths," Peso said. "What do I do?

Min Kao wasn't sure what to do. If it had been some other illness, they could've laundered the rags. But with the pox, everything had to be burned. Now he would have to send the boy out to buy more, and with money so low, he was hesitant to do so. He considered the extra clothes in their wardrobe trunk. There wasn't much, but they could use it, he supposed. Or would Jingwei be upset at him?

"Can I please see Luli?" Peso asked, his eyes hopeful.

Min Kao shook his head. The boy had thus far been spared, but he wouldn't tempt fate. Peso was looking ragged now that Jingwei wasn't well enough to remind him to comb through his hair or wash his face, and he was probably hungry. But the boy was loyal, of that there was no question. He did whatever Min Kao asked him to do and never uttered a single complaint. Even through the long hours of night, he remained curled on the other side of the door, only catching moments of sleep as he remained ready for instructions.

"You cannot go in there, but I want you to stand here at the door and keep an eye on them. I will go make up a new poultice and some broth."

Peso seemed satisfied with that, and he settled himself in the doorway. Min Kao moved around him and went down the stairs, already hearing the boy begin to talk encouragingly to Luli.

Downstairs, he looked toward the front door and noticed Peso had left it unlocked. What did it matter, though? Business had all but dried up because of the flag that marked them as contagious. Min Kao was afraid to let his thoughts go to how much money they were losing or even how they would survive in the months to come. Or how they would rekindle their business. So much hung in the balance now that the smallpox was threatening everything he held dear, but he had to take it one step at a time.

He went behind the counter and began to gather the things he would need to make a new poultice. Their supplies were getting low, and he would have to send Peso to the outskirts of town to bargain with the farmers. He wasn't sure if that was a task the boy could do, or if he would come back penniless with nothing but ditch weed. It all depended on the honesty of the farmers or if they were desperate enough to trick a boy.

So many decisions, and he didn't have the energy to make any of them.

Sighing, Min Kao pulled out a small bag of herbs and shook bits of it into the stone mortar. He added more ingredients, then lifted the pestle to grind it all together.

He hesitated. Was he forgetting an important component? He wished he could ask Tao Ren, but the man was nothing short of delirious when awake.

Suddenly he doubted himself. What was it he was about to do?

He felt a wave of dizziness and set the pestle down. He put his hands on the counter for balance. When had he last eaten? Or slept? He tried to think.

The bell over the door rang, and he looked up, surprise already registering that a customer would venture in by choice. He hoped they came with a big order and a pocket full of cash.

But it wasn't a customer.

His heart gave a lurch, and he blinked a few times to be sure his mind wasn't fabricating a ghost from his past.

The visitor remained. Silent and staring.

"What are you doing here?" Min Kao finally asked.

"I'm here to help you save your family," Wei said. "Word on the street is that you are about to lose them."

Min Kao studied his brother.

Wei had aged much too quickly to be normal. He looked like hell and Min Kao wanted to tell him to turn and leave. To go back to whatever hole he was selling opium and prostitutes from and to keep to his own soiled business. But in that moment, all he could do is remember the brother he used to know—the boy who stood by him in many unfortunate circumstances. The brother he'd shared a womb with and, no matter how much animosity brewed between them, would always care for.

Ignoring the traitorous tear that ran down his cheek, Min Kao felt the last of his energy leave him, and he lowered himself to sit on the stool. His heart pounded in his chest, and he was too overcome to speak.

Finally, he looked back up at his brother who, if the roles had been reversed, might not have been willing to swallow his pride. But then, his brother didn't have Jingwei or Luli. Or even know true paternal affection as

Min Kao did from Tao Ren.

Min Kao didn't have riches, but he had so much more.

His pride be damned. His next words came out in an exhausted and desperate whisper.

"You are right. I need you, Min Wei."

Min Kao stood guard over Luli's bed, watching every move the old woman made as she shuffled from patient to patient. It was getting hard to breathe, for the large horse's trough that Min Wei's men had carried up had been lit on fire and was now sending billows of fumes into the air from the fumigation process. They'd opened the only window in the room as well as the downstairs doors, but it was hard to breathe. And crowded.

His brother had come with an entire brigade to help, it seemed.

"What is in there?" Min Kao asked, holding a cloth tighter over his nose as he pointed at the trough with his other hand.

The old woman ignored him for a moment, but when Min Kao asked again, she paused to look at him. Her face was startling with its stark paleness and the penetrating, deep eyes set in a nest of wrinkles and old pockmarks. Obviously she had beaten the sickness herself some time before.

Wei stood leaned in the hall, too afraid to come inside the sickroom, but he met Min Kao's gaze and shrugged.

To be honest, the woman quite frightened Min Kao, and he was glad that Luli was sleeping deeply and wouldn't see her face. Even Tao Ren had barely stirred at all the activity and commotion. Jingwei was the only one who'd awakened, but after she'd looked around and saw Wei and the strangers, she'd closed her eyes again as though she didn't have the strength to inquire about their presence.

"Sulfur," the old woman began naming as she counted off each finger as though bringing the ingredients to memory. "Seeds of the carambola. Wood."

Carambola was a fruit he'd eaten as a child. Min Kao had always known it as star fruit, and he didn't know where they would've found the fruit tree anywhere near San Francisco. It didn't matter, though. He was desperate enough to try anything to heal them.

Wei said the woman was the most renowned Chinese healer in the West and had cost him a lot of money to bring to Chinatown. As for the men who did the heavy lifting, they looked to be from the bottom of the barrel, but his brother only had to speak a few words, and they jumped to do his bidding. He'd sent one to the market for clean linens to put on the beds and to be torn for bathing.

The woman had bidden the other worker to hang a makeshift curtain between the beds of Jingwei and Luli, and of Tao Ren. As soon as it was done, she ordered him to bring up freshly boiled water. It was clear she planned to bathe the sick, and as soon as the water was ready, she waved everyone out of the room.

"Out, out," she said. Then she pointed at Min Kao. "You. Eat and then sleep. Don't argue."

Min Kao nodded. He would go down and eat something, but he would not sleep—not until the old woman gave word that the tides had turned and they would all survive.

In the hall he stopped to wash, then followed Wei down the stairs. The other men were behind them, and once they all stood in the shop, Wei ordered them to go out for noodles and bring some back.

In the furthest corner of the room, Peso slowly swept the floor. Now relieved of most of his duties, he was doing what he could to stay busy.

"Peso, have you eaten?" Min Kao asked.

The boy shook his head.

"We will have noodles soon." Min Kao went behind the counter and sat upon the stool. Suddenly he felt like he could sleep for a million years.

Wei pulled up another stool, and they were face to face.

"You look different," Min Kao said to him. He didn't expound on what he meant, but he had a feeling that Wei knew he looked ragged.

"It's a tough life out there," Wei said, grinning sideways.

He didn't admit to the fact that opium and white liquor probably had a hand in his peculiar premature aging, Min Kao noticed.

"And how is the House of Lai?" Min Kao asked.

Wei nodded. "Good. Desperate times calls for desperate measures. The whites want us out of here, and our men are finding less work. Illness is spreading. Times are hard, and yes, we help them forget. Therefore when all else fails, our business still does well."

Min Kao looked over at Peso to see if he was listening, but the boy was preoccupied in his own thoughts.

It turned Min Kao's stomach that his brother took advantage of a man's bad luck to hook him on the pipe. He didn't like the callous side of Wei. It reminded him too much of someone else, though Min Kao tried to forget the man who'd both sired him and betrayed him by leading him to believe their business in America was nothing unsavory. Still, he needed to know, so he asked the question on his mind.

"And Father? He is still the man in charge?"

"He thinks he is," Wei said, shrugging. "I let him believe what will keep him content. But I report what I please, and believe me, I am compensated very well for running the business. In a few years' time, I may even branch off alone. I now have a gambling house that he knows nothing of. Soon it will be making a healthy profit."

Min Kao hated to bring up their mother in the midst of such vile conversation, but he couldn't help himself. She hadn't answered his last letters, and he worried for her health. He longed for news of her. "And Mŭqīn?"

The door opened, and Wei's man came in, carrying several covered bowls stacked in a tier of baskets, chopsticks tied on top. He brought them to the counter and set them down, then retreated back outside.

Wei set one of the bowls before Min Kao and loosened the chopsticks. "Now, Brother, you must eat, or you will be weakened enough to catch the pox, too. Then what will your little family do without your loyal vigil?"

He was right, but Peso needed his first.

Wei saw where he looked and called the boy over. He gave him a bowl and chopsticks and sent him away.

Peso disappeared into Tao Ren's small alcove under the stairs. Something about Wei's presence unnerved Peso, Min Kao could tell.

The boy had a good sixth sense about him.

"You come get more if you need to," Min Kao called to him. He then lifted his bowl and sipped at the hot broth. It was delicious, and he was thankful to finally have sustenance. He used the chopsticks to rake noodles into his mouth, barely even chewing before swallowing quickly.

As the food filled his belly, he began to feel drowsy, so much so that his eyelids threatened to fall at any moment, putting a curtain over the dismally empty shop that only a week before had been bright and brimming with activity.

His body felt weighted down, as though he were trying to walk through knee-deep mud. He looked at Wei. Could he trust his brother to watch over his family while he slept? If Wei were the brother he'd grown up with, he would never harm anyone intentionally. But Min Kao wasn't so sure.

Wei patted Min Kao's shoulder. "Have no fear, Brother. You still have my loyalty and can trust me. Why else would I be here?"

He had a point. And what choice did Min Kao have? He was depleted. Emotionally, physically, and yes, even financially.

With a slight nod he alerted Wei that his offer was accepted. Words of gratitude would have to come later, after the outcome of the ordeal was revealed. All their lives, Min Wei had found a way to come out on top, gaining whatever he wanted. For once, Min Kao wouldn't begrudge him this gift. Instead, he'd pray that this time would prove to be like every other and that his brother would emerge the victor over the deadly smallpox that had hold of everything Min Kao held dear.

With the decision made, his body could do no more. He laid the bowl on the table and then his head upon his folded arms.

Without strength enough to even carry himself to a bed, he finally allowed his eyes to shut, welcoming the sweet oblivion of the black curtain that fell across his vision and swallowed his fears.

CHAPTER EIGHTEEN

IT WAS NOT THE BOOT of an evil white man, Sun Ling realized. She touched the soft brown moccasin as if it was a lifeline to safety.

"Help us," she begged. The sound of the other horses was coming closer, but these visitors had arrived silently, barely making a stir.

Dubuda smiled down, then slid silently from her horse. She squatted next to Wan Li and Sun Ling, taking in the young man's injury.

The Indian man that sat atop the other horse looked about the same age as Dubuda, and Sun Ling wondered if perhaps it was her husband. His attention was on the woods behind them. He said a few words, and Dubuda stood. She pointed in the direction of the creek. The young warrior nodded, then slid down from his horse.

Dubuda took the sash from around her middle and worked it around the body of Wan Li. Her Indian partner tied a small rope around Wan Li's feet and the plywood, securing him from rolling off.

Dubuda grabbed Sun Ling by the shoulder, gestured at the reins of both horses, then at the creek.

Sun Ling understood. She was to lead the horses, and they would take Wan Li.

A few more shots from a rifle spurred them into action, and Dubuda took the end of the board, the other Indian the top, and without a sound, they crept toward another trail and disappeared into the trees.

Sun Ling tied one of the horse's reins to the tail of the other horse, then took the reins and followed the Indians. It was slow going, as the horses first balked at their new guide, but with some clicks of her tongue and reassuring whispered words, they obeyed. She marveled at how quiet they were and wondered if it was because they had been raised by Indians. She'd always thought Dulin was soundless during their midnight excursions, but the horses she led now were amazing with the softness of their steps.

As she tread carefully, she kept her sights on Dubuda. She could barely make them out, but she remained calm and caught up to them at the water. At least five or six feet across, it was no small stream, and Sun Ling was grateful to see the old Indian man there, sitting in the well of a canoe. She was surprised to see that he was wearing a white man's jacket and pants and not the traditional Indian attire he'd worn the night at their camp.

He saw them and quickly moved to the back of the small boat, gesturing silently for them to hurry.

Dubuda and her partner lifted Wan Li on the slab and, together, waded into the water and balanced him across the canoe. There was just enough room at the head of the canoe for one more person, and they beckoned Sun Ling to climb in.

She only hesitated a moment. Dubuda was her friend—she was sure of it. The girl had arrived like an angel of the night, and Sun Ling felt she could trust her.

She waded through the water and climbed in.

Once she was in, she realized she'd lost her bag. But it was too late to worry, for only seconds later, the old man began to paddle, and they were moving quite swiftly down the stream. Behind him, she saw Dubuda and her partner jump upon their horses and take off in the opposite direction.

She put her hands on either side of Wan Li, holding tight to the plywood to keep him steady. He had stopped moaning, and Sun Ling held onto the hope that he'd simply blacked out.

As they moved through the water, Sun Ling thought of Bei Ming and the other men. She'd heard no more gunshots for the last few minutes, so she clung to that thought and envisioned her friend free and clear from the murderous mob.

The mob had no qualms about venturing into the woods to look for Chinese lumberjacks, so most likely they'd wreaked havoc in town, too. The Chinese of Truckee had to be under siege. John would be beside himself. She thought of the laundry being burned out again, feeling pity for Jack Yan and all he'd had to overcome simply for the right to live and prosper.

John would be scrambling to get to her, she was sure. She hoped he wouldn't be caught in the crossfire or become too agitated when he found Bei Ming without Sun Ling. There was no use worrying over it at the moment, as she wouldn't leave Wan Li with the Indians, despite her confidence that Dubuda was her friend.

She thought of her father and wondered if in some way, the young Wan Li was representative of her own father and the fight he was going through for his own life. Perhaps because she couldn't be there for him, she was doing penance by sticking with Wan Li and doing what she could to help him survive.

The minutes ticked by, and the sash tied around Wan Li to bind his wound was soon dark with blood. Sun Ling said another silent prayer to the gods for Wan Li and her father—that they would both pull through and be returned to those who cared for them. Life was so fickle, and in the quiet of the stream, with only the sounds of night around them and the steady slice of the old man's oar through the water, she stumbled over many regrets.

If only she made it and her father was still there when she returned to San Francisco, she would spend less time on her mission and more time with him. She might even marry the man of his choice if that would make his last years on earth satisfying ones.

As she pondered all these things, she felt the canoe being smoothly grounded. She looked up and saw they were at the edge of a small campsite.

A few young Indian men rushed out of the brush and pulled the canoe higher upon the bank. One held out a hand to Sun Ling, and she took it, then climbed out. Next they took hold of the plywood and carried Wan Li up the bank and into the camp, setting him beside a small campfire.

Sun Ling stood helplessly aside, ignored as a young Indian woman rushed to Wan Li's side and dropped to her knees, examining him closely.

When the maiden lowered her ear over Wan Li's mouth and listened, then looked up at the two men and nodded, Sun Ling was so weak with relief that she dropped to the ground.

Others rushed around, and soon, she could no longer see Wan Li through the half-dozen Indians that surrounded him. She wasn't sure how they were administering to him, but whatever they did was better than being left in the woods to bleed out, so she remained silent and let them work.

Soon Dubuda was by her side and bent down, looking into her eyes. She beckoned Sun Ling to follow, then led her back to the creek to wash. Since the tunic Sun Ling wore was long, she slipped out the moccasins and then the pants, leaving them laying on the bank. She stepped into the water, relishing the coolness of it on her ankles.

Dubuda joined her, then worked to pull the tunic over Sun Ling's head, tossing it on the other discarded clothes.

Next, Dubuda lay her back into the water and gently rinsed the blood that had found its way into Sun Ling's hair, then scrubbed at it with handful of fragrant leaves. After every trace of Wan Li's injury was gone from her body, Sun Ling climbed out of the water and up the bank.

She was glad that Dubuda brought her a soft shirt and motioned for her to put it on. With the fresh shirt donned, Sun Ling looked around, taking in the camp that was beginning to be more evident in the first rays of light that filtered softly over the trees.

Sun Ling suddenly felt the fatigue of the last few hours. Dubuda sensed it, too, and led her to a small hut that was made from what appeared to be wild cattails tied together around a circular frame.

Sun Ling crawled inside and found herself atop a soft fur. She looked back at Dubuda, who folded her hands under her head and leaned to one side, signaling sleep. After one more peek toward the center of camp to try to see Wan Li, Sun Ling gave up and agreed. She needed to rest or she'd be of no use to him.

She curled into herself, and laying her head upon the fur, she wondered if she could possibly be dreaming, and in reality be bleeding in the woods beside a dying Wan Li? Was Dubuda only a wishful vision?

If it was only a hallucination, she preferred it over the ugliness that had taken over the world, pitting one man against another simply for the color of his skin and the shape of his eyes. Yes, she decided. She preferred to dream. To pretend that all was well.

She closed her eyes.

Sun Ling was awakened by delicious aroma of something waved under her nose. She sat up, rubbing her eyes as she tried to determine where she was.

Dubuda was holding out a bowl and smiling broadly.

First, Sun Ling was confused. Then the events of the previous night came flooding back, and she stood, looking out the doorway for Wan Li.

"Where?" she asked, trying to see around Dubuda.

She could see the old man from the canoe outside, and he'd changed into traditional robes and was shaking a bunch of feathers and beads over Wan Li. He chanted a comforting song or a prayer—she wasn't sure which.

"Is he still living?" Sun Ling demanded.

Dubuda nodded and motioned for Sun Ling to sit back down.

Sun Ling took this to mean that Wan Li had made it through the night. She breathed a sigh of relief, then sat.

But her relief was short-lived, for she remembered her father. If only she could know what was going on in the Chinatown of San Francisco. She longed to be at his side, reassuring him and encouraging him to fight the fever.

Dubuda handed her the bowl, and Sun Ling put it to her lips, taking a sip of the soup held within. She recognized the taste of rabbit and realized that the fur she'd slept on was also a series of rabbit pelts sewn together.

Now that it was light, Sun Ling could see Dubuda's face clearly. It was covered with red clay, possibly to block the sun's hot rays. Earrings made of bone dangled from her earlobes, moving with each gesture of her head.

The girl watched her, nodding each time Sun Ling took a sip of the soup as though feeding her made Dubuda exceptionally pleased. Eating wasn't an effort, as it was a delicious blend of spices, meat, and broth.

Why they were helping her and Wan Li, she didn't quite know. She thought of her father and hoped he'd also survived the night. He would be so captivated by what she was seeing; his interest in other cultures and medicines had always been healthy. Unlike the white men, he respected every culture, and when she was a child, he had emphasized that every people group had something the others could learn from.

The day was already swelteringly hot. The sun was high in the sky, telling Sun Ling it had to be noontime.

She looked toward the trees, wondering if Bei Ming was alive and if John was searching for her. She didn't know how she could make Dubuda understand that she needed to get a message to Jack Yan or John to let them know she was alive and well, but she needed to do so.

After she'd drained the last drop of broth and eaten the meat from the bowl, Sun Ling returned it to Dubuda and gestured toward Wan Li.

Dubuda nodded, and Sun Ling went out of the hut and approached Wan Li. His eyes were closed, but she saw the rise and fall of his chest that was wrapped in cloths that were clean, not saturated with blood. Beside him was a piece of pottery that cradled several pieces of buckshot. The old Indian had stopped his dance and now squatted next to Wan Li, his eyes closed, too, as he continued to chant.

On the other side sat yet another bowl, filled with a porridge-like concoction. Hopefully some sort of powerful plants and herbs.

Sun Ling felt relief. The boy was alive. Just how bad off he was, she didn't know. Now she worried for Bei Ming and the two Chinese men, running for her life. What had become of them? And John—had he tried to intervene and stop those out to harm those they consider inferior? If so, had he put himself in danger? She didn't even want to think about what might've happened to him. She couldn't go there in her mind.

Dubuda came alongside her and motioned for Sun

Ling to follow.

They passed a few long-haired boys shooting rocks with a bow, and a very fit young man carrying in a catch of several trout hanging from a dangling line. The sweat glistened off of his body, and Sun Ling looked away after noting he had the largest muscles she'd ever seen. She should've blushed at his naked chest, but she was too busy trying to determine what the markings were alongside the many scars, to react properly.

It was a different environment than she'd ever known. She could feel the peace within the tribe, and everyone turned to watch Sun Ling, their eyes widened with curiosity as she and Dubuda walked to the edge of camp.

They stopped where a group of women sat in a circle, weaving baskets.

Dubuda sat on the dirt beside the others and beckoned for Sun Ling to do the same. Then she picked up a bundle of willow stems and began working with them.

Sun Ling watched, fascinated as the girl worked quicker than the others, and so much more gracefully, pulling the willow in and out until, in no time at all, a pattern began to show. Some of the others stopped their weaving to watch, too, and Sun Ling got the notion that Dubuda was the most gifted of them all.

Dubuda paused, then tried to hand her work over to Sun Ling.

"Oh no," Sun Ling said, shaking her head. "I can't."

The women laughed, their soft voices mingling together in a song of sisterhood. Dubuda began to work again, her eyes rising and falling from the beginning form of a basket to Sun Ling, seeking her approval.

Sun Ling nodded, forcing a smile upon her face even through the thoughts that raced around, her worry for the others and her need to return to town and see for herself what sort of damage was done.

She looked around and once again, realized she had no

idea even in which direction Truckee lay. At the mercy of the kindness of the Indians, she would have to wait until they determined it was time for her to go.

CHAPTER NINETEEN

WHILE MIN KAO STOOD GUARD, watching his family sleep, his mind stuttered between racing and stopping in befuddlement as he struggled to remember just what it was he'd been thinking of only a moment before.

He felt a bit improved after snatching a half-hour's rest, but his body ached with soreness from his vigil.

The old woman was downstairs, preparing the area to be able to make bone broth when the rest of her supplies arrived. She'd made clear that every other trick she'd tried was having a minimal effect against this latest deadly strain of the pox, and the broth was their last resort.

Wei was out, obtaining the meat they'd need. It was going to be expensive, part of the ever-mounting debt to his brother that was adding up—another worry of Min Kao's.

Thinking about it, Min Kao realized he shouldn't have been surprised by the suggestion of the tea. Before the officials had hung the flag, he'd had at least some customers, men coming and going to work and stopping by to purchase anything they could to first prevent the fever from coming, then when that didn't work, to battle and find a cure. Family members—or neighbors when there was no family—came to Tao Ren to tell them what to do and how to do it if and when the fever struck.

People were desperate to believe in anything they could that would save them, but the broth wasn't something that Tao Ren offered or recommended.

From her perch on top of the headboard, Kitten meowed, her distress over Jingwei's listlessness evident in her refusal to leave her side.

"I know, Kitten," Min Kao murmured. "I feel the same way."

The cat jumped down and coiled against Jingwei's back, her tail twitching before she settled down and closed her eyes.

Min Kao knew nothing about the broth, other than it was made by boiling a cut of rump meat—bone included—and then simmering for a few hours with water and salt. Tao Ren had declared not only that its reputation as a miracle cure was a myth, but also that, in his opinion, in was dangerous to ingest. Sure, they could've made much money from selling it to unsuspecting customers, but they were an establishment built on honor and integrity.

However, desperate situations called for desperate measures, and Min Kao was willing to try anything. He was terrified. Luli had fallen into the deepest sleep yet, her chest barely rising and falling.

If he lost her, he didn't know—

"Baba," he heard.

He looked over at Luli and saw her eyes were open. He felt his hope soar and went to her quickly, sitting beside her on the bed. Picking up her tiny hand, he rubbed the few fingers not covered by the offending blisters.

"You're awake," he said, his voice thick with tears.

"Where's Mama?" Luli said weakly.

"She's sleeping right beside you. Look, Kitten has curled up next to her to give her comfort."

Luli's eyes appeared to be less foggy. They were no

longer yellow around the edges, either. His chest tightened with fear. Could this be the last stage of the fever, when the patient looked better for a short time before their death?

"Luli, how do you feel?" He laid a hand on her head and was shocked to find it cool for the first time since her illness began.

"I'm better, Baba," she said. "The nice lady took my fever away."

His brow wrinkled. So she had seen the old woman through her delirium and didn't even seem frightened of her.

As though on cue, the old woman opened the door and stepped in. She brought a pan of fresh water and a clean cloth, putting them on the floor beside Luli's bed. She peered down at her.

Luli pulled back, putting space between her and the woman.

"Hmmph. You are awake," she said gruffly. "How do you feel?"

His daughter looked confused. "Who is this, Baba?"

"It is the nice lady who took your fever," Min Kao said. "Remember?"

"No," Luli said, shaking her head slowly from side to side. "The nice lady who came to me was prettier, except she had a birthmark around her eye."

Min Kao was taken aback, unable to say a single word.

"The girl was delusional," the old woman said, then felt her head. "Hmm…but the fever appears to have left her. We may be in the clear on this little one."

Luli struggled to sit up. "I told you, the nice lady came last night, and she kept her hands on my head until the fever left. She said that it wasn't my time to go yet—that I needed to be here for you, Baba. She also said Mama will wake up soon."

"Did she say anything else?" He was almost afraid to

ask.

"She said she left a present for me. A beautiful flower. And you are keeping it safe until I'm older. Do you have it? Can I see it?"

Min Kao felt shaken. The birthmark. And a flower? It had to be his mother. *Luli's mother*. The flower was the brooch she'd given him as a farewell keepsake to Luli, so many years before in China. Made of jade, it held much value, and Min Kao had stored it in a safe place and never shown it to Luli, so she could have known nothing of its existence.

He nodded. "Yes, of course. I have the flower."

The old woman looked at him, her eyes curious. "You know whom she speaks of?"

"I do."

"Then it is someone from beyond the curtain?" she asked.

Even though Min Kao knew what the woman meant, his heart refused to accept it. While he believed his daughter, even knew she had the gift of communicating with those from the afterworld, that would mean that his mother—

No, he couldn't accept that.

The old woman bustled around the bed, coming to stand before Min Kao, peering up at him, her face grim.

"If she is seeing ghosts, then she is not completely in the clear. We must find a human tooth. We'll need to wrap it in paper and burn it to ashes, then mix it with wine to give the child. Can you give me one of your teeth?"

The door opened, and Wei walked through. He stopped, looking around the room and smiling when he saw Luli was awake.

"Well, there you are, little rat," he said.

Luli didn't reply. She looked from Wei to Min Kao, a confused expression on her face.

Min Kao went to him and clutched his tunic. "I need to talk to you."

Wei shook him off, then straightened his shirt. "What is it? Why do you look angry? One of your loved ones is awake. I have stocked up on expensive beef rumps, so now we can feed the broth to the old man and Jingwei. We've had one miracle, why not two more?"

"Wei," Min Kao hissed at him, leaning in so that Luli couldn't hear. "Is our mother—is she—"

He couldn't finish the question, but Wei searched his eyes, then hesitated before he nodded.

For once, his voice held a touch of compassion in words he gave his brother.

"*Dui*, she is dead," he said.

CHAPTER TWENTY

S UN LING SAT PROUDLY UPON the horse, following the elder Indian through the main road of Truckee. As they passed small houses and then businesses, people stepped out onto the rickety porches and stared, their astonishment evident in their open mouths, widened eyes, and pointing fingers. Obviously they'd never seen a Chinese woman dressed in deerskin, a turquoise feather in her hair, and riding beside an Indian brave.

"Let them look," she muttered, raising her chin higher, feeling every bit the Indian princess she knew she looked like.

They stared, but they would not try to hurt the Indians. Why should they? The government had successfully driven most of them onto reservations, bringing the tribes to their knees in submission so that they would not starve, now that their rivers and woods were being depleted. That Dubuda and her small tribe had thus far avoided being rounded up and taken from their land was a miracle.

They hadn't told her any of this, though she had come to find out that the elder spoke a bit of English. Sun Ling remembered most of the information that John had shared, words that she hadn't really pondered until she was in the midst of such an interesting and peaceful people.

Only the night before, she'd witnessed the birthing of a new addition to the tribe. It was her first time witnessing childbirth, and she'd felt the miracle of life as the baby emerged and then was passed to her. Holding it in her arms, she felt the ache of something she couldn't quite name.

Sun Ling hadn't known what they'd wanted her to do with the baby, so she'd kissed the small forehead, a blessing of sorts, then placed it in the arms of his mother. Now she knew why Jingwei was so committed to her work as a midwife, as the miraculous moment the child took its first breath was one Sun Ling would never forget.

Her time in the camp, though worrisome as she waited, was also peaceful and enlightening. She'd learned to weave, too, though her basket left a lot to be desired. Dubuda had held it up and acted as though it were a masterpiece, then tied it to the side of her hut, arranging it between others that were much more beautiful.

Dubuda and the other women had also gifted her with beaded necklaces, and they tinkled with each step of the horse. Her ears held the very bone earrings worn by Dubuda, and in her new bag—made from rabbit hide and decorated with turquoise beads—was another set of moccasins that she would probably give to Jingwei.

The best gift of all was the knowledge that the Washoe people were her friends. To have such acceptance from those so different than her was an amazing gift.

Before they turned off toward the part of town where the Chinese lived and worked, they passed a saloon, and two men stared at them, their expressions grim. The taller one spit a long stream of tobacco on the road as he locked eyes with Sun Ling.

She ignored them and pushed her mounting anxiety aside.

As they approached the Chinese part of town, her heart fell at the sight. The people of Truckee had indeed tried to burn out the Chinese.

While there were many still smoldering piles of rubble, not every building was affected, so she held out hope that Jack Yan's laundry still stood. As they rode, she kept her eyes open for John, knowing he must be beside himself with worry.

It had taken three days before Wan Li was well enough to sit up, speak, and eat on his own. Every minute had been torture to Sun Ling as she waited and signed with her hands, until Dubuda finally gave in and spoke to the elder, who agreed to lead her back to the town.

Wan Li still remained with the Indians, but Sun Ling had every confidence he would be treated well and would fully recover.

They passed another structure burned to the ground. Sun Ling couldn't remember what had been there, but she knew someone must have taken a gigantic loss.

The elder stopped and nodded for Sun Ling to go around him and lead the way. She did, and when they were almost to the laundry, she held her breath. She would come to it before the rooming house where John would hopefully be waiting, and her gut clenched.

She turned the corner, and her breath left her all in one whoosh. The laundry was still standing, but it wasn't unscathed. The front window and door area were blackened, but the structure still stood, and from what she could glimpse inside, it was at least inhabitable.

They stopped their horses and John ran out, meeting her in the street.

"Sun Ling! My God—where have you been?" He looked her over, then turned to the Indian. He was frantic and breathing hard.

"It's a long story and we can get to that later. You must thank our friends so they can return to their camp.

They swooped in and saved Wan Li and I before the men could get to us. But where is Bei Ming? Did she make it?"

John nodded, catching his breath before putting his hands on her waist to help her down. "She is fine. They are still cleaning and trying to get reorganized."

Sun Ling slid off the horse, straight into his arms, as their gazes locked.

"I—I was frantic. We have looked everywhere for you, Sun Ling. They must've taken you far across the river."

She couldn't help but feel a flicker of joy at his concern. "I don't think so. There was a river, yes, but we didn't cross it. I am just relieved that they were so willing to help Wan Li, and I'm sure they waited to bring me back until they could be sure the uprising was over."

"I was petrified," he said under his breath. "You took at least ten years from my life."

"For that I apologize, but as you see, I am fine," she returned, trying to compose herself. She did not want him to know how worried she had been about him, too. She had to keep their conversation guided away from them. "I felt I had to do whatever possible to save that young man's life."

"I should've never left you alone."

Her face burned, and her heart thumped out a rhythm from being so close to him. Sun Ling moved out of his grasp. Her waist felt hot where his hands had been. She ignored the fluttering in her stomach as she put a few feet of distance between them. She couldn't even think with him that close.

"It appears you did the right thing," she said, looking at the laundry. "Are Jack Yan and—"

"Sun Ling!"

Before Sun Ling could finish her question, Bei Ming hustled out of the shop, holding her pantlegs up as she hurried to meet them.

"You made it," Sun Ling said to her as they embraced.

With a rush of Cantonese, Bei Ming pulled back and began to ask a myriad of questions, only stopping when she realized she hadn't given Sun Ling a chance to answer.

"Wait," Sun Ling said, looking past Bei Ming to the Indian. "I must tell him goodbye."

She went to the Indian and put her hand on his moccasin boot, squeezing it briefly. He watched her, his expression gruff.

"*Xie xie*," Sun Ling said, knowing he didn't understand the words but would know what she meant.

John joined her.

"My deepest gratitude," he said, then reached into his vest and began unbuckling a belt that Sun Ling hadn't noticed on him before. From it hung a pistol, and he handed the entire thing up to the Indian, holding it in the air.

"Where did you get that?" she asked John.

"The same place I'll get another tomorrow. I've learned that in a town such as this one, a man should not balk at being armed. But please, convey to him that I want to give it to him as a gift of my gratitude. For keeping you safe."

"I think he will understand, even without the words," Sun Ling said.

The Indian was admiring the gun, and he met John's eyes briefly. After John nodded and held it up a bit higher, the man took it. He showed the first smile Sun Ling had seen from him when he took the belt and fastened it around his thick waist, then adjusted it until the gun hung comfortably.

He slid off of his horse—more gracefully than a man of his age should've been able to—and faced both her and John.

Sun Ling smiled at him, hoping her gratitude for his hospitality was evident.

He nodded at her. Then he turned to John. Reaching down, he took both their hands and then held them together, hers tightly against John's. He nodded once more, a solemn gesture of finality, before releasing his grasp.

With that, he hopped back on his horse, then grabbed the reins of the one Sun Ling had ridden in. Pulling the horse around, he began to follow the trail they'd come in from.

Sun Ling pulled her hand from John's as though it were on fire. He smiled slightly, his familiar crooked grin making her feel like herself again.

An onslaught of cursing from some passing cowboys brought reality flooding through her. People were watching. And she had no time to waste. Not even for John.

"John, did Bei Ming tell you? I must get home to my father at once," she said.

He nodded. "Yes, we've got a lot to talk about, but first, let's get you inside so you can tell me exactly how you came to be riding into town looking like an Indian maiden."

CHAPTER TWENTY-ONE

A S THE COACH ROLLED INTO San Francisco two days later, Sun Ling perked up, and the nervous energy returned full force. Even though they'd made better time than she could have imagined, the return trip had still felt excruciatingly slow, leaving her with too much time to think. Her father's face had barely left her thoughts for a second, despite her ongoing battle to put her worry aside.

She also kept remembering when the elderly warrior had put her hand to John's. The memory of it burned in her mind and caused her cheeks to flame. She couldn't wait to be out of the small carriage and away from his intense stare.

Thankfully, this time John had ignored Clyde and hired a more competent driver for the first leg. They had not even stopped to stay overnight anywhere, just switched carriages as needed and stole snippets of sleep along the way. He'd promised to pay the drivers handsomely for their swiftness, and most of the journey was now a blur. On top of it all, Sun Ling's exhaustion made everything feel surreal.

"Do you think that Bei Ming will eventually marry Jack Yan?" John asked, breaking the silence.

"I suppose she might," she answered. "She seems very committed to helping him get things going again in the laundry, and they get along quite well."

It really hadn't surprised her that Bei Ming had asked if she could stay behind with him in his shop. San Francisco was dangerous for her if the tong she was connected to ever tracked her down. At least in Truckee there weren't tongs that Sun Ling knew of, or even associates of them. Only a mob of vigilantes who thought they owned the world.

When John had relayed to her the extent of the uprisings, Sun Ling felt sick at her stomach and lucky to be alive. He'd pieced together that the group of men who called themselves the Caucasian League had met at the house of the appointed leader, dressed in black, gathered their firearms and cans of kerosene and coal oil, and then slipped out of town to look for the cabins occupied by various Chinese woodcutters.

At the first cabin they'd come to, the men had covered the roof in oil before setting it aflame. When the Chinese men inside tried to flee, one man was shot in the stomach.

His comrades carried him into the darkness, hiding until morning, but unfortunately the man succumbed to his injuries and died.

That news made her realize how lucky she and Bei Ming had been, because the vigilantes were in too much of a hurry and had just thrown torches in the building, which had given them time to grab Wan Li and get out, though if it weren't for Dubuda and her tribe, Wan Li's fate would've been the same as Ah Ling's.

Sun Ling peeked out the window and saw they'd turned down the lane with her father's herb shop. She prayed he would forgive her for taking so long to return.

John had apologized numerous times to her for not being there when she'd needed him, though she'd never expressed anything but understanding. The picture he'd painted of what had transpired in town was startling in itself. Not only were many of the Chinese homes and businesses set afire, but he said townsmen had rushed through the streets, screaming out that the Chinese must go, hurling stones at them as they tried to escape the flames.

And the state-of-the-art fire engine the town liked to flaunt? John said they'd only used it to protect the few white businesses that were scattered within the burning Chinese ones.

"Are you thinking of Wan Li?" John asked. "You've barely said a word for an hour."

She nodded. "Yes, him, and the other man, as well. Ah Ling. They will never get justice, will they?"

John stroked his moustache. "For now, there will be no more uprisings because a congressional commission is on their way to investigate. The town officials are worried, even though their supposed Caucasian League is rumored to have grown to over three hundred members from the surrounding communities. They and their actions are about to be scrutinized. And it's a long shot, but it is possible that the culprits will held accountable. However, I've already heard they have hired Charles McGlashan to defend them, and he doesn't usually lose a case."

"And who is he?"

"Some time ago, I think around 1846 or 1847, there was a group of people that got stranded in a winter storm as they were trying to cross the high Sierra Nevada area. The Donner party. Have you heard of them?"

She nodded. It was a tragic story that still made the rounds. The families had been forced to resort to cannibalism to survive.

"Charles McGlashan is the attorney made famous from the publications he wrote about them. He has a lot of pull in the judicial system now. He claims that a Chinaman can be hanged for killing a white man but a white man cannot be hanged for killing a Chinaman."

"It's despicable, is what it is," Sun Ling said.

"I've promised Jack Yan and the others that I will return to stand beside them and even represent them, if needed. I may need you," he said, raising his eyebrows at her.

Her pulse quickened.

"It is my hope that Wan Li will press charges against the entire group until someone steps forward and takes responsibility for almost killing him. He should have some sort of compensation because he will no doubt have complications with his health for the rest of his life."

Wan Li would survive, and then hopefully he would move on to somewhere that he could recover and start over. Somewhere that he could build the future for he and the girl he loved in China—or if he was smart, he'd just go back there and make a life where he could be accepted without strife. Why would he want to suffer any more at the hands of vigilantes like those in Truckee?

"We're here," John said, leaning forward as the carriage came to a stop.

The first thing Sun Ling noticed as she looked out the window was the yellow flag indicating a pox alert. The sight of it made her dizzy with fear, even though she already knew there was illness there.

John opened the door and climbed out. Then he held out his hand to Sun Ling.

"Be careful," he said.

As soon as her feet touched the road, she felt a moment of dread, then relief that John was with her and she wouldn't have to face anyone alone. The feeling was ironic, for at first she hadn't wanted him to come. He'd never been to the shop before, though he'd met her father once briefly when she'd taken him to Adora's house and sat in the garden with him. But there wasn't time to drop him off first, as Sun Ling couldn't wait another moment to go to her father.

They walked to the door, and Sun Ling hesitated, her step faltering as she tried to calm herself.

John reached down and squeezed her hand. "It will be fine."

She pulled her hand loose, unwilling to let anyone see her being inappropriate with a man not her husband—and a white one, at that. People talked, and she'd learned a long time ago that her relationship with John and Adora was one that already had some speculating. She wouldn't give her father's neighbors any more fodder.

Before she could put her hand on the knob, the door swung open.

"Ah, the prodigal daughter has returned."

Involuntarily, she shrank back against John. While she'd expected Min Kao to greet her, she was taken totally off-guard to be face-to-face with his brother, the man who had caused her much pain on her arrival to San Francisco years before—the man who'd sworn to have revenge against her, out of some ridiculous notion that she'd turned Min Kao against him.

"Wei." She composed herself, straightening her shoulders and raising her chin. She adjusted the stylish but dusty bonnet she wore and brushed against the wrinkles of her white cotton day dress. It was simple, yet the cranberry-colored ribbons she'd adorned the sides with, along with the lace trim around the neckline, gave it a very reputable appearance. She didn't look to be a poor Chinese girl sitting in a squalid jail cell, as she had been the last time she and Wei had crossed paths.

Sun Ling was no longer that girl. And she would not allow him to see how shocked she was that he was there. What did it mean? Had they all died, leaving Wei like a vulture to pick through the pieces and see what of value he could salvage from his brother's life? Sun Ling couldn't imagine any other reason that Min Kao would let Wei back into their lives.

She felt overcome with fear, the thought of losing her family almost strangling her. But she held her emotions inside, her expression impassive.

Wei crossed his arms and stepped back, allowing her to enter. He was dressed in a tailored Western suit made of fine material, but she couldn't help but notice how much he had aged in the years since she'd seen him last. As she stepped into the shop, she felt a tingle of satisfaction that perhaps the universe was somehow repaying Min Kao's wayward brother for the wrongs he'd committed.

"I see you've still got the Lane family at your beck and call," Wei said, his voice dripping with acid as John moved to stand beside Sun Ling.

"And I see with the illness that has befallen Sun Ling's father, you've shown up to see how it might be to your benefit," John answered, his eyes narrowed at Wei.

Sun Ling looked around and saw no one familiar within the four walls of the shop. Even her father's stool was empty, propped against the wall as though waiting for its master. The small table where Luli studied and played was now piled high with plump bags marked *rice*, *sugar*, and *flour*. Gone was the array of glass bottles and bowls that Luli pretended to mix potions in. There were a few other people in the shop that she didn't recognize, including a haggard old lady behind her father's counter, standing there as though she owned the place.

"Make them leave," the old woman said to him, the hard dialect of her Cantonese nearly unintelligible. "We've no time for the gentry and his kept woman to be sightseeing here."

Sun Ling's shock turned to anger. "I beg your pardon."

Who were these people who'd taken over her father's

shop? She meant to get to the bottom of it and quickly. Then she would find out what had become of her father, Min Kao, and Jingwei. Even little Luli. Sun Ling felt a rush of protectiveness for all of them. She'd been there for his brother and Luli more than Wei had. What gave him the right to now descend on them in a time of need? From what she knew of Wei, he would do nothing for anyone unless it resulted in some benefit to himself.

Simply, Wei was not a good man, and he was not welcome in her father's house. But she would deal with him and his cohorts later.

She left John's side and strode past Wei, then slammed her bag on the counter.

"Where is my family?" she demanded.

CHAPTER TWENTY-TWO

SUN LING HELD BROTH TO her father's lips. Their gazes met over the rim. Relief couldn't even come close to describe the emotion that surrounded her when she took the stairs and found him still alive in the room with Jingwei and Luli. He'd barely stirred all day, though, and Sun Ling was beyond worried.

She stared down at his brow. The furrows were worrisome and deep, from pain or uneasiness—she didn't know. He'd been through so much, and she had not been there. It pained her to think of it.

Wei had explained to her all that had happened, and though she'd have rather turned her back to him, she listened as he catalogued everything he had done to save his brother's family. The old woman, it seemed, was some sort of healer, who had cost Wei a fortune to entice to leave her shop where she saw many patrons, to focus only on three near-death customers.

Sun Ling only half-listened, and before Wei had even finished with his self-congratulatory accolades, she'd taken off to see for herself. She cared not that she'd exposed herself to the pox. If it were to get her, it would be penance for not being there with Min Kao to nurse their family back to health—with her father as any faithful daughter should be.

"You must go home and sleep," Tao Ren said, his face

etched with concern.

"I will sleep downstairs, Baba," she replied. "I want to be here when Jingwei awakens."

That wasn't the only reason she didn't leave, and he knew it. Her guilt clung to her like a bad smell. Beside them, Luli played with her rag doll, but next to her lay Jingwei, still in a deep sleep that the old medicine woman claimed to have put her in.

"It will help her recover," she'd said, then at Baba's request, cataloged a list of ingredients that she was using. He wanted to be sure the woman knew what she was doing. She'd obviously passed the test because he nodded to give her the go-ahead.

"Mama will be fine," Luli said. "The nice lady told me so."

In the two days and one night that Sun Ling had been there, she hadn't had a chance to talk to Min Kao and get his account of the last two weeks that the pox ravaged those under his roof, but as soon as she could, Sun Ling meant to question him about this 'nice lady' that Luli wanted to talk about constantly. But for now, there were more important things to discuss with her father. While she was in Truckee, she'd done a lot of bargaining with the gods, promising all sorts of things if they only allowed her father to live. And if she knew anything, it was that one didn't break oaths made to the heavens.

"Baba, I must ask your forgiveness for not being here when you needed me," she whispered, leaning over him so that Luli couldn't hear. Everyone else was downstairs eating the lunch that Wei had sent his errand boys for, finally leaving them alone in the room, so now was the time for her to get some things off her chest.

"No forgiveness needed, child," he said, his voice frail. "It sounds as though you were in quite the predicament, yourself."

He was right about that. Sun Ling had distracted her

father during his awake moments with her stories of all
that had happened in Truckee, including her adventure
with the Indians. He had been very distressed to hear
how the Chinese were being treated, but he'd smiled
weakly at her account of bonding with Dubuda and the
other women in the tribe.

"I would never have believed you would be such a
child of adventure," he'd said, his eyes showing a twin-
kle again for a few minutes as he'd listened. "I've fought
to hang on for you, and I am so relieved you made it."

But today, things weren't going well.

While only the night before, he'd seemed greatly
improved, now he struggled again, falling in and out of
sleep, and at times speaking in confused fragments.

Sun Ling needed to find the words that would bring
him back to her completely.

He struggled to sit up, then reached out and took Sun
Ling's hand. "I need to talk to you, Daughter."

"I'm listening, Baba," Sun Ling said, unable to keep
the worry from her voice.

He swallowed hard before beginning again. "You
need to forget the past so you can embrace your future.
Buddha tells us that each morning we are born again,
and what you do today is what matters most."

"I agree," Sun Ling said. "And that is why I am going
to be a better daughter, starting now."

He smiled gently.

"Sun Ling, you are already the best daughter a man
could ask for. Why are you so troubled? If it is forgiveness you seek, and will bring you peace, then you have
it."

"*Xie xie*, Baba," Sun Ling thanked him. "But that is
not all. Only I have the ability to give you the desire of
your heart in your final years, and you've asked me to
comply too many times. I shall agree to it now. I will
marry the man of your choosing, and give you a grand-

son."

When the words were out, Sun Ling almost couldn't believe she'd said them. She swallowed past the lump in her throat. An arranged marriage of duty was not what she'd dreamed of, but she was willing to do anything for her father to truly be satisfied with her as a daughter. In a world where females had little say, only a man's word was considered final. But Sun Ling also had honor, and above all, she wanted to please her father. She would keep her oath, even if it meant changing the very woman she had been striving to become.

He smiled gently. "I think we both know that fate has spent years pulling you towards someone of *your* choosing, if you would only admit what your heart knows is true."

Sun Ling stared down at her father. Could he be talking about John? Was her father, a man known to cling to traditions and honor, giving his blessing for her to consider someone outside of their heritage?

"I only want to please you, Baba," she said, sighing deeply as the moment became even heavier.

He shook his head and a tear ran down his old cheek, writhing its way through the crags and lines of wisdom.

"Daughter, don't you know that my heart's desire has only been to be reunited with you, and to have your forgiveness for the unconscionable thing I did in ever sending you to Hong Kong?"

The guilt in his eyes was like a knife in Sun Ling's gut. She couldn't bear it.

"Baba, you did what you felt necessary for me to have a better life. You did not know what would befall me at the hands of that family, and I do not hold you responsible. But either way, you have my forgiveness."

He coughed, and the sound of it struck Sun Ling, from how painful it must be. She needed to talk to the healer woman about a lung remedy. Why wasn't the old woman up there working now, instead of wasting valuable daylight?

"Now that we have both extended forgiveness for the other's perceived wrongdoings, do I also have your oath that—" He paused to cough, covering his mouth for a moment before finding his voice again. "That you will find peace and happiness, and slow down your evening escapades?"

She bowed her head. "I will try."

He squeezed her hand. "Remember, Sun Ling—our lives do not begin only at the moment of birth; and death too, does not imply the end of everything. I am very proud of you."

"Why are you talking like this, Baba?" Sun Ling asked, concerned at his change in mood from the day before. She did not want him to speak of death.

Before he could respond, she heard a rustle of bed-clothes behind her.

"Mama!" Luli said.

Sun Ling turned to find Jingwei staring at them. The relief that filled her made her dizzy with emotion. "You're awake," she said, pulling her hand from her father's before going to Jingwei's bedside. She poured her a cup of water from a pitcher kept on the bedside table.

She held it to Jingwei's lips while she took a sip. Then another and another.

"Min Kao?" Jingwei asked, once she'd had enough water.

"He's downstairs having a bite to eat, and he has not been struck with the pox."

"But you and I were, Mama." Luli stroked Jingwei's forehead, making Sun Ling smile at the tenderness that passed between them.

Yes, they had beat the pox, but they hadn't come out unscathed. Jingwei would have scars upon her face—

the pockmarks were deep and vivid. Luli, however, would likely only have a few on her arms, as those on her cheeks were already healing well.

Downstairs, a voice bellowed with laughter, and Sun Ling recognized it as Wei. She wondered how much Jingwei remembered of her convalescence, and if she knew that Min Kao's brother was involved. Over the years, they'd discussed Wei occasionally, and Jingwei had expressed the hope that he would stay away from them and Luli.

"How do you feel?" Sun Ling asked her.

"Better," Jingwei said, even as turned her attention to Luli.

Sun Ling could see a mother's worry as Jingwei scrutinized her daughter's youthful skin.

"I will go tell Min Kao that you are awake. He will want to see for himself," Sun Ling said. "He will be much relieved that you have all pushed through, now, and I'm sure we will plan a banquet to lay at the feet of the gods and thank them for this miracle."

Jingwei nodded and smiled weakly.

Luli looked up suddenly. "And Ye Ye says we are fighters because we were able to beat it. He said to tell you how proud he is of you, Mama, for being the victor."

Sun Ling hadn't heard her father say that. Was Luli making it up?

She stood, and a shiver ran through her, quite like an electric current except it washed her with warmth before dissipating. She looked over to where her father lay. His eyes were closed, but his face didn't hold pain or worry. Instead of the evidence of the long illness he'd carried, there was nothing but a peaceful gaze.

"Baba," she called. "Are you still awake?"

He didn't answer, and she went to him. Kneeling by his bed, she took his hand in hers, and she was struck by the heaviness. It was still warm, yet it didn't feel like her father's hand. It felt—well, there it was—lifeless.

With fear in her throat, she lay her head on his chest.

She heard nothing.

For a minute, it stayed that way. Then an unnatural high keening hit her ears.

It was a terrifyingly haunting sound.

Sun Ling cringed and kept her arms over her baba, protecting him. Only after she realized the sound came from her own soul did she accept the fact that for her father, there would be no banquet of thanksgiving.

PART THREE
UNDER THE STARS

CHAPTER TWENTY-THREE

MIN KAO CLOSED THE LEDGER and sighed. The beads on the worn *suanpan* that lay next to it caught his eye. No matter how he added and subtracted, begged or borrowed from the long lines of numbers, sliding the beads noisily around the counting frame until the clacking reverberated in his head, nothing would make the sums look better. The smallpox that had invaded their home was long gone, barely a pockmark upon his daughter's face to remind him of his terrified vigil. Even after several months, the loss of Tao Ren still burdened him, emotionally and financially, and the consequences still affected their livelihood.

The day the old man had died, something in Min Kao changed, dampening his hope for the future. Possibly because, on top of Tao Ren's death, he'd also learned his own mother had passed, too, this time during yet another childbirth—something that, at her age, shouldn't have happened at all.

Now Min Kao grieved that he'd never have the chance to show his Mǔqīn how well he'd upheld his oath to protect Luli.

However, if Luli's gift could be counted on, even in death his mother was witness to their lives and had even contributed to pulling Luli through her bout with smallpox. Now the illness was gone from their home, but the collateral damage would take years to recover from.

To be sure, the interruption it caused to their business had left them at the bottom of their coffers, with customers reluctant to return, many choosing another herbalist with more maturity and experience. No matter that Min Kao had the honor of having been under the strict tutelage of Tao Ren, the people wanted someone at least twice his age to direct them in matters of their health.

Outside the shop, Chinatown was booming, even pushing past the invisible boundary between Stockton Street and the lower part of Nob Hill. The whites tried to keep the Chinese boxed in but his people were smart and with tenacity and ingenuity, they found ways to expand. At times they built inward and upward, and now the streets were packed with even more stores, boarding houses, temples, restaurants, gambling halls, brothels, and even a smattering of theatres.

The atmosphere felt as though someone had bottled up China and brought it across the ocean to the western shore. It was loud, colorful, and rampant with all sorts of exotic wares and shows. The intoxicating smells that blew in off the docks blended with the familiar and pungent sizzling of oil frying up Chinese delicacies on many street corners.

Min Kao felt like everyone was flourishing except him. It was frustrating. He was honest and hard-working, yet he fought to make ends meet enough to pay their rent and put food on the table. He wanted more for his family. Jingwei and Luli deserved better.

His brother had tried to help again, coming to him after the grand funeral Sun Ling had organized for her father.

Min Kao still doubted that Wei's resources were gained legally and ethically, thus rejected his offer, maintaining that his integrity was not to be bought. And he had no inclination to ever see his father again.

However, some days he pondered whether he'd spoken too rashly to his brother. Only the month before, they'd sold the finest piece of Jingwei's jewelry, a heavy jade bracelet given to her by Sun Ling.

Min Kao still felt guilt from that transaction, though it had given them the funds needed to stock the shop's herb inventory again.

Sun Ling had brought them another girl the night before, and a woman the week before that. Jingwei had settled the new girl into what once had been the sickroom, introducing her to the other woman. Even gave her alternate clothing and a hot meal of rice and vegetables, taking from their already-low pantry.

The cost for their missions was something Min Kao had always looked past, knowing it meant a lot to his wife for her to be able to make a difference in the lives of girls who found themselves in unfortunate circumstances. Not only did it help Jingwei to come to terms with her own past as a bonded servant, but she thought of it as her way of thanking the gods for giving her a better life.

But now he thought it bordered on obsession.

Min Kao was going to have to talk to her and explain that unless Sun Ling started to contribute even more financially—as in, take up Jingwei's share of the cost to feed, clothe, and set these women off on new lives—then it would have to stop.

It wouldn't be easy to get through to his wife, but she had to see that they barely had enough to feed their own family. Luli and Peso both needed shoes. Books for school. And it was going to take years for them to build their business back to where it was before, if it was even possible. With the smallpox hitting them so hard, Tao Ren's shop had lost respect throughout the Chinese quarter. People thought he should've been able to keep the illness at bay, at least for his own family and self.

"Uncle?"

Min Kao looked up to find Peso holding out his hand, a stack of bills in it.

"What is this?"

"I'm been making deliveries from the docks, and this is my take from this week," Peso said, smiling broadly.

"You weren't at school?" Min Kao frowned. He thought of Wei, then, growing up as an eager boy always trying to turn a coin, no matter how he had to make it. "And did you earn this fairly, without criminal conduct?"

Peso looked taken aback. "I didn't steal it, Uncle. Every bit was given to me for a job well done. Nothing unsavory about it."

Min Kao searched his face and saw truth. He felt relief.

"Still, it is not your responsibility to keep us afloat," he said.

Peso shrugged. "I want to help. I'm not a boy any longer."

He was right about that. Min Kao couldn't believe how tall Peso had grown in the past months. He'd obviously gotten his sturdy build from his Mexican father, though the angular planes of his face still held a strong Chinese familiarity that fit with his ability to speak fluent Mandarin. He was a handsome lad—and smart, too.

Peso could even converse easily in Cantonese, the more prevalent language in Chinatown, which a huge help to Min Kao who, even after nearly a decade of living around so many Cantonese, had not picked it up so easily.

Now Min Kao could add 'generous' to the boy's list of attributes.

"I can't take that," he said to him, pushing the bills back toward the boy.

Peso straightened to his full height and pushed it forward again. "Yes, you can. And there will be more, especially if I can save up for my own horse and wagon. There are so many people coming off the ships and not nearly enough draymen to carry their belongings to their new abodes. The Chinese coming in don't want to trust the white devils, and the whites don't want to feel as though they are being servants to the Chinese, so they price gouge to make up for it. I'm young, and no one takes me to be a swindler, so they easily choose me from the crowd."

"How are you carrying it?"

"You remember old Lau who owns the laundry? His boy gets all the deliveries done early in the morning, then I rent his horse and wagon for the rest of the day, and he gets half of my profits."

"And what do you get for a delivery?" Min Kao asked.

"The foreigners charge three dollars, so I give a bargain at two. Lau gets one dollar of it, and I can usually do at least three runs in an afternoon. Sometime only two, though, depending on their destination and amount of belongings."

Min Kao was surprised, but it sounded as though Peso had a bit of business sense to him.

"You can drive a wagon?" he asked, unable to visualize the boy behind the reins of an unruly horse.

Peso smiled broadly. "Not only can I, but some say I'm really good at it. It's really not so hard. If the other drivers would only learn to earn the respect from their teams without assaulting them with words and straps across their backs, they'd find it easier, too."

Min Kao let out a chuckle, imagining Peso whispering encouragement to a horse before each trek. That part wasn't surprising, as he'd learned quickly that the boy had a much gentler spirit than most. Perhaps that was why he and Luli were so close. She saw how vulnerable and trusting Peso was.

"But school—"

"I am terrible at school. And other than Luli, I have no friends there. They don't see me as Chinese. I'd rather stay away and do what I can to help the family."

Min Kao wanted to protest more, but Luli had told him of the abuse heaped on Peso for his mixed heritage. He wasn't accepted as Chinese, and even the Mexicans turned their back on him and treated him badly.

The boy had stuck with it, holding his tongue as he struggled through the lessons, only because it had been a rule set in place when he'd arrived under their roof. It was clear though that unlike Luli, who loved her classes, Peso wasn't happy there and had most likely learned very little.

And they really needed the money.

"Perhaps I can help," Min Kao said.

"No, you can't. Don't forget about your back," Peso said, shaking his head.

The pox hadn't hit Min Kao, but carrying Tao Ren up the stairs and spending hour upon hour bent over his family, tending to them as every muscle clenched in anxiety, had taken its toll on Min Kao's back. It had never been the same. He'd spent many sleepless nights trying to get comfortable and failing. Delivering goods would require lifting of heavy trunks, crates, and barrels. He could not possibly do it. And someone needed to mind the shop, even if only a few customers came per day.

Peso stood before him, waiting for approval. If Min Kao ordered him to give up his business, to go back to school, then the boy would most likely comply. But was that what was best for his family?

He sighed, then put his hand over the money. Slowly he plucked a few bills from the top and then slid the rest back to Peso.

"I will not take all of your hard-earned pay. You can give a percentage to the family coffers and save the rest for your future. One day, you'll be ready to leave here and make a life of your own, and I want you to be financially prepared. Unfortunately, I'll most likely have nothing to offer."

That reminded Min Kao that one day, he would need to provide a dowry and a wedding for Luli. Time was moving too fast, and he was beginning to feel like a failure in the paternal role he'd taken on for her.

Peso nodded, then bowed his head. "I am grateful for every moment you've allowed me to be here, and I understand there will come a time that I shall have to go."

Min Kao frowned and put his hand atop Peso's. "Wait," he said. "Look at me."

When Peso met his eyes, Min Kao began again.

"I'm not saying I ever want you to go, Peso. But when you become a man, you'll meet a girl who you'll want to make your wife. Then it will be your desire to make your own way. It happens in every household. With every son."

When Min Kao said *son*, Peso looked up, tears filling his eyes.

"Now tell me more about this drayman job and the people you've met coming in from China. Which provinces do they hail from? What sort of treasures do they bring?"

Peso swallowed hard, obviously trying to control his emotion before speaking. "Just yesterday I saw a carved wedding bed being carried off of a ship. The top lattice was intricately carved with magpies. It was so large, it took six men to move it down the gangway and onto a wagon. It was so grand that I was tempted to follow the wagon and see where it ended up. If only I could have something like that one day."

Min Kao smiled at the sparkle in Peso's eyes. The boy had ambition, of that there was no doubt.

CHAPTER TWENTY-FOUR

JINGWEI LEANED OVER LULI'S SHOULDER, watching her as she carefully measured out ten drops of the oil they'd distilled from the clary sage flower, and then added it to the vial. Luli moved methodically, taking care to be exact since Jingwei lingered behind her to supervise.

"How will this work, Mama?" she asked, putting the rubber stopper into the vial and setting it upon the shelf with the other concoctions.

Jingwei straightened, putting her hands on the small of her back to ease the discomfort of bending for so long. As Luli grew in beauty, she was flourishing in inquisitiveness, making her the perfect student for studying alternate ways of healing. Luli was quickly learning that extracting the oils from flowers, grasses, fruits, leaves, roots, and trees was using nature in its most powerful form.

"The mother that is having trouble breast-feeding because of insufficient milk will put a few drops on the palms of her hands, then massage it onto her breasts in a circular movement, starting under her arms and working inward toward her cleavage. If she does it once a day, it will make her stronger, then her milk will come in better, and both mother and child will be soothed."

"I hope she remembers to wash it off before trying to

feed her baby," Luli said.

Jingwei smiled. Of course Luli would think of that. She was becoming more and more fascinated with the subject of men and women coming together to make a life. A few months before, she'd asked Jingwei why she didn't have siblings. It was a question that Min Kao and Jingwei had known would come one day, but she was still unprepared. The truth was, Jingwei still envisioned herself as a mother to a brood of children, not just one and she could never explain why that was not to be.

"What will we make tomorrow?" Luli asked.

Just this one formula to extract oil had been strenuous. They'd begun by placing the petals in goat fat—which in itself had been a trial to find—then they'd waited until the oil was pulled from the petals into the fat. After that happened, the rest of the process was tedious and time-consuming.

"We won't be putting anything new together tomorrow." Jingwei's supplies were limited, though the flowers that Sun Ling brought to her from Adora's garden were a huge help. The truth was, many of the plants and flowers she needed just didn't grow in San Francisco. Even the pink-rimmed petals of the clary sage flowers were from a plant brought in from Central Asia, sold at the farmer's market. Jingwei had been lucky to get her hands on it at all, and it had cost her more than she wanted Min Kao to know.

"If we have time, I want to teach you about how the oils from lemon, lavender, and a few others, can together be a remedy to assist convalescence. A few drops into a warm bath can make our new mothers feel less nervous and stressed."

The remedies they were making had not brought in much income thus far. While Min Kao claimed to be supportive, he resisted putting any of it for sale where the customer could see it, as he felt it was a dishonor to stray from Tao Ren's medicines.

Jingwei was therefore practically giving away her concoctions to the mothers she tended, experimenting with them to tweak her formulas. Her love of mixing perfumes had given her the idea to use the flowers, leaves, and stems for other things, as well. Whether it would lead to much, she didn't know, but it was something she enjoyed and that she and Luli could do together. Making memories.

Luli stood and turned, embracing Jingwei tightly.

"*Wo ai ni*, Mama," she muttered accolades of love.

"And I, you," Jingwei replied.

She and Min Kao didn't have much, and it was true, they struggled even more than most since much of their customer base had dropped off after Tao Ren's death, but they all cared for and respected one another, each working to do what they could to contribute, and that was worth more than any rich Californian could claim.

Jingwei kept that in mind on the days she was tired from her ministrations as a midwife, or from dealing with the girls that Sun Ling delivered to her. She somehow found the energy to spend some time with Luli, teaching her all about flowers as Jingwei's mother had done with her, handing down the knowledge from one generation to the next.

And for her years of hard work, the ladies at the mission had stepped in to provide Luli with the tutelage that Jingwei couldn't. Through them, Luli was learning to speak a much better version of English. She was also being schooled in the art of calligraphy. Even learning poetry and reading from the English classics.

Yes, Luli would outshine them all, when it was all said and done. Jingwei was ever so proud of her.

"I'm going out to see if Peso is back from the docks yet," Luli said, then skirted out of the room.

Jingwei went to the silk box that held what little jewelry they had left. She opened it and peered down at the brooch that symbolized who Luli really was. She plucked it out of the box and held it in her palm.

Her hand trembled, moved by a current of electricity that passed through until it frightened her, and she let the brooch drop back into the box.

The piece had felt alive with energy.

Jingwei thought of the woman who had come to Luli during her illness. Did Luli somehow realize that it was someone very special to her? Did she ever suspect that Jingwei wasn't her birth mother?

It pained Jingwei not to tell Luli the truth, but Min Kao said she wasn't ready. Jingwei didn't think he'd ever feel Luli was ready. He wanted to keep her an innocent little girl, but the truth was, Luli was growing more rapidly than either of them were prepared for.

Already she turned heads on the street, even with Peso always protectively at her side. There was just something about her, a quiet maturity that hinted Luli was special. Others—not just them—picked up on it and gravitated toward the girl.

Only the year before, Luli had slipped and read someone, giving them the message passed to her from their loved one.

After Luli told the woman her child was there, trying to speak to her, the woman had fainted away. When she'd come to, she said her daughter was swept over the rails on the ship bound to America, and they'd never recovered her body. The child wanted her mother to stop worrying about her, to go on and live life. Luli, being the compassionate soul she was, had felt the anguish the woman carried with her and had not been able to walk away without trying to take her burden.

Since then, a few more residents from Chinatown had come sniffing around, trying to see if the rumors of a soothsayer in the body of a teen girl was true. Min Kao had run them off, but Jingwei wondered how many more out there had encountered Luli outside of the shop and if their daughter had ignored their warnings and complied with pleas to speak to the dead.

It terrified Jingwei.

"Jingwei?" she heard Min Kao call from downstairs. His voice wasn't right. He sounded as though something were wrong.

She took a deep breath to calm her nerves, then headed out of the room and down the stairs. As she descended, she heard a woman's voice. Not Sun Ling's, but that of someone else. As soon as the main room came into view, she was struck by a feeling of déjà vu. Her memories went back to the moment so long ago on the ship bound from Hong Kong, the exact second that she'd taken Luli into her arms and felt that connection that would never leave.

She felt it again.

This time it came as she stopped and took in the scene presented to her. There was a woman there, indeed. It was the leader of the mission. In her arms she held a small baby wrapped in a blue cloth, his skin dark eyes like coal.

Confused, she looked at Min Kao, only to find that he held another child identical to the first—though the bundle he held against his chest was wrapped in a pale pink.

Luli stood beside Min Kao, the tiny fingers of the girl infant wrapped around her thumb.

"What is going on?" Jingwei whispered.

The woman turned to her and smiled hopefully. There was a large basket at her feet, piled with blankets. Next to it, a bag of bottles and a jar of milk.

"Jingwei, meet the two newest additions to your family, if you'll have them. They are orphaned, and strict instructions were left that they be delivered to you. With the years of your dedicated service, I can't agree more that you would be their best option for care."

Min Kao was shaking his head. "I've already told her, we can't—"

Jingwei held her hand up to interrupt him. She spoke to the woman. "Don't you have ladies from society clamoring to adopt them?"

"I feel these orphans should remain with their own people. You will need to find a nursemaid, but you are still the best option," the woman said.

Jingwei felt her breath quicken. Orphans? Their own people? She remembered the young woman she'd been administering to weeks before, her belly larger than normal for a pregnancy of that stage. She'd disappeared before delivering, and Jingwei had thought she'd decided to return to China and the safety of her own family.

Could these be her children? And if so, what of the husband she'd claimed to have? Jingwei had never met him, but the girl said he was a storekeeper. Was he gone, as well? What could have happened to them both?

"Jingwei," Min Kao said, a warning in his tone.

She left the last stair and came to stand between the woman and Min Kao, unsure which child to touch first. She looked down into the dark eyes of the boy, and he locked gazes with her. The woman pushed him into her arms, and Jingwei felt the warmth of him against her chest, acknowledged the strong beat of his heart.

He was a fighter.

"Jingwei, please," Min Kao whispered. "It's impossible."

The woman's smile faded, and she looked concerned, her glance going from Min Kao to Jingwei.

"Mama, can we keep them?" Luli said, her eyes hopeful.

Jingwei looked down at the face of the infant girl, the roundness reminding her of Luli when she was that small. The lips so rosy, yet chapped as though missing her mother's breast. She needed a mother. Not just any mother, either. Jingwei could feel the connection, even without touching. It was there, almost palpable in the air between them.

It couldn't be denied.

"Min Kao," Jingwei said softly, looking at him.

He shook his head. "How?"

They didn't need to speak of their dire circumstances. Words weren't needed to remind her of how close to destitute they were. Jingwei didn't want the woman to know.

"We will find a way," she said, pleading with her eyes.

He sighed, long and heavy. "We just can't. You know this is true."

She wished for more words to convince him, but she could see his mind was set. But she had to at least keep them long enough to see them settled. She knew someone she could call on for nursing, too. She turned to the woman. "I will care for them while you look for another place. I can get a nursemaid immediately and may know a childless couple who will take them."

She beckoned for Min Kao to hand the other child over. He did, then helped her until she had both babies balanced in her arms. She felt breathless with longing. They felt so right there—so perfect. Almost as though they filled a part of her that she had not known was empty.

Luli put her arms around the three of them, and as soon as Min Kao had shown the mistress out the door, he joined in. Jingwei savored the moment, as suddenly, deep within her soul, she knew that with the arrival of the tiny two, the gods had laid out a new path for her and Min Kao follow.

CHAPTER TWENTY-FIVE

AFTER A LONG DAY OF sewing, Sun Ling's hands were tired. She remained in the kitchen with Bessie during dinner, but she forbade anyone to talk above a whisper or make any racket that would inhibit her from hearing the conversation around the family table in the next room. Normally, she would sit with them, but with the captain home from an extended journey, she chose to steer clear of his steely gaze.

But their table talk was too interesting not to eavesdrop.

John was home for a visit, and Sun Ling could barely conceal her relief to see him. And she wanted some time with him to talk. For now he vented, voicing his frustration about the most recent campaign against the Chinese, some sort of inflammatory pamphlet being distributed.

As he talked, Lian moved quietly around them as she served. Sun Ling really owed Adora for talking her mother into yet another hire, and honestly, having Lian with them brightened the dim attic. She was a sweet girl who was eager to pay back what she felt was a huge debt owed to Sun Ling. And she knew to keep the details of their initial meeting private, too.

"More water, please, Lian," Mrs. Lane said, then nodded toward her glass to indicate what she wanted.

John continued to talk—ranting about the committee he referred to as a farce.

"What do you expect, Son?" The captain said, talking around the huge turkey leg he'd just put to his mouth. "Chinatown is less of a community than it is a den of iniquity. With all the opium, gambling houses, and prostitution, it's no wonder that the fine citizens of San Francisco want to have it eradicated."

"Papa," Adora scolded, and Sun Ling saw her glance toward the kitchen.

You tell him, Adora, Sun Ling thought. What about the herb shops, laundries, and the multitude of other less-savory businesses? And the families? What of them?

She needed not worry the captain's insults would go unchallenged, because in the next second, John slammed his glass down on the table so hard Sun Ling was surprised it didn't shatter.

"That's not true, and you know it," he said. "Yes, they have their fair share of the unsavory side of life, but so do we. Many of those houses of ill repute you talk about are filled with white prostitutes, not Chinese. After all, your own colleagues are seeking out consolation from the fallen women who land in Chinatown, Father."

"Oh, chile," Bessie whispered, stepping back a least a foot and shaking her head. "Things gonna get nasty now."

Sun Ling peeked around the doorway just in time to see Mrs. Lane jerk upright in her seat as though a puppet pulled by a string. Her face was paler than even normal.

"I will not have this sort of talk around my table," she said, glancing up toward Lian and Julia.

"Mama, this is an essential conversation," Adora said. "You just may need to send Julia for your smelling salts, because John has some important issues to speak of."

Without prompting, Julia scuttled out of the room, most likely glad to be out of the line of fire in case talk turned to the Irish. Now only Lian stood along the sideboard next to the table, unable to understand the English but obviously aware of the tension. Still, she held her ground and waited, prepared to serve the next course.

The captain slowly swallowed what he held in his mouth. He looked up and met his son's eyes. Then he turned to Adora and shook his head. "I don't know what I ever did to make my own children such heathen-loving fools, but I'll tell you this, I'll not allow you to speak ill of the upstanding and respectable men who run this city."

Behind him, Lian began to tremble at the low, threatening tone he'd taken.

"Of course you won't," John said. "Because for the last decade, you've had most of them in your back pocket so they'll look the other way when it comes time to pay taxes on your shipments. Yes, Father, we understand completely what your stance is."

Even Adora looked shocked, and Sun Ling knew John had gone too far.

The captain paled, then pointed a finger at John. "How dare you? Are you truly so thickheaded as to speak of my business in front of your mother and sister? You know nothing of what I do, because you have never cared to be involved. All high and mighty you are—too good to follow in the steps of your seafaring father."

"Julia—where is my medicine?" Mrs. Lane called weakly.

Sun Ling rolled her eyes. The mistress's medicine was the laudanum she'd come to rely on to get herself through her days. She was addicted, and with it, she shut everything else out, but everyone in the house pretended otherwise.

"And after everything I've done to work and put you through school, ignoring your presumptuous attitude that, because of my trade, I am somehow beneath you…" the captain muttered, then took a long drink from his glass of whiskey.

Lian quietly left the room—where to, Sun Ling wasn't sure, but it was most likely the back porch where she could hide from the sudden discord. She was still as timid as a rabbit, but she'd need to learn to ignore the commotions in a house such as the Lanes' if she planned to stay long.

"Would you like to take this to the library?" John asked his father. "Away from the women?"

"I beg your pardon. I want to be a part of this, too," Adora said, indignation making two round red spots appear on her cheeks. She fiddled nervously with the one of the fifteen buttons Sun Ling had just finished sewing on her new bodice that afternoon. Made of a fine bluish black velvet, the bodice was lined with a simple brown cotton, making it one of Adora's easier requests.

"I've had enough." The captain stood, letting his napkin fall into his bowl of pea soup. "John, I'll ask you to refrain from visiting your family home if you cannot show me the respect due as your father. I know you are still grieving the loss of your wife, but I'll not stand for your insults."

John shrugged, appearing unaffected by his father's words, but Sun Ling saw the tic in his jaw that the mention of his late wife caused.

"And you," the captain pointed at Adora. "I've been patient with you long enough. You let a good man get away with your aspirations to be some sort of writer. Now you expect to be a part of every conversation, whether suitable for young women or not. I've made up my mind; you can keep scribbling in your diary all you want, but you will choose a husband before the season is over. I'll not be responsible for a spinster daughter all my days. All these women's rights you want to preach about day and night, and the silly trousers your Chinese maid makes for you—you'll make this family the laughingstock of the town."

Sun Ling wasn't surprised that Adora didn't throw a fit. Gone was the flighty girl she'd met on the ship, and in her place, a woman. One with a new air of maturity.

Adora stood and sighed loudly, then straightened her shoulders and glared at her father. "It's not scribbling that I do, but I'm sure you'll never understand that, Father. And I've never worn the trousers outside of this house except in the stables, though I've had a mind to. But I thought your goal was for me to be content with life? Doesn't every father want his children to find their purpose? Would you have me be a simpering fool and marry someone I don't love just to appease your sensibilities?"

"Yes, I damn sure would," the captain said, then strode out of the room.

The tears started, one running down the slope of Adora's cheek. But they were silent, a blessing for them all that there were no longer such audible tantrums in the household.

Sun Ling gave up her need to remain unseen and went into the dining room. It was rare indeed for the captain not to do anything and everything to please his only daughter, and his outburst was shocking, even to Sun Ling. He had to know, didn't he, that he was a part of the reason Adora had been so spoiled and hardheaded in the past? Perhaps he wanted to keep her that way. Obviously he hadn't noticed that Adora had matured and no longer made such a fuss about her hair and clothing or obsessing over parties and gossip—but instead spent time doing activities to build upon her intelligence.

His pompousness made him oblivious to what was happening right under his nose. Even his own wife barely left her bedchamber when he wasn't around. The captain was a poor patriarch of the family, in Sun Ling's opinion.

"Don't pay him any heed. He doesn't mean it," she said, putting her arm around Adora and ignoring the petulant expression worn by Mrs. Lane at her sudden appearance.

"No, he does mean it. He's ashamed of me because I won't conform to his idea of what a woman should be," Adora said. "He thinks that because I read novels, I'm addled in the head. It doesn't cross his mind that a woman can have a brain, too."

"Well, this was a lovely family dinner," John said, a wry grin sneaking across his face. "I suppose Father hasn't noticed, I am a middle-aged widowed man, and you, Adora, are a ripe old age of twenty-eight years. I'd hardly think that makes us children. But then, he wants to be blind to everything else, why not to his own brood?"

Now the room was charged, with a tension that Sun Ling felt deep in her stomach.

"Oh, John, how could you?" Mrs. Lane said. "I wanted a nice, civilized dinner. You've even scared off the help."

"No, Mother, how can *you*?" John said. "Don't act like you don't understand the importance of this issue. The Chinese are good enough to stitch your clothing, wash your laundry, clean your home, and work your gardens, but when your husband sides with those who want to run them out of this country, you have nothing to say? Where is your spine? Is it pooled in the bottom of that cup that you claim is your medicine?"

"John." Adora hissed a warning.

His mother was quiet, but the quiver in her chin said enough. Gone was her moment of being stronger than usual, of speaking out. Now Sun Ling was dismayed to see she'd bowed her head and returned to the quiet shell she normally hid under. The mistress wore one of Sun

Ling's creations—a long fitted jacket with three-quarter length striped sleeves over a matching striped skirt. She'd chosen a pale peach color, against Sun Ling's urgings, and now her wan face blended with the outfit. Even the yellow sprig of nosegay tucked into her collar did nothing to brighten her looks.

Pity was what Sun Ling suddenly felt for the woman. She was obviously not well.

John stood and went to her. He bent beside her chair, reaching for her hand.

He held it to his heart. "I apologize, Mother. Please, forgive me. I'm exhausted, and I do not wish to take my frustrations out on you. It's just that—that—well, you know how stubborn Father is. He is a man of much means and, if he wanted, could add a sane and respected voice to the fight for equality. That he continues to behave this way is astounding to me."

Mrs. Lane blinked back tears. "Son, we didn't send you to law school to spend all your time defending lost causes. Can you not focus on other, more profitable cases? For me, John?"

"Mother, please," Adora said. "John is doing well on other cases, too. We talked about this. Every attorney worth his salt takes on charity work within the community."

John stepped back and sighed. He held his hand up to quiet Adora. "Don't call what I do charity. It is no such thing. I am doing only what is right. What is fair. And no, Mother. Not even for you can I focus on other— more profitable—cases, just to fill my pockets. At least not until I've done my part to defend people who are guilty of nothing more than coming to this country—at our request, mind you—to help us build our railroads, dig our dams, and construct our buildings. But I'll not bring this battle to your table again. For that I'm sorry. Causing you grief is never my intention."

He turned then, leaving Sun Ling to comfort his sister. Sun Ling hoped he didn't leave the estate altogether. The last time he'd stomped out, it had taken two months before he returned. She had missed him then and didn't want to go that long again without having him as a confidant.

CHAPTER TWENTY-SIX

SUN LING STOOD AT THE counter, waiting for the order of shredded pork with fragrant sauce. The tantalizing aroma of ginger, garlic, and scallions being tossed in the enormous cast iron skillet made her mouth water and, for a moment, took her mind off the fact that after the Lane family spat, John had left, neglecting to meet her in the garden for their usual catching up. No one knew when he'd return.

An afternoon with Luli and her innocence was just what she needed.

The aproned cook threw in the bamboo shoots and ear fungus, flipped it around a few times to cover it in the delectable sauce, then turned it over and divided the concoction into the two bowls, pouring it over the sticky rice.

Finally, the order was handed over, and Sun Ling took it to the table, setting one dish in front of Luli before settling down with her own. She handed one set of chopsticks over and then used her own to rake the contents from her bowl into her mouth, closing her eyes and lifting her chin to the heavens in appreciation for the simple yet familiar fare.

"*Měiwèi de*," Luli muttered, mirroring Sun Ling's thoughts.

"Yes, very delicious," Sun Ling agreed. She was glad

she'd decided on the small shop for their monthly afternoon outing. Sometimes she took Luli to one of the few foreign eating shops that accepted Chinese patrons, settings she could use to teach the girl western dining etiquette, things she'd need to know in the white world. But today she'd felt the need to stay around her own people. As if by a magnetic pull, she'd found herself drawn to the little side street where they'd found the tiny shop bustling with the locals.

"Thank you for bringing me," Luli said, grinning at her. "This is much better than tea and finger sandwiches."

Sun Ling smiled back, then stared at Luli over the bowl. It seemed just overnight she'd transformed from an innocent toddler to a girl with her own mind.

"So tell me what is going on with the babies?" she asked between bites.

Luli sighed dramatically. "They are up all through the night! One is put to sleep and then the other wakes. The nursemaids only come in the day, and we give the babies a bottle at night, but there is never any peace anymore."

Spoken like a true big sister, Sun Ling thought. "And your mother—she is handling it well?"

Luli's head bobbed as she sucked in a stray piece of rice. "She loves it. You should see her, Auntie. I've never seen her so happy."

"And you are fine with that? Not envious of the babies yet?" Sun Ling couldn't help but worry that Luli felt her role had changed too much.

Luli shrugged. "I guess. Baba lets me help with them, and sometimes Peso and I take them out for a walk. Baba made us up a crate with wheels, and we put them down into it."

"Your mother lets you take them from the store?" Sun Ling raised her eyebrows.

"Just a few paces back and forth in front of the window."

"And has she found anyone appropriate to take them in?"

Luli shook her head. "Not yet, even though at least a half-dozen women have come by the store to see them and offer to take one or the other. Mama refuses to separate them."

"Anyway, how are classes?" Sun Ling asked, setting her plate back down on the table and moving the subject back to Luli. Their lunches were meant to be all about her, not the babies.

Luli shrugged again. "Good. I'm the top student in my class, but since Peso doesn't attend any longer, it's boring."

Sun Ling nodded understandingly. Jingwei had told her of Peso's new job delivering luggage and goods from the big ships to the homes of those disembarking. She'd talked of how he was bringing in a bit of income now to help them along. Sun Ling had offered Jingwei a loan, but her sworn sister had declined, stating it wasn't Sun Ling's responsibility and that she'd already done enough by allowing them to keep the herb shop that her father had built.

That was never even a question. It had been clear that Sun Ling's father loved Min Kao like a son, and Luli as a granddaughter. He even loved Jingwei. Even though the question was never asked, Sun Ling knew that her father's wishes would've been for them to stay. And what in the world would she have done with the shop, anyway? It wasn't like she ever had any plans to live in Chinatown.

"You know, he's here today," Luli said suddenly, smiling as she put her bowl and chopsticks down.

"He?"

"Ye Ye."

Sun Ling felt a chill run over her. She knew of Luli's

ability, and it never failed to frighten her, but thus far, Luli had never once tried to give a message from beyond the curtain to the family. However, since the day her father had died, Sun Ling had felt his presence. He had not moved on to the afterworld, even after the extravagant funeral she'd given him. The thought that he was not settled weighed heavily on her.

She felt a sense of relief that perhaps she'd finally find out if her suspicions were true.

"Are you sure it's him?" Sun Ling asked.

Luli nodded. "Absolutely. And he knew you'd question it, so he said to tell you he was there the afternoon your mother taught you the rules of dying material. She told you that the softest yellows come from the petals of the *jú huā* flower, and that the bark from a tallow tree is good to use for dying black cloth."

Sun Ling remembered those exact words coming from her mother's lips and knew that she herself had never repeated them. Only her father had been witness to the lessons she held so dear to her heart, teachings her mother had passed down to her.

It *was* him.

She moved her eyes around the room, over Luli's shoulder as though she could pick her father out of the shadows. But she saw nothing.

"What does he want?" she finally asked.

Luli swallowed hard. "Are you sure you want to know?"

Sun Ling nodded.

"I really don't want to give this message," Luli said, looking over Sun Ling's shoulder, her voice pleading.

She wasn't talking to Sun Ling.

"Tell me, Luli. What does he say?" Sun Ling had to know.

Luli let out a long sigh, then dropped her head. "He says he's disappointed in you. I am sorry, Auntie."

Sun Ling felt all the air rush out of her. All her life, she'd only tried to make something of herself so that her father would be proud. Even when he'd sent her to Hong Kong, she'd done her duty, knowing that he had put his good name on the line.

"Does he say why?" She had a feeling she already knew and was almost afraid to ask. She hoped he wouldn't tell Luli too much.

"He says you are not moving forward. You are not allowing yourself to be happy."

Sun Ling's face burned with shame.

"And what am I to do?" she asked, longing to look into her father's eyes and ask him herself. He'd always passed down the most fitting wisdom.

Luli was quiet for a moment, her stare off in the distance.

"He wants you to stop your mission and accept the gift that fate has offered," she said, looking confused. Then her expression changed and she held her hands in the air. "I don't know what Ye Ye's talking about."

"But I do," Sun Ling said. The word *gift* rang in her ears and sat like a rock in the pit of her stomach. "If I do these things he's advised, will that bring my father peace enough to move on to a better place?"

The last thing she wanted was for her father to be wandering the earth as a lonely ghost. The thought of it made her heart heavy with pity. And even shame. Once again, she'd caused him pain.

Luli hesitated, looking past her. Then she nodded. "Under the stars, Auntie. He said under the stars, you will know."

Under the stars? Sun Ling looked out at the clear blue sky, unsure what it was she would know if and when she was under the stars. But even in life, her father had made it clear that he didn't approve of her late-night missions.

"Tell him it will be done," she said.

She would have to find some other way than the clandestine rescues to fulfill her sense of duty. Her baba was right—the work was getting too dangerous. It would grieve her deeply, but putting a stop to it should put her father's spirit to rest. That much she could do. In the matter of the gifts offered, that was not up to her.

CHAPTER TWENTY-SEVEN

SUN LING SAT AT THE scarred wooden table, soaking in the warmth and light of the sun while she finished the stitching on a day dress for the mistress. Bessie worked at the counter, occasionally belting orders to one kitchen helper or the other as they prepped for the day's meals.

"Scrub those tators," she said to the girl at the counter, then turned to the gardener who'd come in for a drink. "I need parsley, and plenty of it."

He fled, his intimidation by Bessie's size and volume of voice evident. She ran her kitchen with an iron fist, but Sun Ling knew that under it all was warmth and kindness and a motherly affection for all.

"Where is Lian?" Sun Ling said, realizing she hadn't seen the girl all morning.

Bessie shrugged, but something on her brown, doughy face looked sneaky, as though she knew something and didn't want to spit it out. But Sun Ling had no time to coax it from her, as she needed to put away one task and start another. Her mind flitted from one thing to another, but always touched back to the thought that John was due in that afternoon. He had another meeting to attend to in San Francisco and had sent word to Adora that he'd be by to check on things in his father's absence.

The captain was on another long journey to Asia, and

that meant there would be at least another month before he returned. They'd seen barely hide or hair of the mistress since the last family dinner when John had run out, as she claimed to have come up with a new cough. The truth was that she barely stirred until it was time for the captain's return, in which she then was re-energized in the tasks she felt prudent to welcome her husband home. Only upon the week before and days leading up to his projected arrival did the mistress allow her girl to take more time with her hair and other primping. It was then that she did her best to cover the dark circles and add color to the sallow cheeks. She would also plan an extravagant banquet of treats for his first dinner back— puffed pastries, fine slabs of meat, and every variety of garden vegetable cooked to perfection and accompanied by their best bottles of wine, as though welcoming home a hero.

It infuriated Sun Ling that he never noticed the condition of his wife. Didn't the captain see how frail his wife was? Or notice her pallor from too much time indoors? Or was it that he simply didn't care?

Sun Ling finished the last stitch and gathered up the dress, then her tools, and stood.

"I'm going to the attic to freshen up," she said to Bessie, who raised an eyebrow back at her.

The woman knew John was coming.

Sun Ling's cheeks burned with embarrassment at the silent acknowledgment.

"I plan to go to the silk market today," she said, defending herself.

"Sure 'nuf?" Bessie said. "How about picking me up some of that ruby red fine stuff and make me some new drawers?" Then she threw her head back and laughed, her bellow echoing in the big kitchen.

"Oh hush, Bessie," Sun Ling said, then headed for the attic stairs, her arms laden with her load. She'd have to press the dress before presenting it to the mistress.

She climbed to the attic and set the dress and her sewing kit upon her bed. Her status in the house had changed—she was barely even considered help—but she still chose to remain in the attic with the others.

A sudden pounding on the stairwell startled Sun Ling. "What is it?" she called down.

"The young master is home early," Bessie called out. "And he's all in a ruckus. You'd better come down and see what you can do to calm him."

She gathered her skirts and took the stairs quickly, wishing Adora hadn't gone to one of her secret writers' meetings. She was really the best one at calming John, though Sun Ling also had some tricks to settle him. She wondered what it was this time—another Chinese being targeted? A new law to keep the Chinese from gaining a rewarding life?

Whatever it was, they'd work through it.

She ran through the kitchen and out to the back courtyard, where John was still near his carriage, giving orders to the stableboy to care for the horses who had been ridden too hard. Sun Ling's heart soared, so happy she was to have her dearest friend back. She'd missed John, as always happened when he stayed away for more than a few weeks, or honestly, more than a few days.

But now he was here, and it made the day brighter.

Just as she started to speak, another carriage arrived, and Adora stepped out, her hand up and mouth open to greet her brother. But it was her appearance that stopped Sun Ling in her tracks. Adora had obviously not been to a writers' meeting, for what sort of writerly meeting would have resulted in the complete shearing of her long, gorgeous curls, Sun Ling couldn't fathom. She'd also traded her long skirts for a set of the trousers that Sun Ling had made her for the stables, but this time, she'd worn them in public!

"Oh Adora, what have you done?" Sun Ling said, covering her mouth.

Adora smiled and used her hand to cup the short locks. "I've simply made my outward appearance match who I am on the inside."

John turned, his eyes going from his sister to Sun Ling. He shook his head, then he did the unexpected. Instead of chastising her for such a rebellious act against society and something that was sure to send their mother into conniptions, he bridged the distance between them and took her in his arms, embracing her for the longest moment.

Sun Ling stayed back, letting them alone.

When he let Adora go, John sighed loudly.

"What is it, Brother?" Adora said, looking up at his face, searching. "Why are you sad?"

He took a deep breath, and then he said it.

"It's Father, Adora. He's been lost at sea."

CHAPTER TWENTY-EIGHT

SUN LING TOOK HER TIME bathing, enjoying the privacy of Adora's room, granted easily to her in exchange for a promise to accept the request of a dinner out with John. Sun Ling had said no at least a dozen times, but Adora finally convinced her, urging her to just continue being a confidant and friend to John as he traversed the mire of legal issues their father had left behind.

Only a month had passed since news had arrived of the captain's demise, and the house was still in mourning, black draped over every window and barely a whisper of human life within. The mistress had not left her chambers since the funeral, and even Adora had found it hard to get back to her routine once the mourning period had passed. She still respectfully wore the dark attire when out of the house, but at least now Sun Ling was starting to see some of her sass return.

Sun Ling admittedly enjoyed John's company, and his conversation. Perhaps it would help her out of the somber mood she'd carried lately, completely unrelated to the master's passing. She honestly felt nothing about his sudden death. She thought him a poor husband and an unsympathetic father. She showed quiet respect to the family but to truly mourn him would have felt hypocritical.

As she poured the flower-scented water over her breasts, she inhaled deeply, taking in the new scent Jingwei had created. She was becoming a master at mixing the perfumes, making Sun Ling wonder if there was anything her sworn sister couldn't do.

But enough of that—today was a new day. She lifted each knee, washing behind them before moving to her feet. She would try to leave the melancholy behind.

She let herself indulge in a rare moment of daydreaming, pretending it was her bedchamber and she was the mistress of the house. One of these days, she would make good on her threat to leave the attic and find her own accommodations. She definitely had enough funds saved from all the seamstress work she'd provided for Adora and her circle of friends over the years. She thought of the ring sewed into the bottom of the dragon dress she'd brought over from Hong Kong so long ago. Back then, she'd thought for sure that she'd have to use it to survive. But fate had changed, and the valuable ring—and the dress—lay untouched at the bottom of a locked chest in her father's home.

The chest, with its symbolic etching of a phoenix rising out of ashes, still held a few reminders of a past long buried.

She paused, thinking she heard a sound, but when no one came to the door, she leaned back and closed her eyes, taking in the quiet.

Adora had taken off after morning tea, most likely to one of her secret meetings again. Sun Ling didn't know what the girl was up to, and she hoped it was something clandestine, perhaps even a secret beau. If he was of acceptable lineage, it would make her mother very happy and hopefully ease some of the tension in the house. But on the other hand, if she was off with someone of questionable background, the scandal would keep Mrs. Lane to her bed even longer.

If the mistress would only stop or at least curb her addiction to the reddish-brown bitter laudanum, Sun Ling felt she would be better off. Mrs. Lane had Adora and the servants believing the concoction was necessary to ease her rheumatism and help her sleep, but Sun Ling suspected that it was really her crutch from the reality that her life had become a bore.

Though the mistress was obviously genuinely saddened by the death of her husband, Sun Ling had never seen affection between them.

Sun Ling stretched, sleepy from the warm water. She considered if she would have time for a nap, but she discarded the thought and stood, then climbed out of the tub. She dried her skin, then pulled on the chemise and worked herself into her corset. Jingwei couldn't understand why Sun Ling wanted to torture herself with such contraptions, but she didn't understand that with the fashion Sun Ling liked to wear, the undergarments were a necessity.

Finally done with the chore of getting into what wouldn't even be seen, Sun Ling climbed into the dress and pulled it up, fastening the buttons along the front. She looked in the mirror and was pleased. It was a new dress, and for this one, she'd chosen to place a red silk against a pristine white bodice and underskirt. She was thankful she was not expected to don black. The red was striking, especially against her long, dark hair. While not even close to an Asian fashion, the cut and color of the dress reminded her of her heritage.

However tempting it would be to feel the freedom of loose hair, she would not succumb to the thought.

Sitting at Adora's vanity, she worked expertly to maneuver the heavy locks into a sleek twist, then pinned it low to her head.

If she were still in China, her hair would have been left undone as a sign that she was yet unmarried. But here, she chose the mature styles, and tried to pretend she cared not that she was nearing the age that she'd be considered a spinster.

She glanced down at the jars and pots of color on Adora's vanity, but quickly dismissed them. She'd never worn makeup and had no need to start now, though she did reach up and pinch her cheeks for a bit of color.

Quickly she crossed the room and knelt to pick up her suede boots.

Pulling them on, she studied the embroidered pale peach-colored flowers that ran up both sides of the black footwear. A gift to herself at the last Chinese New Year, she never regretted for a moment that she'd splurged, especially when she remembered the look on the face of the snobbish shop owner who'd tried to show her the door, murmuring that she was obviously in the wrong establishment. But she hadn't turned down the cold, hard cash Sun Ling had laid on her counter, had she?

Leaning against Adora's bed, Sun Ling pulled the laces of the boots tight, then tied them. The boots couldn't be seen under the long skirt she wore, but Sun Ling would know they were there, and that would give her enough confidence to get through a meal at a western restaurant.

Or, at least, she hoped it would.

The carriage was freshly cleaned, and the coats of the horses shone from an obvious brush down. Sun Ling had wanted to stop in and offer Dulin an apple, but since she didn't want to smell of the stable, she'd refrained. Now she sat across from John as he rattled on about mundane subjects, trying to cover the sudden awkwardness between them.

"Where are we going?" she asked when the smooth lane turned into a bumpy plank road. She held on to her bonnet she'd donned at the last moment, hoping it didn't come loose.

John hadn't commented on her outfit. As for him, she'd noticed he'd switched up his usual all-black attire to brown tweed trousers and a yellow silk vest. His normally tousled hair was combed to the side in a neat angle that made him look more mature. She much preferred the less trendy John to this new, uptight one, though she appreciated the extra effort he put forth for being seen in public.

"The Oakdale Clam House," he said. "You do like seafood, yes?"

She nodded. Growing up as house help in Hong Kong, she'd seen the cook create many dishes with seafood from the harbor, though she doubted the Californians would be using the same techniques as the Cantonese. When Cook was able, she'd saved some of the leftovers for Sun Ling and Jingwei, enough for them to taste but never enough to fully experience.

"I received a letter from Bei Ming," she said, smiling at the memory of the happy words on the paper.

"How is the Yan family?"

"Growing yet again," Sun Ling said.

Jack Yan and Bei Ming had married, and now she was expecting another child. After all the unrest in Truckee, a truce of sorts had been called between the committee and the Chinese.

One by one, each man accused of being a part of the riot and killing on that fateful night had been exonerated, with a cannon shot at word of each acquittal and leading the town to celebrate in short bursts over a week's time.

John had done all he could, but ultimately the Chinese had lost, and though they would never forgive the townspeople, they'd settled into daily life once again.

"At least one good thing came out of our efforts there," John said. "One day, there'll be a mass of Yan children taking over that town. Then the committee had better watch out."

Sun Ling laughed at the picture he painted, of a long line of Bei Ming and Jack Yan's children parading through the main street, their faces grim with retribution.

She didn't remind him that another good thing had happened because of their efforts. And because of the Indians, of course. Young Wan Li had healed completely, then taken the money given to him by the so-called lady's charity society in Truckee, to return to China.

Last Sun Ling had heard, he had married that girl he was so moon-eyed over in a wedding that could be envied, and he too was working on building a family.

"How long do you plan to stay in town this time?" she asked, speaking up over the hollering of Clyde trying to keep the horses on task.

"I have to be back to Oakland by the end of next week. That means I have to rush through more meetings about father's holdings." He ran a hand through his hair, upending it from the tidy arrangement and putting it back to its natural look.

Sun Ling hid a smile. He might have been a fancy up-and-coming lawyer, but he still had the mannerisms of a boy.

"And what sort of case are you working on now?" she asked. "I mean—other than sorting out your father's affairs."

He waved a hand in the air. "It's been slow in Oakland. I've been handling mostly land grants for a month or two."

She nodded. It sounded tedious.

"But I did get to San Jose for a conference and was delighted to observe the famous Clara Foltz in action," he said, his voice taking on a more excited tone.

"Foltz?" Sun Ling thought the name familiar, but

couldn't place it.

"She is the first women to be admitted to the California bar."

"Oh, yes. Adora was going on about her. Didn't she take on the legislature to change the wording of what a lawyer can be? She argued an attorney shouldn't be listed as a white male, but as *any person.*"

He grinned. "Close enough. There's still talk of overturning it, as the men are worried that her being allowed in will open the gates to women becoming jurors and then, God forbid, even judges one day."

"That's doubtful," Sun Ling said, frowning. It was a man's world, and though she thought Ms. Foltz admirable for finding a place in it, the thought of a woman being a judge one day was just too far-fetched to fathom. She and Adora had talked about it at length, even debated the possibility. Adora considered it conceivable, even in her own lifetime. Sun Ling told her she was naïve, and they agreed to disagree.

"Well, needless to say, my sister is enamored with her because Mrs. Foltz began her career as a writer and contributor and now is in law school. Who knows where it will take her next? If our own father hadn't been so obstinate on a women's place being in the home or as a teacher, I do believe Adora could've found herself a career more fitting to her constitution."

Sun Ling agreed. Adora just wanted her voice to be heard in the loudness of the world. One day she might want to settle and be married, but she hadn't met that day yet. To the contrary, though she'd been deeply grieved by the loss of her father, Sun Ling could sense a new Adora emerging, one free to speak her mind.

The driver pulled them up in front of the small restaurant, and John leaned forward, one hand on the door. "Ready?"

Sun Ling's breath caught in her throat at the scene outside.

A group of men all stood on the porch of the building, laughing and leaning on the rail as they took their after-dinner smokes. Of course they were all white. Sun Ling should've expected it, but she still suppressed a shiver of panic. A few ladies sat at a table by the door, their dresses fanned out around their feet as their heads bowed toward one another, mouths taking turns moving rapidly as they most likely exchanged the latest gossip. John had assured her that the proprietor was friendly to the Chinese, but still Sun Ling felt out of place.

She wanted so badly to be like those ladies—to be one of them.

"You look very fetching, Sun Ling," John said softly, seemingly reading her mind.

Sun Ling looked down at her dress, at the fine gloves on her hands.

Yes, she did.

Feeling a burst of confidence, she nodded. "I'm ready."

John let the driver pull the door open, and he disembarked first, then held his hand out to her. Sun Ling hesitated once more, then lifted her chin and carefully climbed down, taking heed to hold her skirts from the dust of the road.

She tried not to notice that the men had stopped laughing and the women were also silent, all staring their way as she and John made their way up the ramp leading to the door. Keeping her eyes on her feet, Sun Ling let John lead her inside.

Once again, the onslaught of conversation came to a lull, then silence fell over the room. A man dressed in long coattails, a towel over one arm, and what appeared to be a menu in his hand, approached them.

"May I be of service?" he said, bowing.

"Table for two," John said cheerfully.

The man looked first at John, then Sun Ling.

"Two?" he looked uncertain.

"Yes, two," John's voice dropped a few octaves, losing the cheer. He reached into the pocket of his jacket, extracting a folded bill and furtively holding it out to the maître d'.

Sun Ling looked away, her cheeks suddenly feeling as though they were lit on fire. She hoped John would not have to ask for the owner to come rescue them.

Thankfully, the maître d' furtively pocketed the bill, then led them to the furthest corner, to a table next to what appeared to be the kitchen doors. It was small, set somewhat crooked and looking almost as though it were an afterthought, or a station set up to roll napkins or sort silver.

"This is all you have?" John asked quietly.

"It's fine, John," Sun Ling whispered, praying he'd sit down so they could stop being the center of attention.

He hesitated, let out a long and frustrated sigh, then pulled out the chair for Sun Ling, offering it to her. She sat, hopeful that conversation would begin again and people could stop looking at her as though they'd just arrived from another planet.

And it did.

Slowly people began murmuring around them, their voices rising to a normal level. Waiters moved again, glasses clinked and silver clanked.

Sun Ling felt relief wash over her.

John still looked grim, but he sat down and looked at the maître d', holding his hand out. "Is that your wine list? Do you just want me to guess what's on it?"

The man handed it over and stood waiting. Sun Ling dared a look up at him and found him examining her embroidered boots before he quickly looked away. She'd garner a bet that he wondered why she wore shoes that possibly cost more than he made in a month's pay. He probably thought John had bought them.

"Just bring us your best house wine," John said, closing the booklet and handing it back. "We'll start with clam chowder and move on to the chef's menu." He didn't offer a token of kindness to the man as he quickly diverted his attention from the book to Sun Ling's face.

When he left them, John attempted small talk. He spoke about the weather, about the surge in prices of goods his father had been bringing over from Asia, and other trivial tidbits. Sun Ling tried to concentrate, but the mood was broken.

The wine came first, and the maître d' poured. Sun Ling took great pains not to grimace when she took her first taste. She'd never drank wine before and, by the sour taste it left in her mouth, wasn't sure if she ever would again. When the clam chowder came out, their spoons tapping the porcelain bowls became the only sound from their table. It wasn't tasty, at least nowhere near as good as Cook's clam chowder back in Hong Kong, but Sun Ling nodded and smiled as though it were the best thing to ever touch her lips.

John pushed his to the center of the table, barely any gone from the bowl. The maître d' returned, his expression inquiring.

"I've had clam chowder here many times, and this isn't up to par," John told him. "Take it back and bring us your cioppino."

Sun Ling felt her cheeks burn again, but she didn't look around to see who was watching them. John discussed selling his small apartment in Oakland while they waited for the maître d' to return. He'd already rid himself of the small estate he and his wife had shared, so where he was going to live was a big question, but not one she wanted to ask. Speaking of living arrangements would just feel too personal.

When the man set two steaming bowls down and then backed away, Sun Ling peered down into what looked like a thick stew.

"Try it," John said. "I can't promise, but on a normal day it's amazing."

"What's in it?" She stirred the concoction, snagging a crab leg on her spoon.

"Well, crab legs, obviously. And vegetables, calamari—you might even find a few mussels and clams, depending on their take from the docks today."

She took a spoonful and was pleasantly surprised at the blend of spices and seafood, at how good it tasted. She smiled at John.

"See—" he began, then was cut off when the word *chink* made it to their table. He looked around, his face thunderous as he tried to figure out who it had come from.

The other diners didn't look their way. The disembodied voice wasn't to be pinpointed. In other words, someone was cowardly.

"I apologize," John turned back to her and said.

"For what?"

He nodded his head toward the other patrons. "For them. For those outside. Hell, for all of San Francisco's stuffed shirts. They are narrow-minded and short-sighted—that's all I can offer up for an excuse."

"They don't want Chinese in their restaurant," Sun Ling said softly.

"They can be damned, then," John said, his tone raising an octave. "You are more of a lady than any of their tongue-wagging social-climbing fishwives."

Sun Ling touched his arm. "John, please."

She heard someone at the closest table gasp and when she looked, an elderly but quite stylish woman was staring at them—her attention on Sun Ling's hand on John's arm, to be more precise—and she'd covered her mouth in shock.

Sun Ling knew they shouldn't have come to the

restaurant together, appearing as a couple. Just months before, the California civil code passed a new regulation that prohibited the issuing of marriage licenses between whites and anyone of color, including what they referred to as Mongolians. No, she and John weren't a couple— but it was easy to assume untruths, and she immediately regretted not insisting they have a chaperone.

The man who dined with the woman stood and made a show of straightening his shoulders, then pulling the edges of his jacket together as he tried to cover his paunch. He was a mature man, much older than John, and his handlebar mustache still held the remains of the crackers he'd obviously nibbled on while waiting on his main course.

He turned to them, staring bold-faced at John, his hands on his hips.

"Is there a problem?" John asked. He picked up his napkin and blotted his own mouth. He looked calm. *Almost too calm.*

The man reached down and picked up a newspaper that lay folded on his table. He strode over to them and slapped it down beside John's bowl.

"I'd say yes, there is a problem. We come here every weekend to enjoy a leisurely, civilized dinner. Not to eat within view of some savage," he said, nodding his head toward Sun Ling.

She looked down at the paper and saw a cartoon on the outer page. A Chinese, his face garish and comical, lay relaxed against a chaise. He held to his lips what was most likely supposed to be an opium pipe.

John took one look at the paper and pushed it off the table, letting it flutter to the floor.

Sun Ling put down her spoon, suddenly not hungry. She wished she could melt into the floor right there. To be ridiculed in public was one thing, but to be humiliated in front of John made her wish she was invisible.

"You'll pick that up, sir," the portly gentleman said.

"Like hell I will," John replied.

The man huffed and puffed, all eyes in the room upon him as others watched the situation, waiting to see how it would end.

He stood taller, pulling his shoulders back. "I believe I speak for the entire town when I say the Chinese are a cancer that must be cut out of San Francisco."

"You don't speak for me, and I'm from this town," John said quietly, but loud enough that others could hear. He didn't flinch under the man's stare.

"Then perhaps you just look the part of the dandy but are no more than a penniless fool," the man said, crossing his arms over his chest. "For if you were business-minded, you'd realize like the rest of us do that Chinese are pricing us out of the labor market. Our men can't compete with the low wages they'll work for."

"Then pay better wages and get the workers you want," John said, shrugging. "But don't blame the Chinese for being loyal, productive, and less greedy."

The man's flustered, his eyes darting back and forth as he thought to come up with an intelligent retort.

"Let's save him the trouble, Sun Ling," John said, standing. He held his arm out to her, as though she were a fine lady deserving of such a thing.

He helped her up then reached into his pocket and withdrew a few bills, throwing them onto the table.

"We shall go to dine where we don't have to cavort with pigs and a meal will be a treat, and not a chore," he said, holding his arm out in a grand gesture for her to lead the way.

Sun Ling complied, suppressing a smirk as she walked by the now blustering man. She took them right out the door, and thankfully, the carriage was near enough to walk to. When John handed her up into it, she never felt such relief at being closed away from the night air.

He climbed in after her and sat across, then smiled.

"Thank you for keeping your cool, and helping me to keep mine," he said. "You have more class than all of them fools in there put together. I'm sorry I didn't get you the fine meal I promised."

He bowed his head, putting his fingers to his temples.

At first, she didn't know what to say. "I'm truly no longer hungry," she offered.

He looked up. "Neither am I. We can skip dinner for now, but no one will make us miss what I've planned for the latter part of the evening." He knocked on the roof of the carriage, and the driver went into action.

Sun Ling didn't know what John had planned, but whatever it was couldn't be more entertaining than the way he smiled at her from the other seat.

"I am intrigued," she said, smiling back.

CHAPTER TWENTY-NINE

SUN LING COULDN'T TAKE IN her surroundings fast enough. She'd never dreamed she'd be able to set foot inside a theatre, and though John had maneuvered her around the marquee and refused to tell her what was playing, she cared not what it was. Just being there was treat enough, and she couldn't wait to tell Jingwei and Luli about her experience.

"Is this your own box?" she asked, looking around the small enclosure. She was not aware that he was a part of the theatre scene.

"No, I've borrowed it for the night. We're early, as I'd expected to be at dinner for a while longer."

Sun Ling was glad it wasn't yet time for the show to begin. She was also grateful for the drawn curtains keeping the people on either side from seeing into their box. She had a feeling they would not approve of John's choice of her as a guest, noting as she scanned the crowd that not another single person of color was anywhere to be found. Both she and John had deigned not to talk about the obvious glances of disapproval they'd had to navigate through just to get to the box.

"This is splendid," she whispered.

After taking in the intricate architecture of the pillars, the scandalously expensive chandeliers, and the rows and rows of plush velvet seating, Sun Ling visually devoured the different costumes and fashions the ladies wore. She was thankful that she'd worn the red silk dress, noting how well it fit with the dramatic atmosphere of the playhouse. At least in fashion, she was able to keep up with society, though she doubted any of the ladies would give her credit for that.

She would not let that thought ruin her evening. Her skin practically tingled with anticipation, and she had to remind herself to take a breath.

"You look very fetching this evening," John said softly.

Sun Ling thanked him but didn't turn his way. She couldn't, for it was proving impossible to peel her eyes from the drop curtain on stage. It was painted with an elaborate, panoramic scene of the San Francisco Bay and must've taken the artist a massive amount of time to complete.

"Have you ever imagined seeing the bay from this standpoint?" John teased.

Actually, she had seen the bay from a similar standpoint, and that day was forever etched in her mind. They'd successfully left the trauma of Hong Kong behind, but she'd been exhausted from their voyage, depleted beyond comprehension because she'd almost lost someone so dear, but she'd also been full of dreams.

"Reminds me of the day that Jingwei and I arrived."

"You've both had quite the journey," he said. He reached over and patted her hand, then tucked his own back into his pocket again.

He was right. Their journey was one full of hardship but also many rewards. The banks of California weren't what Sun Ling had expected, but despite the ordeals they'd been faced with and conquered, Sun Ling had found not only her long-lost father, but also her purpose. For almost ten years now she'd given her life—every bit of resources and energy she could muster—all in the name of protecting oppressed women. She and Jingwei were sworn sisters and that was something special, but she was now also an integral part of a secret sisterhood that she'd built slowly, one rescue at a time.

But now, suddenly the passion was beginning to waver. She'd felt it for a while but had not wanted to acknowledge it. Could it be that fate was trying to tell her it was time to move on and follow another course? What it would be, Sun Ling had not a single idea, but for the first time in a very long time, she considered a different future.

"Jingwei named the babies," she whispered, her eyes on a young man moving through the rows, selling peanuts.

John turned and looked at her, raising an eyebrow. "And what does that mean?"

"I think we both know." Sun Ling smiled.

There it was—she realized it as soon as she'd uttered the declaration about the twins. Jingwei and Min Kao had moved along in their life, building their family by whatever means they could. And together they stood, valiantly taking on every hardship put upon them. The herb shop was struggling, but Min Kao refused to shut it down, his loyalty to their remaining customers and her father's memory unwavering.

Even Luli and Peso were moving forward. Peso was building his tiny company bit by bit, each day making more money and winning over new customers. He simply needed a hand up, and he would be off and running, the youngest entrepreneur that Sun Ling had ever met.

"I will give Peso the rights to use Duli for his business," she said, proud of herself for coming up with at least part of the solution to help Jingwei's family. "Duli will appreciate getting out of the stables more frequently. Now I must find a wagon."

John winked at her. "I know of a secondhand wagon

that can be bought for a song. I will purchase it for Min Kao, and he can partner with Peso. They can make payments to repay me. That should settle your worries."

He was right, but there was one more thing that she would do for them. Jingwei still had the dragon dress, put up for safe keeping. It was time to bring it down and show her what was within it. The ring would be put to something useful and bring them all good fortune.

An investment in family. And the dress, fit for an empress, would be handed down to Luli, with much affection.

With those decisions made, Sun Ling felt relief for their future.

Min Kao could keep the shop going, and with two avenues of income and the funds from the ring, things should be much easier.

She thought of how Luli would be as an adult. The girl was proving to be not only a gifted soothsayer, which they kept as confidential as possible, but also an apt student to the teachings that Jingwei was giving her about flowers, oils, and their healing abilities. Each afternoon that Sun Ling spent with Luli, she walked away wondering how they'd all been so lucky that Min Kao had carried her away from a bleak future in China, making her the center of their universe. Now that Luli was getting older, Sun Ling had to ensure her future was solid.

"I must find Luli a place in a better school," she said. "The white schools are bound to begin accepting Chinese if they can speak English, don't you believe?"

"The show is about to begin," John said, nodding toward the stage. "We can talk more of that later."

Sun Ling could hear more patrons behind them in the hall, and they made their way to their own seats. A few seconds later, after a flurry of rustling skirts, someone pulled open the curtain closest to John.

"Mr. Donaldson—" a man began, then stopped when

his gaze fell on John and Sun Ling.

"Lane," John said, extending his hand. "Harvey Donaldson is a client of mine and loaned me his seats for the night."

The man looked at John's hand, then at Sun Ling. Slowly he leaned back again and closed the curtain.

John let his hand fall into his lap. "Hypocrite."

"How so?" Sun Ling asked.

"You heard about the Transcontinental Express train that arrived here last week for the first time?"

She nodded. Of course she'd heard about it. The entire town was buzzing about the miracle that now one could leave New York and be in San Francisco in a mere eighty hours, all the while sitting in an opulent and relaxing cabin as the world sped by outside the window.

John scowled. "Well, he's a huge stock holder and is going to make millions from it. As you and I both know, most of the hard work was completed upon the backs of the Chinese. I suppose they're good enough to make him rich, but he can't fathom one sitting so close to him in his own theatre box."

"It's really quite all right, John," she said. "I do not want you to get offended so frequently on my behalf."

To the contrary, she was becoming accustomed to fighting for every right, and it no longer incensed her for someone to look down their nose at her. Did she agree with their viewpoints? Absolutely not! But since her father's death, she was beginning to understand that she could not change the behavior or attitude of those around her, but she could change the way she reacted to it. She could also refuse to let their idiocy steal her joy.

"I will always be offended on your behalf, Sun Ling," John said.

She was saved from giving a reply to such an intense statement. The stage curtain began to rustle, and a hush moved through the crowd until all eyes were set forward.

John nudged her and pressed a paper in her hand.

Sun Ling looked. It was a leaflet, and across the top in bold letters, it read, "From the Hong Kong troupe, the California Theatre presents *The Thorns*."

Before she could register her surprise that they would be seeing an Asian-inspired play or even contemplate the show name, the curtain began to rise, and Sun Ling was struck silent.

On the stage, a woman sat at a dressing table, dabbing a brush in a jar of powder before streaking it across her face. She wore a long robe of gold, the wings of a phoenix embossed in black threads shining across her back. In the mirror, Sun Ling could see the reflection of heavy gold jewelry shining from her wrist and ears.

From stage right, a door opened, and a young girl dressed in a drab-looking tunic and wide-legged pants came scurrying in, her back bent from the efforts of carrying a large bucket. She sat the bucket behind the woman and beckoned for her to turn around.

The painted lady obliged, turning to face the audience, she delicately placed both feet in the bucket, and the girl began to clean them.

As the girl worked, the lady chastised her for being too slow, too rough, then too gentle. She continued on with a litany of tasks that should be done before the girl retired, and she talked loudly of the master of the house and his impending visit to her bedchamber later.

Sun Ling could feel John's eyes on her, and something niggled. First it was the set that mesmerized her, the attention to detail taken to emulate the chambers of a rich Cantonese family in a way that was true to life. Then the girl playing the part of a bondservant held her attention and brought about pangs of empathy. But when she let her eyes wander up the legs of the woman and linger on the face, her realization was so sudden that she gasped.

"Chin Lee," she whispered, her voice heavy with awe. Even under the heavy makeup and dark wig of long hair and nearly ten years since she'd seen him last, she would've recognized him anywhere.

Finding such a solid link to her past sitting directly in front of her was startling, to say the least. She looked at John. "You knew?"

He nodded. "Since Ralston, the owner of the theatre, drowned last year, the theatre has faltered, and they have begun accepting most any troupe. I heard this was coming, and I wanted to surprise you."

Sun Ling shook her head, amazed that she was sitting there, as John's guest in a fancy uptown theatre and watching her old friend and confidant play out the life she'd led so long ago. The experience was surreal, and as the storyline unfolded and Chin Lee perfectly played the part of Yu Qi, one of the master's concubines, the crowd was entranced.

For her, the bickering portrayed between Chin Lee and the actor that played Yan Die, the other concubine—and actually Chin Lee's birth mother—was familiar and nothing to be astounded at. But for the white society crowd of San Francisco, the dramatic day-to-day depiction of a master, a surly wife, two jealous concubines, and their oppressed servants was obviously of great interest.

Yet, Sun Ling enjoyed it immensely. It wasn't the story that kept her mesmerized—it was the revelation that Chin Lee had left Hong Kong to become part of an international troupe. Watching him perform with such ease and confidence filled her with joy. She had thought he would have to reluctantly take on the role of master of the house upon his father's demise, and she was proud that he'd stood strong and chased his own dreams instead.

"What do you think?" John whispered.

She sighed, a smile playing across her lips at the sudden argument between the concubines over who was master's favorite. It was hard to believe, but Chin Lee's portrayal made her feel wistful. Not for the life of a bondservant that had been her cruel reality, but for the reminder of things she'd left behind.

In the last few years, not only had she declined to wear Chinese fashion or follow her old customs, but she'd even blocked the good memories of a life from long ago. How long had it been since she'd thought of her childhood home? Of the people in her village? Even— she took a deep breath, tasting regret—of her mother?

Jingwei had tried to tell her that it didn't have to be one or the other. That she could have it both ways— could embrace the future even as she held onto her own culture.

It had taken so long for Sun Ling to see it, too. With her past being played out in front of her, Sun Ling felt her life had come full circle, and she could see clearly it was time for a change. "I think you just gave me the best gift anyone could give," she replied to John.

Sun Ling walked beside John, holding onto his arm as they traversed the uneven walkways of Bush Street. Her head was swirling with emotions from the last few hours. In her free hand, she carried the leaflet with Chin Lee's name upon it. In her heart, she carried the sweet memory of their brief meeting backstage.

"You aren't angry?" Chin Lee had asked, his face crestfallen after his initial surprise of seeing her there.

"At what?"

"That I'm using your life, even the name you had for them," he said, referring to the Thorns in Hong Kong.

Sun Ling took his hand. "Oh, my friend. It was your story, too. And I am happy you were able take a bad memory and make it into your fortune. I cannot tell you how proud I am of you."

Chin Lee had taken his wig off and scrubbed most of the paint from his face, and though he was now a grown man, Sun Ling saw evidence of the young, worried boy he had once been. His father had never approved of his acting, nor his feminine ways, and had nearly suffocated them out of him. But Chin Lee had won. And the bully who had been his father had lost. Chin Lee was free to be who he wanted to be.

Now Sun Ling hoped that the master was somewhere around, his unsettled soul lurking from the afterworld to see his son indeed had more of a spine than he'd given him credit for—that he'd had enough to carry him away from a life he didn't choose or want, and into one that fit who he was.

She and Chin Lee had embraced and parted with promises to write one another. Sun Ling still felt fresh with tears at saying goodbye.

John nudged her and told her to look up.

It was a clear night, and the stars shone brightly, flanking the moon as they twinkled out a silent song. For the most part, no one paid them much attention. Those still out on the town, strolling along or riding in the carriages, either hadn't looked close enough under her proper dress and hat to see Sun Ling, or simply had other things on their mind.

It was a welcome respite from the constant condemnation.

At the end of the street, John guided her toward a small bench and urged her to sit. He settled in beside her, leaving enough space between for her modesty to remain intact.

"I will take you home shortly, but first I'd like to talk

to you," he said.

"John, I can't thank you enough," Sun Ling said, her words filling the slightly awkward pause in conversation. "It ended up being a magical evening. Truly, it was."

"Please, Sun Ling. Don't thank me," he said. "It is I who am grateful for your company. And also for all that you have done for my family in the last months. Adora has told me how you've stepped up to fill my mother's duties since she took to her bed."

Sun Ling had not known that Adora had relayed everything to John, and heat filled her face that they'd been talking about her. However, it wasn't such a bad change of position. Adora had not wanted the responsibilities it took to run the house and keep everyone and everything on schedule. She'd practically begged Sun Ling as well as offered her a substantial raise in pay. Sun Ling hadn't minded—was even enjoying it, to be honest—and the staff respected her enough to allow it, as well. Cook was thrilled, as she knew Sun Ling would let her get away with anything.

Sun Ling was no longer a ladies' maid for Adora. Along with the work she did designing and sewing dresses, she actually enjoyed playing at being the mistress of a fine manor.

"I'm only doing what needs to be done until your mother is fit to resume her duties," she said.

"I don't know what we ever did to deserve you," John said.

"Deserve me?" Sun Ling felt confused. Adora and then John had been the ones to change her life, even to save it. She'd been the lucky one.

"Sun Ling, it's like you… like… like you fell out of the sky and into my life. Who am I to question God as to why? But with your presence and strong convictions, you opened my eyes and gave me a way to become a better man." He ran his hands through his hair, as though he struggled with something internally. "A better human being."

Sun Ling didn't know what to say. He looked so stricken. And he stumbled over his words, an unusual thing for him who was usually so self-assured.

"You were already a good man, John," she whispered. "But that you use your resources to help my people means more to me than I can say."

"I have a confession. I discovered the travesty that my father hid within his business. His role in transporting the Chinese for selling. I ask your forgiveness. I beg it."

Sun Ling could see his anguish. "If you must have it, then yes. But it wasn't you, so it isn't required."

"It was done under our family name and I'll spend the rest of my life trying to erase the stain and make up for it." He said, then put his hand over her.

With his touch, a shock coursed through her. It started in her toes, and even the tips of her fingers tingled. She was surprised her hair didn't pop out of its chignon and stand on end.

He sighed, long and heavy. "The truth is, I am nothing but a shell unless you are at my side."

"Now that's just not true, John." She pulled her hand out and patted the top of his. "You could continue to do the same work whether I was with you or not. It's getting easier every day to find an interpreter. The ladies at the mission are doing a fine job in teaching English to newcomers."

He stood and towered over her. "You aren't getting what I'm trying to say."

She searched his face, then shook her head. "I suppose I am not. I apologize, but if you can simply come out and say what it is you want—"

"Sun Ling," John said, interrupting her. He dropped to one knee in front of her, and reached out and took her hand. "Can't you see it? Don't you already know?"

A couple passed by them, and Sun Ling was too stricken to look. What would they think? John was on bended knee. In front of her! She felt tongue-tied, and her insides were quivering as though a dozen butterflies had been let loose there.

When she didn't reply, he smiled. "I tried to deny it. I've suppressed it since the day I met you, standing there in that black silk dress, the golden dragon crawling up your collar. You were so lovely and graceful, yet so fierce. I'll never forget that moment. And here, under the stars, I am confessing that you have my heart."

Now Sun Ling felt faint with shock. Was this really happening to her? As her mind tried to keep up with what her ears and eyes were experiencing, she realized that his words mirrored her thoughts. She'd never allowed herself to believe that John could feel anything for her more than a professional companionship and sense of responsibility.

Because of that, she had also suppressed her own longing.

He rose and took the seat beside her.

"In a few weeks, I will be selling my apartment in Oakland to move back to San Francisco. I'll move into the house to oversee my father's business until I can get a reliable partner in place. That means I'll need to find you other living arrangements, if you agree."

Now Sun Ling was very confused. She straightened, her spine ramrod stiff. He was so perplexing. But if he didn't want her in his family home any longer, that was fine. She didn't need his help. She was a self-made woman and could just go along and self-make herself somewhere else. She could feel her pulse pounding, and her face flaming.

She lifted her chin and steadied her voice. "Other living arrangements would be fine. I apologize if I have overstepped any boundaries. I will find my own new quarters. But I will need time to school Adora on what she will need to do in my absence. She has not a clue how to keep that house running."

He turned to her, putting his hand to her chin and guiding her to look at him.

"Sun Ling, I will find someone to fulfill your duties, but it is only temporary. What I'm trying to say is I'd like your permission to court you properly. And if I am to court you, it would not be acceptable for you to live under my roof."

She stared at him, hearing the words but taken so far aback that she couldn't quite grasp them.

"You want to court me?" she asked after a long pause.

He took her hand. "Not only do I want to court you, but I want to marry you."

Sun Ling felt hope soar. With it, a myriad of feelings were unleashed. All that she'd felt for John—and tried to bury deep inside—came gushing out, front and center. She fought to keep it all under control.

"I am decidedly sure that I love you," he said softly. "I also think you are fond of me, too."

She wished she could speak the words, but they were too foreign. In her culture, love was shown but rarely spoken. But with his declaration, her heart felt it would explode with emotion. She thought of Jingwei and Min Kao, knowing now what it was that kept them so strong and loyal to one another. This feeling—it was something she'd never known. Her entire body felt warm and light—so weightless that if John was not holding her hand, she might float away.

He took a deep breath and squeezed her fingers. "I can't promise you it will be easy. And I can't promise we won't face conflict and ridicule. But what I can promise is that I will be there for you every day, doing my best to convince you that we are meant to be. That not race, culture, or prejudice can come between what fate has brought together."

"But legally. They will never allow—" She faltered.

He put his other hand up to silence her. "The laws will change, and you'll see. Before long we will be able to marry. At least possibly in New York. After a lengthy courtship, of course. But no matter what obstacles we may face, I can promise you this: I will be devoted to you. I will treat you as an equal. I will be tender, and I will be kind. Of all this, you have my word."

He went silent then, giving her time to reflect on his words. She could see his face, etched in the moonlight, the planes and hollows so familiar to her now. He was a good man. A caring man. She respected him. More than that, he never strayed far from her mind.

She thought of her father's wishes. Was John's declaration what he had wanted her to accept? To acknowledge? Had he known all along what would be coming?

Under the stars, Luli had said.

As she considered it all, a sense of peace fell around her, a blanket of solace covering every insecurity she had about who she was—the color of her skin and the shape of her eyes. Reflected in John's eyes, she saw appreciation. He cared for who she was on the inside, and she, him.

She thought of all the time they had wasted.

With all the knowledge in front of her now, she knew what she must do.

She nodded, one miniscule motion to indicate that she agreed. They would be bound, forever together in commitment and strife. Friends, partners, and one day, possibly more.

For so many years, she'd felt she must do her part to move the world and push it along where she felt it needed to go. Where it should be. Now, for the time being, she wanted to relish the new path her life was taking—to drink in the revelation that she was wanted.

She squeezed John's hand back and wished, for one simple moment, that all would stand still.

FROM THE AUTHOR

WITH THIS STORY, I HOPE to show the world how unfairly the Chinese suffered to find their place in a land dominated by whites. Much of the examples of oppression and prejudice depicted in *To Move the World* was pulled from true life stories. For example, the Truckee Massacre did occur and was far more deadly in real life, as was the efforts to drive the Chinese out of Los Angeles.

I feel that only when our history of discrimination and racial unfairness is recorded and shared, for people to learn, acknowledge, and regret, will we then be fully acceptable of embracing the person next to us not for the color of their skin, but for the quality of their soul.

If you'd like to know more about the early struggles of the Chinese in America, I encourage you to read the fascinating book titled *Driven Out*, by Jean Pfaelzer.

As for Luli's gift, the legends of soothsayers in China are just as popular today as they were in the far past. Years ago, I was waiting in the car in the parking lot of a train station in Suzhou, China. A woman came to my window and was about to try to communicate with me when my driver came dashing back to the car, jumped in, and drove us quickly away. I asked him why he was acting so erratic and he told me the woman was a soothsayer and wanted my money in exchange for a reading. He added that if I refused, she could curse my family. The terror he felt was palpable and the memory has stuck with me and most likely resulted in my creation of Luli's character.

I would like to apologize if the use of the words Indian,

Oriental, or coolie are offensive to you as a reader, and a human being. This was a subject discussed thoroughly, and in the end, I chose to use those words because they were the most commonly used during that time period in those communities. As we now know, they are no longer (and should've never been) acceptable. In the circumstance of Indian, my research has shown that the term Native American also has issues and dangerous connotations tied to it that have to do with the environmental movement. Currently, my resources at this time, show that some prefer to refer to themselves as Native or Indian, while others would rather be known by their tribal affiliation. I won't give you examples of what is the correct term now, as it is subject to change, and you would need to do your own research at the time of reading this.

If you enjoyed *To Move the World*, posting a positive review on Amazon and Goodreads is one way to show your appreciation and help me gain further visibility for my work.

I would love for you to go to my website at www.kaybratt.com to sign up for my newsletter and be the first to know when new books are released, and to join in the fun of giveaways, free books, and contests. What should you read next? If you want to stay in China-inspired fiction, you may want to check out my *Life Of Willow* duology. It is a fascinating look into modern day orphanage life and what it's like to feel as though you belong to no one. In the first book, Somewhere Beautiful, the reader will follow experience a story of loss and loyalty that will have you following three teens as they battle their way through life's obstacles in the search for the always elusive happily ever after.

Or if you haven't already immersed yourself in the Tales of the Scavenger's Daughters, it is a fan favorite, and consists of five full-length books. Whichever you choose, my biggest gratitude goes out to you. As always, my readers are the reason I can continue doing what I love, and I thank you for your support.

I hope you enjoy a sneak peek of the first book in the *Life of Willow* duology, starting on the next page, or go *www.kaybratt.com* for a full list of other Kay Bratt books.

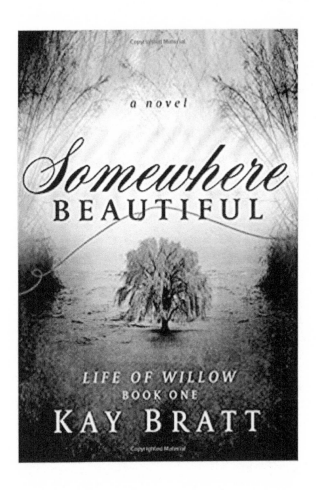

PART ONE
TYRANNY

WILLOW

EVERYONE HAD THEIR OWN PERCEPTION of hell. For Willow, hers was living behind the cold walls of the government-run orphanage. She folded her pitiful excuse for a pillow in half and then half again before finally giving up. She might as well get out of bed because she sure couldn't sleep. But the dream was still there, lingering in the muddy corners of her drowsy thoughts. As usual, the experience left her stomach feeling hollow and her head dizzy with pictures she couldn't make sense of. Swirling leaves, a snippet of sky, and a feeling of cold and loneliness.

She wished she had a cigarette to still her shaking hands, but they were hidden well out of sight under the concrete stairwell. She'd been busted smoking a few times, and she didn't want to lose outdoor privileges again, so she was being much more careful. With that thought, she caught the slight scent of the morning congee already being delivered to some of the rooms. This morning, it wasn't burnt, obviously, but it still didn't arouse any hunger in her. She'd long grown tired of the same boring, pasty porridge and most days, would rather go hungry.

She looked around at the covered mounds in the rows of beds—satisfied to see she was the first awake again. Not surprising, seeing how she'd been the first asleep.

While the other girls lay whispering to each other about their day—who'd been scolded for this or that, who had received a high or low mark in school, what boy gave them an interested look or suggestive smile—Willow had lain alone and quiet, unwilling to join the camaraderie.

Now she counted heads to make sure no one was missing, and she thought what a deceiving picture it all presented. To a stranger, the matching blankets covering rows of dark-headed girls might look like a page from a fairy tale, but Willow knew there was nothing magical about living in an orphanage. It was a lonely place—simply a place that housed the forgotten. That was the only description she could conjure.

Shivering now from the chill in the air, she remembered that despite her circumstances, today was still monumental. The fifth day of October. It was her sixteenth birthday—or at least the closest thing to a birthday she could claim from her unknown past. It was the day she'd decided would be celebrated each year, because it marked the day she'd been found in the park fifteen years before. They'd estimated her at around nine months old when they brought her in. Willow wouldn't acknowledge the birth date the orphanage doctor had given her. She decided a few years ago that it only made sense that the day her old life ended, and her new life began should be appointed as her new birthday. She couldn't make it official, but she could refuse to accept their attempts at total domination.

The officials had also given her a name that she had no choice in. The orphanage director had named her Liu Mei, a tribute to the tree she had been sleeping under. Last year, she'd overheard the older girls talking about how they and others they knew were adopting English names, and she'd laughed at some they'd chosen for themselves. Apple, Halo, and Echo were just a few that had stood out. She'd busied herself at school looking up the meanings, only to find them even stranger once she knew.

Still, after questioning them as to the English version of her own name, she decided she wanted to be called Willow. At first, her best friend, Kai, had a difficult time pronouncing it, but after a few corrections, he finally got close enough. He purposely dragged out the second syllable, calling her *Will...low...* Although she pretended it was irritating, it was just another quirk that made Kai special to her. The *ayis*—nannies—as well as her brothers and sisters in the orphanage, had eventually accepted the new version of her name when she'd stopped answering to Liu Mei. At least they had given her that—one small victory in her war to gain any piece of independence.

Willow quietly climbed out of bed and poked her feet into her slippers, then made the bed neatly as she'd been taught from a young age. She crossed the room to the line of lockers and opened hers, removing her towel and clothes. In a perfect life, she'd wrap herself in a cozy robe, make her way to a bathing room, and sink into a deep, clean bathtub filled with hot, soapy water.

But it wasn't a perfect world. Quickly, she tiptoed around the row of beds, out the door, and into the large, industrial bathroom across the hall. She was satisfied that, once again, her plan to get up half an hour earlier than the other girls had worked, and she'd get the shower to herself. Since her body had begun to do weird things, she refused to bathe or dress in front of the others, and she'd taken her share of punishment from the ayis for her defiance. But it was worth the scolding and occasional thump on the head to have the privacy she craved. With bathing restricted to once a week in the cold months, she wanted to enjoy it as much as possible.

First, she checked the water to make sure it was

working, sighing in relief when a small trickle ran into the rusty sink. Willow moved into one of the cubicles and, holding her nose against the stench, squatted and relieved herself over the inlaid, ceramic hole. Wishing for toilet paper, she shook her head at the stinginess of the orphanage director, then stood and undressed. She folded her sleeping clothes neatly and piled them on her clean outfit on the sink to keep them from getting wet. Using the only working shower sprayer, she shuddered under the cold water, quickly washing her hair and body with the harsh shampoo, and rinsing off hurriedly before reaching over to shut off the spigot. There wasn't time for her usual daydreams of flowery scents and hot water; she needed to hurry if she was going to be dressed before the others came in to begin their morning rituals. And she didn't want them to see her taking extra care this morning, or they might suspect she was up to something sneaky.

And she was.

Each year since she'd turned twelve, Willow had snuck away from school during their rest period to make the trip across town, sometimes by bus. When she couldn't drum up the bus fare, she walked. So far, her trek had proved fruitless, but today she had even more hope that it would be the day she finally met her mother.

She stepped out from around the mildewed plastic curtain, and her heart jumped when she saw a figure standing just inside the door.

"*Zao*, Willow," her friend, Rosi, called out, smiling widely.

Willow let her breath out. "You scared me, Rosi! What are you doing sneaking around so early?"

Rosi's smile disappeared. "I didn't sleep at all last night. Will you ask Mama Joss if I can sleep with you again tonight, just one more time?"

Pulling the towel tighter, Willow moved toward Rosi.

This wasn't the first time she'd acted strange about sleeping in her own room. Willow had woken only a week ago to find Rosi huddled beside her bed, her teeth chattering from the cold, before she had allowed her to climb in and snuggle under the covers with her. She hadn't said what had frightened her enough to traverse the dark halls out of her room that time either, but Willow knew it had to have been serious. None of them liked to walk the halls at night—there were too many shadows and dark corners.

"Rosi, you know you can't be in my room. I wish you could, but it'll just get you into more trouble if you're caught."

Rosi's lip quivered, making Willow feel sorry for her. "But I'll tell you what. If Mama Joss is on shift tonight, I'll see what I can do."

Across from her, Rosi nodded, her plump cheeks blushing with emotion. "My ayi is so mean to me, Willow. Last night, she took all my blankets."

Willow was getting anxious. Time was running out, and she needed to get moving. "Well, we'll have a talk with Mama Joss about that, too. *Hao le*? Now, I need to get ready for school, Rosi. You'd better run back and be there when they come in to count heads. And you'll have laundry to tend to soon."

Rosi smiled. "*Hao le*. But I wish I could go to school with you, Willow. Then ayi wouldn't smack me on my head all day." She gave a little wave and shuffled out of the room.

Though Willow had sworn off having close friends, she'd sort of taken Rosi under her wing. It made her so mad that Rosi was mistreated and shunned because of her disability—and not even allowed to go to school. It wasn't as if Down syndrome was contagious, but the way people on the outside acted, you'd think it was.

Rosi was only thirteen but to Willow, she seemed just

as smart as other girls her age did. It was sad but before she became older and strong enough to help with the laundry, she'd spent most of her days in one room with others who had serious disabilities. Willow referred to it as the *Nothing Room* because the kids in there didn't have anything to do—they just sat in chairs and stared at the walls all day. It was the saddest place in the orphanage, and Willow was glad they finally let Rosi do something to escape it for short periods. When the ayi had sent Rosi to join the others on the laundry team, many of the others made fun of her. Her flat face and stubby arms and legs never failed to bring about teasing. But Rosi never complained—she just smiled and laughed as though she was in on the joke.

Still shivering from the cool air, she dried herself and put on her school uniform, tying the red scarf around her neck. Despite the fact that she got tired of dressing in the same outfit every day, the uniform at least allowed her to blend in once she got to school. The trek there was another matter. Following along in a single line with the ayi leading the way, she felt as if they were on display. With the lack of parents and the blazing red uniform the ayis wore, everyone knew they were from the orphanage. Some even pointed to them as they paraded through the intersections.

Thinking about it caused her to brush her teeth too hard, and she nicked her sore gums. She'd asked for dental floss many times but always got the same response— *not in the budget*. She spit out a tiny bit of blood, and then brushed her hair back into the mandatory ponytail. Her hair was another source of irritation to the ayis. They wanted to chop it off as they had done all her life. But a few years ago, Willow grew tired of looking like a boy. She had finally insisted she be allowed to let it grow. They compromised when she promised to keep it up and neat at all times, but they eyed it constantly, just waiting for the moment she left it a mess so they could demand it to be cut.

Willow grabbed the clothes she'd worn to bed, quietly crossed the hall, and returned to her room. She opened her locker, put away her pajamas, and removed her shoes and her familiar blue and white school jacket. She'd have to wear it as usual, so no one suspected anything, but she'd stuff it in her bag just as soon as she got away. Before she quietly shut the door, she looked at the small slip of yellowed paper taped to the inside. Mama Joss had saved it when she graduated to a higher room, and she had given it to Willow. The woman's gesture had started Willow's secret treks to the park, for the ayi had even passed along the information of where she had been found. In the orphanage, the ayis were a huge source of details and knew much more than they let on around the higher uppers.

Willow reached up and smoothed the curled corner. To anyone else, it was just a scrap of yellowed paper. But to her, it was so much more. It was *the* paper that hung on her crib in the baby room when she was brought in—her first identification of sorts. At the top was the familiar character for girl. Under that, her estimated date of birth was marked along with her *finding date*—the day she had been found and brought to the orphanage. The character along the bottom always made her frown, as it categorized her as crippled. She wasn't crippled—she had one tiny imperfection with a foot that turned in. Big deal. But she avoided that description and focused only on the finding date. It was the important part to Willow, for in her heart, she hoped that at least once a year, probably on that date, she crossed her mother's mind.

She knew it wasn't healthy to keep going back to the park, but the mystery of her birth mother refused to leave her alone. She and Mama Joss had talked it over many times, and Willow knew she was probably abandoned because of her foot. She only wished her birth mother could see her and know that her twisted limb hadn't stopped her from learning to walk or talk.

The truth was that she was just as normal as the next girl was. However, her parents would never know that—unless her mother finally came forward.

Willow heard a noise in the hall and froze. She hoped it was only a passing ayi, maybe even Mama Joss. But she doubted it, as Mama Joss was usually so silent you never heard her coming. Like a guardian angel, she passed through the halls quietly, many times showing up just when needed to stop an altercation or soothe a raging fever.

The other ayis avoided Mama Joss, but they showed her quiet respect because of her years at the orphanage and what they considered her unnatural ability to heal the sick without real medical intervention. They didn't like it that Mama Joss cut short many of their unfounded disciplinary actions, but with one look from the woman, they usually backed off and left to find someone else to pick on. Mama Joss had saved a lot of innocent hides, but she couldn't be there all the time and from the first day, she'd coached Willow to follow her example and be her eyes and ears when possible. Everyone knew that Mama Joss had a special relationship with Willow. Because of that, most of the time she was left alone. Yes, Mama Joss had been one of the few beacons of hope and light in a place that was so frequently dark.

The day Mama Joss gave her *the talk* changed her whole world. She'd explained to Willow the issue of the one-child policy and told her how some mothers thought the orphanage could give their children a better life or provide medical care that they couldn't afford. After bringing her to the tree she was found at, Mama Joss said it was time for a life lesson. She then took her downtown and showed her the mothers with babies strapped to their backs, begging for coins. The women looked hungry and pitiful to Willow. Mama Joss explained that her mother probably led a similar life before leaving Willow to be found by someone who could take better care of her. Still, it hurt her to think she might have been rejected because of her disability, or just because she was a girl.

By the time Willow landed back in the orphanage after failing to thrive in her last foster home—her third in a series of a half a dozen—she'd returned to the comforting arms of Mama Joss. This time she came back with a new acceptance for her anger against her mother, and maybe even the beginnings of a tiny seed of love she held hidden in her heart.

Things had gotten more serious since then. Now that she was sixteen and had long since been kicked off the adoption eligibility list, finding her birth mother was her only option of ever having a family. Willow rested her forehead against the paper on her locker until the threat of tears passed. She would never give up her search. Even though so far, it had ended with no new information, she just knew her mother was out there somewhere, looking for her.

Her focus scattered when a bird flew at the window just beside her, making a loud thump before it flew back into the sky. So many times, she'd watched birds outside her window and felt envy at their freedom, their ability to fly free to somewhere beautiful, yet now one confused dove wanted in to her confined world? Not likely.

She sighed. Pushing the heavy thoughts to the back of her mind, she grabbed her shoulder bag and scarf, returning to her room to wait for the others to wake and begin their mad rush to get ready for school.

Download *Somewhere Beautiful* Today

BOOKS BY KAY BRATT

You can find them in Kindle Unlimited, too.

BY THE SEA TRILOGY
True to Me
No Place too Far
Into the Blue

THE TALES OF
THE SCAVENGER'S DAUGHTERS SERIES
The Palest Ink
The Scavenger's Daughters
Tangled Vines
Bitter Winds
Red Skies

LIFE OF WILLOW DUOLOGY
Somewhere Beautiful
Where I Belong

SWORN SISTERS DUOLOGY
A Welcome Misfortune
To Move the World

STANDALONE NOVELS
Wish Me Home
Dancing with the Sun
Silent Tears; A Journey of Hope in a
Chinese Orphanage
Chasing China; A Daughter's Quest for Truth
A Thread Unbroken

SHORT STORIES
The Bridge
Train to Nowhere

CHILDREN'S BOOKS
Mei Li and the Wise Laoshi
Eyes Like Mine

If you have enjoyed my work, I would be grateful for you to post an honest review on Amazon, Bookbub, and any other platforms you use for your books.

To those of you who have left reviews, my sincere gratitude is yours.

I would love to connect with you on Facebook, Instagram, and Twitter. Please sign up to my newsletter to be eligible to win fantastic giveaways, get news of just released books, and get a peek into the life of the Bratt Pack.

GLOSSARY

*Aiya (I-yah)*Expresses surprise or other sudden emotion
*Ānjìng diǎn (Ann Jing Dee Ann)*Be quiet
*Bijiǔ (Bye-Joe)*Chinese liquor
*Bu (Boo)*No
*Dui (Dway)*Correct
*Dui bu qi (Dway boo chee)*An apology
Hao le (How-luh)Okay or Yes
Hao bu hao (How-boo-how)Okay or not okay?
*Jóusàhn (Joe Son)*Good morning (Cantonese)
*Kuai yi dian (K-why ee dee an)*Faster
*Laoren (Loww-run)*Form of title used for senior citizen
*Laoban (Loww-bon)*Form of title used for a boss/supervisor
*Měiwèi de (May way duh)*Delicious
*Ni hao (Knee how)*Hello
*Qingwen (Ching one)*Excuse me
*Shào nián (Sh-ow nee ann)*lad
*Suanpan (Swan pan)*Abacus or counting tray
*Xiawu hao (Sha Woo How)*Good afternoon
*Xiao Jie (Sh-oww gee uh)*Title for a young girl or woman
*Xie xie (shay-shay)*Thank you
*Zao (Zow)*Good morning (Mandarin)
*Zaijian (Zie-jee-ann)*Goodbye

REFERENCES

Unbound Voices, A Documentary History of Chinese Women in San Francisco Judy Yung, University of California Press 1999, ISBN: 9780520218604

Driven Out, The Forgotten War Against Chinese Americans Jean Pfaelzer, Random House 2008, ISBN: 9780520256941

The Lucky Ones, One Family and the Extraordinary Invention of Chinese America, Mae Ngai, Houghton Mifflin Harcourt 2010, ISBN: 978-0-618-65116-0

San Francisco's Old Clam House on the Lost Waterfront, Susan Saperstein and San Francisco City Guides. This article is posted in English http://www.sfcityguides.org

Chinese Hungry Ghost Festival, Yu Lan Pen Ghost festival, Lauren Mack, February 25, 2017, This article is posted in English at https://www.thoughtco.com/hungry-ghosts-449825

Yang, Lihui, et al. (2005). *Handbook of Chinese Mythology*. New York: Oxford University Press. ISBN 978-0-19-533263-6 (Source of Jingwei legend)

Wa She Shu: The Washoe People, Past and Present, Manataka American Indian Council, Copyright © 2009 by the Washoe Tribe of Nevada and California. This article is posted in English at http://www.manataka.org/page1070.html

San Francisco Chinatown: Chinese in California, 1850-1920, The Bancroft Library, University of California, Berkeley

[*Workingmen's Party of California, Anti-Chinese Council], Chinatown Declared a Nuisance!* (San Francisco, 1880), p. 5.

How Bone Broth Got its Early Start From 19th Century Beef Tea, Sarah Baird, May 20, 2015 This article is posted in English at http://www.eater.com/drinks/2015/5/20/8626891/how-bone-broth-got-its-early-start-from-beef-tea-in-the-1800s

Bravo, Leonore M. (1991). Rabbit Skin Blanket: About the Washo of the Eastern Sierra Nevada And Their Neighbors, the Paiute. BraunBrumfield Inc. USA

Foltz: first woman admitted to the California Bar, By Rebecca J. Hooley, California Bar Journal, 2012. This article is posted in English at http://www.calbarjournal.com/March2012/TopHeadlines/TH4.aspx

"Report of Special Committee on the Condition of the Chinese Quarter," Municipal Reports, 1885, p. 208.
San Francisco, General Orders of the Board of Supervisors Providing Regulations for the Government of the City and County of San Francisco, 1898, p. 478. Hereafter cited as San Francisco Ordinances.
Chinatown Declared a Nuisance, distributed by the Workingman's Committee of California. This article is posted in English at http://www.sfmuseum.org/hist2/nuisance.html

A Trek to Truckee of the 19th century, Connie Emerson, Sunday, November 5, 2006. This article is posted in English at http://www.sfgate.com/entertainment/article/A-Trek-to-Truckee-of-the-19th-century-2467192.php

Ancient China, Albert S. Lyons, Medical History. This article is posted in English at http://www.healthguidance.org/entry/6333/1/Ancient-China.html

Chinese as Medical Scapegoats, 1870-1905, Historical Essay by Joan B. Trauner, California History Magazine, 1978. This article is posted in English at http://www.foundsf.org/index.php?title=Chinese_as_Medical_Scapegoats%2C_1870-1905h

Wikipedia contributors, "Smallpox," *Wikipedia, The Free Encyclopedia,* https://en.wikipedia.org/w/index.php?title=Smallpox&oldid=768636103 (accessed March 8, 2017).

ABOUT THE AUTHOR

Photo © 2013 Eclipse Photography

AS A WRITER, KAY USED writing to help her navigate a tumultuous childhood, followed by a decade of abuse as an adult. After working her way through the hard years, Kay emerged a survivor and a pursuer of peace—and finally found the courage to share her stories. She is the author of novels published by Lake Union Publishing and under her own label. Kay writes women's fiction and historical fiction, and her books have fueled many exciting book club discussions, and sold more than a million copies around the world.

Kay's work has been featured in Women's World, Adoption Today Magazine, Southern Writer's Magazine, Shanghaiist, Suzhou Sojourner, Historical Novels Society, Anderson Today, and Bedside Reading. Her books have been recommended on LitChat, BookRiot,

Midwest Review, Inside Historical Fiction, Blogcritics, The Shawangunk Journal, and Between the Lines (Atlanta, NPR). Her works have been translated into German, Korean, Chinese, Hungarian, Czech, and Estonian.

As a rescuer, Kay currently focuses her efforts on animal rescue and is the Director of Advocacy for Yorkie Rescue of the Carolinas. As a child advocate, she spent a number of years volunteering in a Chinese orphanage, as well as provided assistance for several nonprofit organizations that support children in China, including An Orphan's Wish (AOW), Pearl River Outreach, and Love Without Boundaries. In the USA, she actively served as a Court Appointed Special Advocate (CASA) for abused and neglected children in Georgia, and spear-headed numerous outreach programs for underprivileged children in the South Carolina area.

As a wanderer, Kay has lived in more than four dozen different homes, on two continents, and in towns and states from coast to coast in the USA. She's traveled to Mexico, Thailand, Malaysia, China, Philippines, Central America, Bahamas, and Australia. Currently she and her soulmate of more than 25 years enjoy life in their forever home on the banks of Lake Hartwell in Georgia, USA.

Kay has been described as southern, spicy, and a little sassy. Social media forces her to overshare and you don't want to miss some of the antics that goes on with her and the Bratt Pack. Keep up with her on her monthly newsletter here: *https://www.subscribepage.com/kay-brattnewsletter*

Or find her on Facebook, Twitter, and Instagram, then buckle up and enjoy the ride.

Made in the USA
Las Vegas, NV
03 July 2023

74192543R00163